The Elementary Cases of
Sherlock Holmes

The Elementary Cases of Sherlock Holmes

Ian Alfred Charnock

**BREESE
BOOKS
LONDON**

First published in 1999 by
Breese Books Ltd
164 Kensington Park Road, London W11 2ER, England

ISBN: 0 947533 97 4

Typeset in 11½/14pt Caslon by
Ann Buchan (Typesetters), Middlesex
Printed and bound in Great Britain by
Itchen Printers Ltd, Southampton

To
D. Martin Dakin
In fond Memoria

Contents

Prelude

The Great Exhibition of '51

I t is 1951. The world has just survived the most horrific war in its recorded history with as its final act of belligerence the explosion of two single bombs whose devastating power of destruction leave one in doubt as to the future of mankind. Here I stand, in a queue – there are so many these days, in London; still the centre of a great Empire whose transformation into a Commonwealth is well under way. What finer example could there be to the mischief makers, warmongers, and the bankrupt of spirit than to witness the proud ruler of the world's largest ever empire actually restoring the land to its indigenous peoples in friendship? No Pharaoh, Caesar or Philip of Spain ever did that. George of England and his two fine daughters will preside over a great example to all peoples of the world and those dreadful atomic weapons will never be used again.

In my pocket I have something which in its way is just as horrible a reminder of the recent conflict because it is of such human proportions – my ration book. Even a child born on this very day would have to be issued with its own ration book. That is a full six years after the war finished, a war which lasted slightly less than six years for we British. No one is safe from modern war.

But I grow pessimistic again, probably my aged bones grumbling. My newspaper tells me that my county, Kent, are doing well against Leicestershire with Fagg notching up another century and some new boy, M. C. Cowdrey, posting his first fifty in the county championship. With those initials he should go far! That should cheer me but how can it compete with the rest of the news? War in Korea, trouble in Tibet, oil problems with Persia, Russo-Polish border shenanigans; is there no end to it all? Even Hamlet appears to be under attack from a Guinness. He should stick to brewing, in which case Macbeth would seem to offer a more suitable if slighter role. I need to escape and where better than 221B Baker Street?

How can a number and two bald words in so mundane a juxtaposition become the 'open sesame' to a world so rich and exciting? I never visited it when Watson and Holmes were in residence; too busy doing other things. My single visit took place years after the partnership was dissolved.

This then is my second visit and as a member of the paying public, part of the celebrations of the Festival of Britain. Here is a mystery already. There is no 221B, just Abbey House standing opposite the side entrance of Baker Street station. Has the Norwood Builder been up to his tricks again? And once inside what a menagerie! The Lion's Mane, Cyanea Capillata, the swamp adder or 'speckled Band', the Giant Rat of Sumatra – how she revives chilling memories for me.

As I wander around this exhibition I feel myself very much on the periphery – as indeed I was all those years ago. I overhear many questions about Holmes and Watson. Why did Holmes not like women? How many times did

Watson marry? Who was the 'Illustrious Client'? Which university did Holmes attend? Where was Watson wounded? What was Holmes's second case? Was there a brother apart from Mycroft who inherited the family estate?

And what of the societies which have sprung up in honour of our heroes, particularly in the United States? We have the Creeping Men of Cleveland, the Six Napoleons of Baltimore, the Trained Cormorants of Los Angeles and the Baker Street Irregulars of New York. There is even one named after Charles Augustus Milverton, the most despicable of all blackmailers – have they no shame?! However, I must admit to being impressed by the way in which so many of these enthusiasts have copied the Master's methods in attempting to unravel these problems: having rejected the impossible, whatever remains, no matter how improbable, must be the truth. The method is right but so many of their conclusions are wrong – they need more data, as Holmes would have said.

It is for poor Watson that I feel the greatest sympathy. On the one hand he is criticized for careless proof-reading, inaccuracy over details, chronology and reported speech, and just plain bad writing as in some of the stories published as the so-called 'Casebook of Sherlock Holmes'. Whilst on the other hand, because Holmes is recorded as having quoted twice from only one of Shakespeare's plays, i.e. *Twelfth Night*, it is taken as proof positive that that was Holmes's date of birth – January 6th. (Although I have always taken Twelfth Night to be January 5th if Christmas Day be the first day of Christmas.) The implication is that Watson has left us a code of great complexity and sophistication in the published cases from which we may unravel the private lives of the great protagonists if we have the eyes to see and the wit to perceive. Yet failure to do so brings opprobrium crashing down on the good doctor's head and he is regarded as, to use his own word, 'dense'. Come, come, Watson cannot be a master cryptographer and a careless proof-reader. He must be one or the other.

But then, what does it matter to either of them? Poor Watson is long gone and Holmes never cared for publicity or recognition.

Now I must confess to a conceit. The greatest thrill that I get from being here is not from seeing these familiar or evocative exhibits, or from overhearing so much enthusiastic if incorrect talk about my old associates. To all here I am simply another enthusiast, whose old eyes have grown cloudy and whose legs need, in fulfilment of the Sphinx's riddle, the supplement of a stick. They all avoid me, no doubt fearing lest they knock me over in the crush; a courtesy for which I thank them.

Yet I possess a rare distinction. It is given to few to be immortal and to even fewer to find the spring of eternal youth and be immersed in it. Both Holmes and Watson are examples of the former, whilst I, a figure of ninety-one years, am an unlikely-looking example of the latter. You see my name is Stamford, eternally to be known as 'young Stamford'. It was I who was Watson's dresser at Barts and who introduced Watson to Holmes with the words: 'Dr Watson, Mr Sherlock Holmes.'

Now, listening to all these theories and with all these ideas ringing in my ears, I am filled with a desire to reveal what I know – and it is far more than many will have realized. Those of you who have read the stories of Holmes and Watson in their entirety have already read some of Stamford's words – and were probably disappointed with them. That is one mystery I can clear up; I owe it to John.

The stories that I recount from the 'Musgrave Ritual' I have arranged in the order that Holmes referred to them.

This is not the strict chronological order but I have left clues *à la* Watson as a challenge to future scholars.

Finally, these thoughts and words are only to be published forty years after my death. So Hail and Farewell – but read on.

Part One

Expositions from the Musgrave Ritual

'Yes, my boy, these were all done prematurely before my biographer had come to glorify me. . . . They are not all successes. . . . But there are some pretty problems among them. . . .'

(The Musgrave Ritual)

The Record of the Tarleton Murders

One thing that I had noticed about Mr Sherlock Holmes from the very earliest days of our acquaintance was his habit of becoming morose or 'in the dumps' as he himself called it. These periodic bouts were easily recognizable by several well-defined symptoms. He would start to fidget, his long fingers constantly active as though carrying out the sort of exercises that proved so disastrous for Robert Schumann. It would have been easy to believe that Holmes was simply keeping his fingers supple for the violin had it not been for the subsequent manifestations of his malaise. His eyelids would become heavy and his movements increasingly leaden, ultimately producing an impression of profound inertia. However, the more observant might have discerned the continuing rapid movements of his eyeballs behind the hoods of his closed lids, suggestive of machinery silently over-revving for want of proper engagement.

He was like this one morning as I arrived at Bart's laboratories. For my part I was feeling somewhat delicate after celebrating a victory in the early rounds of the Hospital Cup. I had added to my already considerable collection of policemen's helmets in the course of the evening's festivities but the late night had wreaked its usual havoc on my habitual reluctance to get up in the morning. Thus I was late for my lecture and found the laboratory deserted apart from the lone figure of Sherlock Holmes stretched languidly from a high three-legged stool on to a long bench which had been rendered almost invisible by the forest of chemical apparatus that covered its surface. I approached; apparently all affability but inwardly infirm of purpose.

'Another all-night sitting, Mr Holmes?' I inquired in my most jovial voice, my heartiness making even me wince.

Two heavy eyelids (drugged heavy?) twitched before slowly drawing back to reveal a pair of eyes, ghastly grey and limpid as millponds in winter twilight. 'Good morning, Stamford,' he replied. 'Yes, you are right whereas I, on the other hand, have been uniformly wrong. You converse with a failure.'

'Put it down to experience, Holmes,' I suggested with that facility that one has when giving, as opposed to receiving, advice. 'Better luck next time, old chap,' I concluded hoping that my attempted familiarity would not be taken wrongly. Nothing could have prepared me for the savagery of his response.

'Luck!' he roared. 'Luck has nothing whatever to do with it.'

'We all need luck, Mr Holmes,' I replied rather weakly; 'the bounce of the ball, the rub of the green . . .'

'Sporting metaphors are not appropriate to the logical processes,' he interrupted impatiently.

I could not let that pass uncontested. 'He who knows nothing of sport, Mr Holmes, knows nothing of life.'

'I fence and box.'

'Really?' I replied, keeping as much wind in my sails as possible. 'I have done neither.'

'Obviously.'

I decided to change tack slightly. 'Perhaps you would like to read today's newspaper?' I held out my copy.

Holmes was dismissive. 'I slipped out at one this morning and got a first edition.'

I feigned uninterest but left my copy on the bench next to him. 'Mine is a second but you never know, there might be some interesting late news.'

He appeared to take the bait and picking up the paper he thanked me. I went over to my locker and extracted a large jar marked 'Reviver' from which I poured a deep draught into a beaker that lay unused on Holmes's bench.

A commanding voice rang out from behind my newspaper. 'What would you say is the most dangerous phenomenon to confront the logician?'

'Something which dulls the faculties – Kentish beer?' I suggested.

'Try again,' the voice ordered.

'Drugs?'

The newspaper remained impenetrable. 'A very widely cast net. Even the most lethal drug has its beneficial qualities. Any other ideas?'

I felt as though I was being examined by the hospital board – and failing miserably. 'Insufficient data, then?'

There was a slight pause but the newspaper remained in place as my interrogator gave his opinion of my latest attempt. 'That's better, Stamford. However, to the trained logician insufficient data is not a dangerous phenomenon, merely a hindrance.'

My 'Reviver' was living up to its name and I was lightheaded with ideas. 'Too much data?'

This time the newspaper quivered slightly. 'You really are a tenacious fellow. I had expected you to have given up by now. Once again you have suggested more of a pitfall to the unwary than a danger to the logician.'

'One more, Mr Holmes?' I pleaded, confident of having a trump card still to play.

'If you must.'

I paused for effect; 'A woman.'

This time the newspaper was lowered and I saw a very rare sight, Sherlock Holmes was smiling. 'You have quite a wit, young Stamford. I must be on my guard in future. You have clearly discerned the second most dangerous phenomenon to confound the logician.'

'Therefore what is the answer?' I begged.

Holmes snatched up the newspaper. 'Coincidence. You don't believe it? Follow me.' The spring had returned to his stride. There was something which had caught Holmes's imagination. He led me down to the mortuary, a place where I was almost a stranger, although I knew him to be a regular visitor to that grim theatre of the macabre, pathetic and absurd. Holmes led me to where the unclaimed corpses lay. They looked like desolate ice flows covered as they were with white sheets, each equally lifeless and apart. He pulled back the sheet of his particular study in that machine-like emotionless way that had sent a shiver down many a student's spine.

The body in question that Holmes had revealed was that of a woman in her middle to late thirties. She was well made and somehow seemed unsuited to her present position.

'I'm afraid that she's probably about two days old now, Stamford, but can you tell me the cause of death? She was found in the Seven Dials.'

I closely inspected the corpse for the usual tell-tale signs on the lips and extremities. They were not present and so I looked for any evidence of foul play. There were none that my eyes could see. In fact. she looked to be in robust good health; a thought to which Holmes responded before I had had a chance to put it into words.

'I agree,' he said. 'Can you see anything strange about her?'

'Isn't that strange enough, Holmes?'

'Look again and explain why you think her to be so misplaced here.' Holmes was a collector who had found a very rare piece that had eluded him for years and whose existence hitherto had been more hearsay than reality.

'The skin is quite pink,' I observed, 'and still remarkably supple for a two-day-old corpse.'

'Good, good. Anything else?'

'She also has a most serene smile on her face.'

'Well done, Stamford. I shall make a scientist of you yet. I expected you to notice the smile first and the other features afterwards. You are obviously no mere sensationalist.'

I shrugged my shoulders in faint thanks. 'The coincidence?' I asked, looking about me expecting Holmes to pull back the sheet from another lifeless form.

'In your pocket, Stamford. The newspaper. Page four, second column.'

I drew the newspaper from my pocket and turned to the page indicated. In bold type at the top was printed: 'Death of a Brave Man'. I continued reading the column aloud:

It has just been announced that the Honourable Clive Melvin Moreton-Ashbee has died at his family home of Sibberton Hall just outside Chipping Oversomer in Oxfordshire. He was found by his faithful servant, Hodgson, seated in his favourite armchair next to a blazing fire in the family hearth.

The Honourable Clive Moreton-Ashbee was a renowned explorer who had travelled widely in the islands of the Far East, in particular Borneo and New Guinea, and also he had undertaken exploration in central and southern America.

He will be most remembered by his country for the generous gift of vases from the Yucatan that he gave to the British Museum last year. Friends will remember him for his ready wit and generous hospitality. (At university he was a co-founder of the Festival Hams whose *raison d'être* was to entertain 'by word of mouth and fulsomeness of food'.)

Hodgson, the faithful butler who had accompanied his master on several of his explorations, summed up everyone's horror at the great loss yet pride in having known such a man when he said: 'Although he was not yet thirty years of age he had lived a life far fuller than many twice his age. When I found him he was smiling as though Death was an old friend whose arm he would willingly take for one last journey.'

'Don't go on, Stamford. We do not need to know what his nanny thought of him, or the opinion of the second under-gardener. It is the coincidence that counts and that will take us to Chipping Oversomer this afternoon. Are you game?'

It was at times like these that Holmes was at his most unpleasant. Here was a story most aptly titled 'Death of a Brave Man' about a man who had, in fact, been one of my heroes for his bravery and charm – not that I had met him. I felt my neck grow red and my fists form. Holmes obviously read the danger signals and his manner softened. 'I'm sorry, Stamford. I have offended you in some way.'

'Yes you have, Holmes,' I returned angrily. Moreton-Ashbee was one of my heroes. He . . .'

'Heroes? He was also a conceited, self-centred, patronizing oaf. As were his two friends Wriggleton and Bellaysarias.'

'What qualifies you to make such judgements?' I returned, with no little heat.

'We were at Oxford together,' he answered calmly.

Holmes could see that I was crestfallen by these revelations. 'I have made it a particular point,' he continued, 'never to have heroes. They have an in-built capacity to disappoint as well as deflecting the logician from his chosen path of dispassionate observation and deduction.'

'Beware of the hero – for he may have feet of clay.'

'Quite so. Now let us see what connection there is, if indeed there is one, between the death of a poor woman in the Seven Dials and that of a rich man at his family hearth in Oxfordshire.'

'What time is the train, Holmes?' I asked.

'Well done, young Stamford. I knew I could rely on my tenacious forward.'

The 1:10 p.m. from Paddington to Oxford via Reading steamed easily through the undulations of a prosperous, contented Berkshire, making light of the Chilterns and stopping at various hamlets that looked as though they were still awaiting the Conqueror's commissioners for the Doomsday survey. We had a light lunch after which Holmes lit up his pipe and conversed on sundry subjects with an ease that was as remarkable as was the diversity of the topics. He talked of astrolabes, the 'lost' chord, phlogiston, Watteau and sash fillesters. It was all most informative and so entertaining that I found myself quite engrossed. Any observation that I made would be duly considered and an honest appraisal given of its worth. I felt as though I was a learned and valued colleague, not a freshman attending his first tutorial. Such was Holmes's charm when the mood was upon him.

As we passed into Oxfordshire and thatch became the commonplace it seemed to concentrate Holmes's mind on the puzzle in hand. We talked of medical subjects. *Rigor mortis, risus sardonicus,* sulphur dioxide, carbon oxides, and diseases of the respiratory and circulatory systems all came under our scrutiny. However, interesting as Holmes was on all these subjects, there was only one subject that I wished him to expand upon – the Honourable Clive Melvin Moreton-Ashbee. It was not until we were on the 'halt on demand' branch line to Chipping Oversomer that Holmes relented and fleshed out his earlier comments as to his college contemporary.

'Moreton-Ashbee, the equally Honourable Thomas Wriggleton and Count Bellaysarias formed the Festival Hams purely for their own diversion.'

'Nothing necessarily wrong in that, Holmes,' I observed.

'As you say, Stamford, but those three had a way of making even a charitable endowment an act of cruel self-indulgence. They had wealth to spare and so did not have to be sensitive to the feelings of others. At first to be invited to a Festival Hams dinner was a prize to be grasped at – in fact so it remained for some until the day they left Oxford, but both Pennington and I saw through them.'

'Pennington?' I asked. 'A friend of yours?'

'Pennington was no friend of mine. If anything we were rivals. You will hear more of him anon.'

Was Holmes smiling to himself as he thought of this rival? A rival in what had he been? Boxing, fencing, academic cut and thrust? Love?

'The Festival Hams' committee – in other words Morton-Ashbee, Wriggleton and Bellaysarias – provided the provender, the guests had to provide the entertainment. At first it was harmless enough with the guests doing their party pieces singing, telling a story or whatever, but these three soon tired of such innocent diversions. They would invite various academics to their dinners. The one criterion, although never openly stated by the Hams, was that these Dons had to have an inability to speak well in public. After dinner they would be invited to speak. At first they were ridiculed in a scholarly way but as the wine flowed the insults became more personal – not that the Hams themselves insulted the guests, they left that to their puppets whose only purpose at these gatherings seemed to be to carry out the base wishes of their mentors. They at least continued to prize their invitations. Curiously, other Dons sought invitations if only to prove themselves superior to their peers. Their attempts always ended in disaster as they became the butts of practical jokes.'

'It seems pretty harmless to me, Holmes,' I cut in. 'You know as well as I do that these academics can be very self-important and need to have their self-esteem deflated from time to time. Well done the Hams, I say.'

'I can certainly see your point but even the most sincere and honest were just as liable to attack as the pompous and the conceited. The Hams would find out any Achilles' heel, the more personal the better, and use that to humiliate their guest, if all else failed.'

This I could understand. The cruelty of my school fellows concerning my childhood stammer was still a barely healed scar. The Festival Hams had gone down in my estimation but their interest in exploration was surely an exonerating feature of their personalities. Holmes soon disabused me of that notion.

'It cannot be disputed that the Festival Hams provided the finance for these trips but they rarely actually penetrated the interiors of the remote areas that their publicity would lead you to believe.'

'In that case how did they gather the results that they were able to publish in all those learned journals? Are you saying that they made them up and deliberately deceived the authorities for whatever reason you care to charge them with?'

'I would not put it past them,' Holmes replied. 'It is the sort of thing that would appeal to their warped sense of humour. However, that is where Pennington comes in.'

Holmes hesitated for a moment before he continued, a smile ghosting across his aquiline features as he thought of his old rival. If this man was a rival, I mused, it was obviously a rivalry that Holmes had relished.

'In appearance he was most striking; standing six feet

eight inches with the physique of a Hercules he was not easy to overlook. He was very dark, his eyes like burning embers and his hair although well groomed suggested a violent passionate nature because it was so thick and full of vitality. I was always reminded of a fanciful vision of the Hanging Gardens of Babylon. Rich, luxuriant growths a testimony to civilization and culture while properly tended but given the freedom to grow naturally and they would overrun everything, creating a new order.'

'You said that you were rivals. In what way was that?'

'As you have probably worked out for yourself, my studies have not been the random fancies of a desultory student but a precisely calculated schema with a definite end in mind. Pennington was like that. He was a man of many talents being sportsman, actor and academic. His studies were many and various from cuneiform to tattoos. It was he who told me about the singularity of various tattoos which has become a special study of mine. When studying various tribes of Indians he even had himself tattooed with some of their markings so that he could appreciate their ideas more clearly.'

'What was his subject?'

'Man.'

'A broad canvas, Holmes.'

'The arc of his arm was wide enough to span it.'

'You keep saying "was". What has happened to him?'

'According to the newspapers he was lost on the expedition to the Yucatan.'

'My word.'

'You will notice that since that expedition the Festival Hams have not ventured anywhere. They have lost the man who gave their jaunts credibility.'

'How was he lost?'

'Once again according to the newspapers, he was swept

away by a fast flowing river. A "white water" river as our Canadian cousins call it.'

At that moment the train pulled into the single-platform station of Chipping Oversomer. Although we were in November it was a true St Martin's summer and we carried our coats over our arms as we alighted from the train. Before we had set out Holmes had sent several wires. The first resulted in a dogcart to take us to the local police station where a copy of the coroner's report awaited us.

The coroner was also there. 'We've been in touch with the Yard,' he told Holmes, his words as clipped as his military moustache, 'and a Mr Lestrade has authenticated your status. Although it all looks highly irregular to me. What is a "consulting detective"?'

'A last court of appeal,' replied Holmes as he swiftly read through the report.

'I think that you will find it a wasted journey, Mr Holmes,' continued the coroner. 'It was a straightforward heart attack. Apparently all the men in the Moreton-Ashbee family have suffered from similar weaknesses throughout the years.'

'But it must have been brought on by something,' Holmes remarked.

'There we are in the realms of theory, Mr Holmes, just as Mr Lestrade said we would find ourselves with you as our guide. I deal in facts. It was a heart attack plain and simple that took off the Honourable Clive Melvin Moreton-Ashbee.'

Holmes's cross-examination was far from over, despite the worthy official's obvious belief that he had answered anything that such an irregular fellow might put to him.

'Was there a smile on his face?' my companion asked.

'More of a grimace I would say,' replied the coroner. 'The newspapers embellished Hodgson's imagination in order to make a more interesting story. If you ask me, what smile there might have been was more in the eye of the beholder.'

'Was there anything remarkable about the skin coloration?' Holmes persisted.

'Nothing at all. He had suffered from malaria for some years, as his friends Wriggleton and Bellaysarias have. The result of an expedition to the Far East, I believe. I have served in India myself and have seen the symptoms a thousand times. Even in such warm weather as this he had to keep close to a good strong fire.'

Holmes pondered this last remark for a moment. 'Nothing else, Major Hicks?'

'Nothing else, Mr Holmes. If there were it would have been in my report.'

'May I examine the body?'

'No, you may not. The funeral is in an hour at Sibberton Hall.'

'Then no doubt we shall see you there, Major.'

With that we were back in our dogcart and on the way to Sibberton Hall, the ancestral home of the Moreton-Ashbees.

'An interesting exchange that,' said Holmes. 'Major Hicks is obviously no fool and a man of experience. I expect his feathers were ruffled when he heard he was to be visited by a specialist from the metropolis and that he had another look at Moreton-Ashbee. There were not one, but two, additions to his report restating his original opinions. I wonder if there were any punctures of the skin. Certain snake venoms can reproduce the effects of a heart attack.'

'Were there any snake bites on the woman from the Seven Dials?'

'No.'

'Then I fear that coincidence has been allowed to fog the capacities of the logician.'

'Perhaps you are right, Stamford, but while we are here we might as well see your hero to his grave.'

The funeral had drawn many people to Sibberton Hall, a fine edifice of warm Hornton stone whose justly celebrated Tudor chimneys dominated the many later additions to the Hall. As expected there were the usual officers of the county as well as the household retainers – Hodgson being the most prominent by his weather-beaten face and his obvious grief. Moreton-Ashbee could not have been all bad if he had been able to inspire such devotion in a paid servant.

There were also many others from all walks of life assembled to pay their respects to this now enigmatic man. Holmes pointed out the Honourable Thomas Wriggleton, a very feminine-looking man, more fop than adventurer to my eyes, and Constantine Bellaysarias, a swarthy man of some self-possession. 'He believes himself to be descended from Justinian's greatest general. He's probably as mad as a hatter. He always was rather unstable,' prompted Holmes. Interesting as these two obviously were, my eye was drawn to the young woman who walked between them. She had that delicacy of bone structure and colouring that spoke of the breeding of a long lineage. 'Wriggleton's younger sister, who is the best of the lot,' said Holmes, once again answering my look, not my words.

After the funeral the sun sank over the horizon and a more seasonal chill spiked the air. Holmes and I put on our overcoats and mounted our dogcart to leave, but before we could start our journey a deep oily voice called out, 'Well, well, if it isn't the misogynist.'

'Good afternoon, Bellaysarias,' replied Holmes. 'I trust that you are well?'

'Never better, Hoomes. I am engaged to be married to Wriggleton's sister, Edith.'

'The name is Holmes, Bellaysarias. As to your good fortune, I congratulate you.'

'Thank you, Hoomes. And who is this man who was making cow eyes at my Edith this afternoon?'

His manner was becoming annoying and I understood more clearly Holmes's criticisms of the Festival Hams.

'Forgive me,' said Holmes, completely unruffled. 'This is my good friend Stamford of St Bartholomew's Hospital.'

We shook hands. It was like gripping a bunch of over-ripe bananas. I instinctively wiped my palm on my coat. Bellaysarias gave me a look of undiluted hatred but, turning to Holmes, continued in his sickeningly syrupy tones, 'What a pity about Clive. Still, at least he lived up to the family motto '"My heart is my strength".' His laughter was without humour. Holmes decided to put a stop to the interview.

'Goodbye. Bellaysarias. I doubt that we shall meet again. My best wishes to your fiancée.'

Condolences, more like, I thought, but said nothing. As we left, Count Bellaysarias and I exchanged one more hostile look and then it was off to the station for the journey home.

The train was a long time coming so we sat in the Spartan waiting room, Holmes smoking his pipe whilst I dozed next to the fire. Through the twilight of my slumbers there came the sound of a horse and carriage being driven by a Jehu. Gravel was sprayed against the station wall as the combination was brought to a halt. 'The train's not due yet awhile, is it?' I murmured to Holmes, my eyelids still firmly shut.

'Not for another quarter of an hour,' he returned.

Moments later the heavy door of the waiting room was thrown open to reveal the distraught figure of Edith Wriggleton. 'Whichever one of you is Mr Sherlock Holmes, you must come right away. My brother is dead!'

Holmes was soon out of his world of contemplation and in moments we were in the young lady's carriage charging headlong towards Sibberton Hall.

'Tell me, what has happened?' he asked Miss Wriggleton in a soothing voice as I earnestly leant forward to offer what assistance I could.

'We are all staying at Sibberton Hall until Clive's will is read. There are no Moreton-Ashbees left. At dinner, Constantine and my brother spoke of you, Mr Holmes, in most praising tones. They said that you were one of the most remarkable men that they have ever met.' (Holmes betrayed no sign of any emotion at such fulsome praise.) 'Apparently you had impressed them with your abilities that had seemed almost supernatural. These words came back to me moments after we had discovered Thomas. Constantine and I had been to the library' (did she flush slightly when she said this?) 'to be alone for a moment or two . . .'

'How long exactly, Miss Wriggleton?' asked my apparently inhuman companion.

'Perhaps half an hour, certainly no more,' she replied. 'When we returned to the sitting room Thomas was dead.'

'Was there any evidence of foul play? Was the furniture disarranged?'

'No, quite on the contrary. Thomas had the most serene smile on his face that you could imagine.'

Was this a coincidence?

'Have you called the police?' continued Holmes.

'Yes, but there is only one constable on duty on the evening shift. Thus he has had to wire Oxford for a more senior official.'

'Was Count Bellaysarias with you at all times, Miss Wriggleton?' asked Holmes casually.

'Why yes, of course,' she replied. 'Surely you do not think

that he had anything to do with the death of his future brother-in-law?'

'One must ask such questions, I am afraid, in such times of crisis,' returned Holmes suavely.

When we reached Sibberton Hall, Constantine Bellaysarias rushed out to greet us. Gone was the mocking cynicism of earlier that day. He was genuinely concerned. 'Thank God you are here, Holmes,' he cried almost hysterically as he put his arm around the slender shoulders of his fiancée.

'Why was it that Miss Wriggleton came to fetch us?' Holmes asked with a disarming charm, although if I had asked the question, as I had wished that I had, I would not have been so charming.

'Hodgson is too far gone in drink such is his upset and I feared to leave Edith in the same house as her d—, er, brother,' replied the now contrite Levantine.

'Has the regular force arrived yet?'

'No, but the local constable is here.'

'I must be able to examine the room and the body with my colleague here without interruption. Arrange it, please, Bellaysarias. One last question before you go. Was it the same room as that in which Moreton-Ashbee met his end?'

'No, that sitting room has been closed for the time being, although the two are identical with french windows and hearths that meet in the same chimney.'

Holmes seemed to find this information most significant and his nostrils dilated as though he were on the scent of an elusive quarry. Several minutes later we were in the sitting room, the constable keeping watch from the door. As we looked at the body the first thing to strike us was the face with its serene smile and the pink hue of the skin. Then we became aware of the great heat from the fire. It was almost overpowering. We examined Wriggleton more closely. 'Signs of a malarial attack,' I said.

'Yes, I thought I recognized the symptoms, but it was only a mild bout, I think,' responded Holmes.

Next he looked at the floor and the french windows, followed by the path and the bushes outside. I could see no clear signs in the dusk's feeble glow. Several times he sniffed the air and finally his nose led him to the blazing fire. He pointed out a cigar at the back of the grate which had not been burnt by the fire but roasted so that it had kept its shape and even the maker's label remained intact. He went to the desk in the room and found a box of cigars. They were the same as the one on the fire. 'Curious,' he murmured to himself. He then saw a very small butt of a cigarette and, picking it up from the ashes of the fire with a set of tweezers, he smelt it.

'This is most peculiar,' he said, without really addressing me. 'I have studied many tobaccos and their ashes and hope to produce a monograph on my findings shortly, but this is one that I have not come across before.' With that he dropped it into a small envelope and was about to put it in his pocket when the constable asked him to replace it where he had found it so that the official force should find the room in the same state that Holmes had. Holmes acquiesced and we joined Edith Wriggleton and Constantine Bellaysarias in the library.

'Well, Mr Holmes, what can you tell us?' implored the dead man's sister.

'There was definitely another person in the room with your brother, Miss Wriggleton. He entered and left by the french windows. He is heavier than I, although somewhat shorter. He is a very calm individual and was wearing a woollen coat of South American origin.'

'I told you, Edith,' cried Bellaysarias excitedly. 'Holmes is a magician!'

Miss Wriggleton, although impressed, was still in control

of her mental faculties. Was that why Holmes had judged her to be the best of the group? 'You are certain that it was a man, Mr Holmes?' she asked coolly.

'It would be a most peculiar woman of a physical type most uncharacteristic of the female sex,' Holmes replied. He thought for a moment and then asked: 'Is there a circus in the area at the moment?'

At first the two listeners were too surprised to answer. It was Bellaysarias who broke the silence. 'You are not jesting are you, Holmes? I admit that I was a little ungallant earlier on when we first met but that does not excuse such flippancy in Miss Wriggleton's hour of need.' He seemed to be increasingly overwrought.

'I have never been more serious,' countered Holmes calmly.

'In that case we had best ask the servants. As you know, none of us are from this area.' He pulled the bell rope and before long a young maid appeared. Holmes repeated his question to her.

'No, sir, not a circus. But there is a mop at Sheepstown-by-Stower,' she replied in the broad burring tones of rustic Oxfordshire. 'Come to think of it, it was in Chipping the other day or so.'

'Mop?' I asked.

'Yes, it is a sort of fair where domestic servants can be hired,' she answered. 'They have sideshows and things.'

Holmes needed no second bidding. We rushed from the room and, borrowing one of the house's carriages, covered the ten miles to Sheepstown-by-Stower. On the way I was able to ask Holmes how he had been able to discern so much about the mysterious figure on whose trail we were now set.

'My lens was able to reveal the woollen strand in the holly bush and his footmarks going in and out of the house.

That he was smaller than me was evident from the fact that his paces were not as long as mine. That he was heavier was clear from the depth of his prints in the firm ground.'

'Why did you say that he was a calm character?'

'Simply that his strides to and from the french windows were the same. Also the heels were more clearly discernible than the balls of the feet. In a runner it is the balls and toes that are clearer than the heels. Having said that, his step showed a rather ponderous figure whose movements seemed restricted in some way. There was a great deal of pressure on the inside edges of the print which suggested a rolling gait. Also the shoes were remarkably broad.'

'A short, fat sailor?' I speculated.

'A very good suggestion, Stamford, and quite possible but clearly a very individual step. We should have little difficulty in recognizing our man when we see him.'

'How did you know that he had got into the room?'

'The cigar and the cigarette. The cigar came from the box on the desk and it had clearly not been smoked for some unclear reason. Such mild green Havanas are usually very popular among those who can afford them. However, the cigarette came from an outside source. Wriggleton had no others on his person, or any of the constituents for that matter if he had wished to make his own, and there were no others in the room. The tobacco was reminiscent of Bolivian mix and the paper was of a rough type usually associated with Central America although, despite my specialized knowledge of tobacco and its concomitants, I confess that I can narrow it down no more than that. This in turn does suggest a newcomer to our shores.'

'Why so, Holmes?'

'He still has a supply of his old papers and mix.'

'But why are we going to a circus or a fair, I should say?'

'People dressed in traditional South American clothes

are rare in north Oxfordshire and therefore apt to call attention to themselves. What better place to remain incognito than with other people known for their ostentation?'

'You have an answer for everything, Holmes.'

'Not quite. First there is the unsmoked cigar. Then we have the problem of the cause of Wriggleton's death. You will confirm that he looked identical to the woman in the hospital . . .'

'Indeed.'

'. . . and so we may eliminate heart failure. There were no snake bites on either, so that can be excluded. There is one other question that I cannot answer,' he concluded becoming very thoughtful.

'What is that, Holmes?' I asked, leaning towards him.

'When we find whom we are seeking will we be exposed to mortal danger, too?'

'You can count on me, Holmes.'

When we reached Sheepstown-by-Stower it was obvious that the fair was drawing to a close. Several forlorn as yet unhired domestics still stood by the road carrying the tools of their trade as advertisements for their areas of expertise. The brooms and dry mops looked in better health than their owners whose prospects of employment became bleaker as the hour grew later. Holmes soon found the head man of the fair whose florid face complemented his garish silk waistcoat. On being asked about anyone with South American connections his memory became dim and the rubbing of his chin with his ham-like hand did little to improve his recollections. I thrust some coins into his hand and his amnesia was proved to be only temporary. He directed us to a small barrel caravan at the far end of the line which had 'Madame Yalta' in faded old letters painted on the side and 'The Great Alcalde' in fresh chalk characters just below.

Holmes laid his hand on my arm and pointed to the names. 'Mark that, young Stamford.'

'You mean the Spanish word?'

'No; the fact that it is newly added and only in a temporary medium. The caravan may look picturesque but its contents could be lethal.' We approached with extreme caution. Holmes knocked sharply on the door and almost instantly it swung open to reveal a very short, stout, heavy-bearded figure illuminated by the flickering light from within the caravan. We tensed.

'What do you want?' screeched the ominous figure in an unexpectedly high-pitched voice. My fists clenched tighter and I saw that Holmes was on his guard ready to pounce at the least sign of enemy action.

'Madame Yalta, the bearded lady, I presume?' he remarked in a tone more relaxed than his manner.

'Yes. What of it?' came the screeched reply.

'Your boss . . .'

'I have no boss,' she corrected irritably.

'I beg your pardon, Madame. The boss of the site told me that the "Great Alcalde" was staying here. Could we see him, please?'

'Who are you?' came the response almost spat from her unseen lips.

'For what it is worth, this is Surgeon Stamford of St Bartholomew's Hospital, London, and I am Mr Sherlock Holmes of Montague Street, London.'

At that there came a great bellow from deep within the small caravan so that it seemed to rock from side to side. 'By all the gods! Let them in, Yalta,' boomed the great voice that seemed too large to be contained by such a small vessel. I half expected to see a genie appear as though out of a bottle.

We stepped into the caravan. It was very cramped and

stiflingly hot. I could just stand upright but Holmes had to duck low. At the far end of the caravan the owner of the booming voice sat behind a low table, his great arms and shoulders made even more massive by comparison with the exiguousness of his setting. His head was equally enormous, covered with a thick mat of long black hair and a luxuriant beard streaked with a rich vein of silver. Through this foliage shone intense dark eyes.

'Don't you recognize me, Holmes? And there was I thinking that of all the people on this earth only you would be able to solve my mystery.'

Holmes looked in disbelief and delight at the figure before him. 'Alexander Knox Pennington,' he said, as though unsure of believing the words that his mouth was saying.

'Of course it is,' Pennington exclaimed, pushing the puny table away with one sweep of his enormous arm. He made to stand and as he did so I expected him to put his head through the roof of the caravan remembering Holmes's description of his great height; but when he rose he was barely taller than myself. Holmes and I exchanged a perplexed glance. 'A disagreement with some fish,' said Pennington, smiling. 'Sit down, sit down. It is good to see you, Holmes, and your new friend. Trevor still in the Terai, I suppose?'

It was obvious that Holmes was very pleased to see Pennington again. Was it hero worship I saw in his eyes? There was no chance of him having feet of clay, I thought, in my typically macabre dresser's way, for he had no feet. His legs ended at the knees.

'Surprised to see me, Holmes?' the mutilated giant asked.

'I had read that you had perished in some fast flowing river in Mexico.'

'Fast flowing? Is that what they said? The snivelling

toadies. The river is called the "boiling river" by the natives. At first we assumed that they called it so because it was hot. I waded in and found it pleasantly warm – it probably had its source near a volcano – but the others simply stood by and watched not daring to join me. Festival Hams indeed. More like Fearful Shams.'

'What happened?' I asked, already gripped by this man.

'Suddenly the water started to bubble as though it was boiling but the reason had nothing to do with heat. The river was alive with carnivorous fish. I shouted for help but my brave companions ran away. I staggered as far as I could but the pain was unbearable and I collapsed into the river sure that my end had come. Suddenly the nipping and tearing at my flesh stopped. I looked up and saw, in full dress, a Mayan war party. They had thrown some meat and nets into the river and drawn the fish away. Their presence was probably another reason for the retreat of my companions. No matter. I was saved but if I had thought myself close to death then it was only because I did not know what was in store for me later.'

Pennington took a sip from a flask and continued his narrative.

'These Mayas were as original as you could wish for. They came from beyond the Itza region and seemed to have survived intact from pre-Colombian days. I was taken back to their city, the journey taking several weeks by which time my legs were rotten.

'They held a council to decide what to do with me. I knew some of their language from my various studies and was able to differentiate several schools of thought on this question. One particularly vociferous party wanted to throw me back to the fish or do the job themselves. Another party with whom I found myself in sympathy suggested saving my life.

'Of the pro-death-to-Pennington lobby the main arguments seemed to be that I represented the hated outsider who had brought disease and death to their once great race. They pointed out that the party I was with had already stolen a large collection of pottery which went to prove the untrustworthiness of the white man. I could see their point.'

I marvelled at his sang-froid. It was easy to see why Holmes admired him, for I was sure that he did.

Pennington continued. 'The party who wished to save me simply said that I was a part of Creation just like themselves who deserved life just as much as they did. Their nobility was simple unadorned and absolutely compelling.

'However, my fate still hung in the balance until one of them saw my tattoos. As you know I had several tattoos at university, but on each trip that I have made since then I have had others etched into my flesh. They took me to be a "man of power" and so sought to save me.

'For several months I wavered between life and death. My legs were amputated at the knees and my body was filled with all sorts of medicines that gave me visions of everything from flying to being an ant. While I was still lying in this shadow world they gave me even more tattoos so that when I finally left them I was able to raise money by exhibiting myself, as I have done here. They also taught me to walk on my stumps. When I eventually recovered I got to learn about my saviours and realized what a lucky man I was.'

'I'll say,' I found myself interrupting.

'Not just to have life but to be in a city which appeared to be undisturbed by marauding Conquistadores. What an opportunity for research! The chance to answer the unsolved riddles of the Mayas was there to be taken. What had caused their decline? How did they manage to build such fantastic structures? What were their beliefs? It was almost too much for me. I could even thank the Hams for leaving me there when they did.

'And do you know something, Holmes? Believe it or not I found myself thinking of you and your wide studies. In particular I thought of you as I found out about their medicines. Nearly all of them were poisons. Taken in the correct dosage and they would stimulate the body and so bring about recovery. The wrong dosage obviously had dire consequences. I found that this was where their great skill lay – in correctly calculating these dosages. Just imagine what went into these calculations; the weight of the patient, his natural immunity, the severity of his condition, the purity of the poison are the most obvious; there are twenty-two others.

'It has been suggested that malaria killed the Mayas but they showed me that they knew of the bark of the Cinchona trees, which is an effective remedy for the disease.'

'That's a coincidence,' I exclaimed. 'There is a student at Bart's, Ross or Rose or some such name, who is very interested in malaria and he mentioned that bark to me not long ago.'

'He needs to go to the Yucatan and be taught by the Mayas, as indeed should many of our modern so-called physicians,' Pennington replied with some feeling. 'The Mayas also showed me tree frogs,' he continued, 'that looked absolutely harmless as they sat on their branches and yet they were fearless of all predators. These frogs made no attempt at camouflage; they were bright yellow or crimson or emerald. It was as though they wanted to be seen by the other animals.'

I cast a sidelong glance at Holmes and saw that he was totally absorbed in Pennington's dissertation, particularly this last topic.

'Presumably they were poisonous and their arresting

colours prevented them being consumed in error by the frog's natural enemies,' Holmes remarked. 'What point would there be in being poisonous and eaten? A Pyrrhic victory is of dubious worth to humans let alone frogs.'

'You understate, Holmes. They are Death itself. To simply touch one is enough to kill a man. Yet the Mayas know how to use this poison in their medicine to relax muscles and alleviate pain. They could have been the Borgias of Mexico but instead they have chosen to heal. It made me very humble and led me to question my values.'

At that he leant back and reached for a box. There were holes drilled into the sides and there was a flap on the front which he opened to reveal, behind a pane of glass, a group of wax-like frogs, a riot of dazzling colours. 'Harmless, almost funny looking, are they not, gentlemen? Yet they are certain death if used unwisely.'

We could only agree with their apparent harmlessness and marvel at their unexpected deadliness.

'Did you use this poison in a cigarette to kill the Honourable Thomas Wriggleton today?' Holmes's voice was like a chill wind cutting through the oppressive heat of the small caravan.

Pennington's spell had been broken. At first he looked anguished but he mastered himself and a broad smile illuminated his face. 'We all said that you were a magician at university, Holmes. I won't ask you how you knew, but I would ask you to believe that I did not intend to kill Wriggleton.'

'Or Moreton-Ashbee and the woman in the Seven Dials?' Holmes added.

Pennington's jaw dropped. 'My God, Holmes. You are a magician! I knew she must have died but I got out quick and got a job here to keep me away from prying eyes.'

'At the moment all the evidence is against you. One

death may be misadventure, two a cruel conspiracy of circumstance, but any jury in England will call three murder.' Holmes looked implacable.

'I admit that it looks very bad for me but this is what happened. I got back to England last week and found cheap lodgings in the Seven Dials until I could get my bearings. I had not come back to kill those who had so basely left me to my death but to forgive them and to cure them. As I said, the serene attitude of those who had saved me had led me to revalue my ideas. After all, as we both know, the Hams are only the products of their own shortcomings and we all have them. I knew that they all had malaria as indeed I had had but the Mayas had cured me. I wanted to go back and forgive the Hams and cure them too.' (Did he intend that pun, I asked myself?)

'It was then that things started to go wrong.

'As you know, the Greeks gave curiosity a human form and it was Pandora, a woman. When she had opened the casket she had let out all the evils that would afflict mankind. When Mrs Parsons's curiosity got the better of her she let out the means of her own death. I had no hand in it but I knew that I had to flee or else reveal my identity which would have ruined my plan.'

'How so? I asked. 'If you had nothing to hide, why hide?'

'In my own mind I had forgiven the Hams. To have been seen to come back from the dead would have raked up the past and done nobody any good. It was my intention to do what I had come to do and go back with no one, except the Hams, any the wiser. My wish is to return to the Mayas and finish my life breathing their pure air. It was no good my forgiving the Hams without their knowing – I had to come back and prove that I meant it.'

Pennington's face was a study in sincerity and humility. Holmes remained impassive although I felt that he wanted to believe Pennington's every word. 'Carry on,' he said, without a trace of emotion.

'Several days ago I managed to get to Sibberton Hall. This "mop" had been in nearby Chipping Oversomer and so it was easy. I approached by the french windows and knocked. Moreton-Ashbee turned round, saw me and died.'

'Did you know that his family have a history of heart disorders?' I asked.

'No, I did not,' Pennington replied emphatically. 'I had always thought him as strong as the next man until he got malaria. His case was more severe than the others and I also liked him more than them. That's why I went to him first. I wanted to make my peace with him.'

'But you hated Wriggleton, if I remember rightly,' interjected Holmes.

'Indeed I did. He was a fop with a waspish tongue of the worst kind. He nearly did have a heart attack when I revealed my identity to him. I had intended to see them all together but the others were in the library at the time. He begged for mercy, tried to scream and generally behaved like the weakling that we both knew him to be. Eventually I was able to tell him my story but as I was doing so a bout of malaria started to come over him, probably caused by my unexpected appearance. I quickly lit one of my cigarettes and placed it between his lips. He coughed but seemed to become better. Then to my horror I saw the pink flush cover his skin and the smile come to his lips. Although the cigarette had my mildest dose – I smoke them regularly to ensure my own complete freedom from the disease – it proved too much for him. I had miscalculated, a thing the Mayas never did. My plan had gone all awry and I now had to escape. I threw the butt into the fire, as well as the unsmoked cigar that had fallen from Wriggleton's hand when I had introduced myself, and made my escape through the french windows whence I had come.'

Holmes pronounced judgement. 'If you go for trial, Pennington, you shall surely hang. What do you say, Stamford?'

'I agree.'

Pennington looked the personification of wretchedness. 'Perhaps we are the playthings of the gods after all,' he brooded. 'It's an old gnome of mine, "never try to unravel the weave of Fate or you will find yourself undone".'

We all sat in silence wondering what to do next. Suddenly the strained silence was broken by the horse outside neighing loudly. 'Oh, I have forgotten to feed her again. Excuse me, gentlemen. I must leave you for a moment,' said Madame Yalta, her voice now less than a screech. She lumbered from the caravan and closed the door.

'There is one way that you can prove your innocence, Pennington,' said Holmes.

'What is it? Anything. Holmes, and I shall do it. Anything.'

'Smoke one of those cigarettes that you gave to Wriggleton.'

Pennington boomed a hearty laugh, and the horse outside seemed to stamp its hooves in response. 'Is that all? Of course, Holmes, of course.' Just as he put one to his lips Holmes took it from him and closely inspected it. Having satisfied himself as to its authenticity and congruity with the one that he had found at Sibberton Hall he returned it. Pennington lit it and inhaled deeply. There was no effect at all.

'I know what you mean about strength of dosage,' remarked Holmes as Pennington continued his trial by ordeal. 'I have known two drops of laudanum kill one person, whereas another can drink it almost neat.'

Pennington finished the cigarette, a look of triumph on his powerful face.

'Another!' Holmes commanded. Pennington took another from his small case and lit up, drawing its smoke into his lungs, but as he did so Holmes darted forward and, snatching it from Pennington's surprised mouth, started to smoke it for himself. I studied Holmes closely but nothing happened. 'I am inclined to pronounce you innocent, Alexander,' he said as he finished it. We all smiled at each other and relaxed.

'Thank God that's over,' exclaimed Pennington. I let out a great sigh of relief. Pennington offered us both a drink but before I could reply I saw Holmes's face suddenly flush a pale pink.

'Quick, Holmes!' Pennington cried. 'Chew these!' He reached for another box but it was beyond even his great span. I leapt up and grabbed a box. 'No! No! Not that box! The other one!' he cried in despair. I gave it to him and he tore it open, giving Holmes a leaf from inside. 'Chew this. It's from the coca plant. One of the most remarkable drugs that the Mayas taught me about.' By now he held Holmes's head in one hand and jaw in the other making him chew but Holmes seemed to be fading fast. 'Quick, you take over here, Stamford. He needs an injection.'

In a moment he was back with a syringe and injected Holmes in the arm. 'We can only wait and hope,' he said, slumping down by Holmes who seemed to be experiencing both idyllic dreams and hideous nightmares at the same time.

'What is in those cigarettes?' I asked.

'A mixture of strong natural tobacco, some crushed Cinchona bark and a minuscule portion of tree frog poison.'

'And that has cured you of malaria?'

'So I believe.'

'What are those Coca leaves?'

'They are the most remarkable leaves that I have ever come across. The Mayas and Incas have chewed on them for years.'

'What happens?'

'They deaden the mouth and stomach to any feelings of hunger. They also act as a stimulant, removing all sense of fatigue and breathlessness. That is why I have given them to Holmes to combat this reaction to my mix.'

'It sounds a remarkable set of properties for just a few leaves,' I said, rather overawed.

'They are indeed remarkable, Stamford. Hunters use them to steady their nerves and to tackle tough terrain. In the old days of the Inca empire that stretched for thousands of miles along the west coast of South America it was possible for a letter to travel from one end of the empire to the other in three days simply by being carried by relays of runners chewing on these leaves. As you saw, I have refined it so that it can be administered intravenously. I hope we are not too late.'

'This Coca plant could be of enormous benefit to mankind, Pennington,' I said, ignoring his last remark.

'As could so much of these vanishing civilizations if we had the wit to see that. However, there is a bad side to this drug. It can become addictive because it stimulates and soothes all in one. I became addicted when the Mayas used it on me to deaden the pain of my amputations. They also cured me of my addiction. That was my worst experience of all. . . .' His voice trailed away at the thought.

Holmes was now sweating profusely, but all we could do was watch and wait. I asked Pennington about the box that I had picked up in error.

'That is my box of temptation. When I resolved on this enterprise to return to England I brought a Yucatan marsh toad with me. You don't know what that is? I am not surprised, it is only to be found in one small area of remotest Yucatan. It defends itself by being hideously ugly and unappetizing to the eye. However, it has a secondary defence system that it only uses when in fear of its life.'

'What is that?'

'It spits venom that does not kill. It paralyses other animals but can drive a man mad. There is no cure.'

'Sorry, I meant the noise outside.'

'Probably just Madame Yalta and her horse. It is her real beard, you know.'

Holmes seemed to be sleeping peacefully and the pink coloration had faded.

'You said that it was your box of temptation?'

'Yes. If I wished to do the Hams real harm it would have been most cruel not to kill them but to send them mad with me as the last remembrance they had of sanity. The toad would have been my instrument.'

A chill ran through me. This man had a cold, calculating mind the equal of Holmes. With his knowledge he could be a very dangerous man.

Without warning, the door of the caravan swung open and Madame Yalta rushed in. 'Quick, there are police looking for you, led by some swarthy sprat called Belly something.'

Pennington looked at me both fearful and pleading. 'You know that Bellaysarias can identify me and that I'll hang as things are. Please help me, Stamford.'

I was convinced of his innocence but I wished that Holmes would wake up and take the burden of decision from me. Holmes slept on and would not wake.

'Quick, quick,' urged Madame Yalta.

'I'll act as decoy,' I decided and leapt into action. 'Good luck, old man,' I said, stopping at the door and shaking Pennington's huge hand. He smiled his thanks and I was away.

'Holmes! Holmes!' I shouted. 'Where are you?'

In a moment the police and Bellaysarias, looking even more wild than when we had last met, had joined my bogus search. After nearly an hour I got back to Madame Yalta's caravan. Pennington was long gone and Holmes was coming round.

'What a remarkable cigarette,' he said, yawning.

'And essence of Coca leaf in your arm,' I added. He looked at the puncture mark in his arm.

'So that's what happens with coca leaves. I must carry out some experiments. I have never felt fitter or more alert. This is indeed a gift from the New World. Where is Pennington?'

I briefly outlined the events of the period during which Holmes had been out of action, including my conversation with Pennington. 'You say that Pennington has now flown? In that case why did he leave his frogs and Coca leaves?' said Holmes, pointing to the relevant boxes on the shelf on the far side of the caravan.

'Perhaps in the heat of the moment he forgot?' I submitted.

'Unless he is expecting to come back later to collect them. Where is Madame Yalta?'

'Helping the police with their enquiries. She agreed to be arrested as the person unknown at Sibberton Hall based on your deductions. She has an alibi and will be free shortly.'

At this revelation Holmes lapsed into thought. 'Pennington said that he had only joined this fair a few days ago and yet this Madame Yalta is willing to risk arrest on his behalf. She may know more than she is saying or Pennington has paid her well.'

'Perhaps she believes his story just as we do.'

'Possibly,' Holmes replied as he rose and approached the boxes of reptiles and plants. 'These are truly remarkable creatures,' he said, as he observed the frogs. 'They are no doubt why this caravan has been kept so hot. As for these leaves – wonderful!' He absent-mindedly removed one from its box, passed it under his nose and slipped it into his mouth.

'Good heavens!' I cried. 'The toad has gone!'

Holmes spun round, his brows an unspoken question. 'The Yucatan marsh toad!' I cried in anguish.

Holmes grasped the situation immediately. 'Quick. Sibberton Hall. Did you not realize that Pennington loved Edith Wriggleton? Bellaysarias is in great danger.'

Our carriage had long gone – on the orders of Count Bellaysarias. Holmes's energy was astonishing as we scoured the area for alternative transport. I suggested Madame Yalta's horse and caravan, and before long we were making our way towards Sibberton Hall although Holmes obviously found the going very slow. I half expected him to jump down and run ahead such was the high pitch of his nerves.

As we neared the end of our journey, dawn was making her blushing entrance in the east. Any thoughts of the beauties of Nature were soon dashed from our minds when we saw Sibberton Hall. It was in uproar with lights in every window and doors swinging open. On our arrival Edith Wriggleton rushed from the Hall to greet us, her hands wringing in despair.

'Alexis is gone. Mr Holmes, you must find him, I beseech you,' she blurted through her tears. 'Hodgson has been out all night but has found no trace.'

Holmes was soon on his track. The Moreton-Ashbee estates were extensive and Holmes frequently stopped to examine the ground and surrounding foliage. Several times he seemed to go wrong and scratched his chin as though deep in thought and then he dashed away off onto a new path. Suddenly all of Holmes's skills were rendered redundant as we heard a low moan, human yet wild. Every so often the moan would transform into a high-pitched scream that stopped us in our tracks.

Finally we came upon Count Bellaysarias. He was crouched on a rock by a small pond, his head twitching as though in nervous reaction to some unseen horror. When he saw the rising sun he screamed and when his eyes fell on the setting moon he moaned and wept. As we approached him he spat at us. Count Bellaysarias had obviously lost his wits.

Undaunted, Holmes advanced on the unfortunate Count, beckoning us to follow as he did so. The Count tried to retreat but we had surrounded him. In the ensuing furious struggle he tried to bite, scratch and gouge his way to freedom but we held firm against his struggles. When at last he gave up the uneven contest a great tear fell from his eye and his mouth gave vent to a torrent of words in a language totally unknown to me, but one word he kept repeating at the top of his voice, 'Tarleton, Tarleton.'

Had the delay in looking for transport made us too late to save him? Had Pennington carried out his revenge? Holmes had already described Bellaysarias as mad and everyone else believed that the strain of the previous few days and his unpredictable temperament had taken a final toll of him. If Pennington had engineered Bellaysarias's madness it was the perfect crime, as he was insensible and said nothing that could connect his condition with Pennington. Neither had anyone seen a strange figure with a rolling gait in the neighbourhood.

Miss Wriggleton remained devoted to her Count but I still held hopes of my own in that direction which finally came to nought over a year later. Did Pennington ever communicate with her again? If he did she never said.

Madame Yalta's alibi held good and she was released shortly afterwards. A police watch on her did not succeed in unearthing Pennington. The police took the frogs and the Coca leaves into custody. They then passed them on to Scotland Yard who, in turn, sent them to Bart's for analysis – Mr Sherlock Holmes carrying out the work.

When we left Oxfordshire, Holmes and I discussed the strange course of events. Coincidence had indeed played a major role and the truth looked as though it would remain elusive as a consequence. Holmes gave his verdict in a roundabout way.

'Did you know?' he asked, 'that when I was up at Oxford I used to go about in disguises following people as part of my training. Only one person ever saw through me because of his own great acting ability.'

'Pennington?'

'Pennington. I think that he has defeated me again and given one of his greatest performances.'

'How so?' I inquired, aghast at this suggestion.

'You heard Bellaysarias say "Tarleton"?' he asked.

'Indeed I did,' I replied. 'But there was no Tarleton, so I assumed him to be raving.'

Holmes drew on his briar through clenched teeth. 'Richard Tarleton was Elizabeth the First's favourite court jester who was the only one who could "undumpish" her when the mood was on her. Some believe him to have been the model for Yorrick and Bottom. In fact I shall call this case the Tarleton Murders because it has "undumpished" me – at least for the moment, until I can carry out tests on those remarkable leaves.'

'Murders, Holmes?' I expostulated. 'But was anyone murdered? Surely the sight of Pennington was enough to drive those craven Hams to their fates? And what proof is there that Pennington returned to Sibberton Hall to confront Bellaysarias?'

'Because the Festival Hams in their conceit felt that they were holding court and only one jester was able to endure them because he needed their money to finance his expeditions, and that same jester was able to keep them amused by his brilliance thus earning from them the Tarleton sobriquet in honour of Good Queen Bess's favourite.'

'Pennington?'

Holmes smiled, or at least what I took to be a smile from that most cold of men – it could have been a grimace of intense irritation – but said nothing. Exciting it might have been but I was not sure whether my companion was my cup of tea. I would have to wait and see.

The Case of Vamberry, the Wine Merchant

Mr Sherlock Holmes was a definite presence. When he first came to work in the chemical laboratories at Bart's, people were curious to find out about him. Thus they were most disconcerted when he turned the tables on his inquisitors by telling them far more about themselves than they had ever revealed to him and, in some cases, to anyone before. This made him the object of a great deal of speculation, much of it idle, but people kept well clear of this mysterious solitary student lest they should make an enemy of him. None dared to cross Mr Sherlock Holmes.

It was easy to appreciate this point of view. Although tall enough at slightly over six feet, his excessive leanness gave him the appearance of even greater height. His grey and black clothes perfectly complemented his gaunt sallow features which with their high cheekbones made him reminiscent of a Red Indian. His hair was black and glossy swept back over his head in the rather old-fashioned English style. This gave him the appearance of greater age and I often wondered whether this was a façade purposely cultivated in order to enable him to maintain a certain distance from the rest of the students. His austerity was intimidating.

However, it was Holmes's eyes that constantly attracted my attention. Sometimes they were as brilliant as quartzin, a polished jetstone which gave his face the look of a bird of prey hovering above its victim before the kill. At other times his eyes seemed a watery lacklustre grey as blank as an unwritten page which made him appear far from the affairs of man. I often wondered what thoughts were passing through his mind. His face gave no clue as to their substance.

Thus, the fanciful were wary of him and felt that Death and Sherlock Holmes were old companions.

It was when he was working on some problem of anatomy in the pathology laboratory that the fanciful notions about him seemed to take on greater credibility. He would work in total silence, his concentration almost tangible. His speed and efficiency as he dissected the cadaver were almost unnatural. He seemed to take on a ruthless animation as though fuelled by some inner fire whose intensity made it dangerous to venture too close to him. I was fascinated by him, despite myself. As I watched him at work, the hairs on the back of my neck would stand up and shivers run down my spine. Add to that the cold bareness of the mortuary, the melancholy hiss of the gas jets as they hoarsely sang their doleful threnody, and the long sharp shadows cast by his figure it was easy to see why some of the students feared him and called him Sherlock Bones, the Vampire Bat of Bart's.

This very strangeness drew me to him. Coming from a comfortable family background that had few sensations of excitement or adventure, I was keen to experience as much of life as I could. It was one of my reasons for choosing medicine as a career and not following my father into the family brewing business. There was more of life in the wards than in any tap room. Also I had thought that I would be doing my fellow man greater service by curing him than by intoxicating him. Life I had certainly seen on the wards but it was myself that I saw in the laboratories in the shape of Sherlock Holmes. My imagination was fired. I resolved to become his friend. Every time I saw him I would bid him a cheery salutation and pass an idle comment as to the weather or what was going on in the world. At first he did not seem to notice me. He only had eyes for his experiments. However, with time he would return my greetings and occasionally smile. He was at his most open when there was no one else in the laboratory to overhear us. Probably he was wary of my motives; I had something of a wild reputation and he probably did not wish to be associated with it. But when he saw that my overtures of friendship were genuine and that I was not doing it for effect, we would often chat for a moment or two before going our separate ways.

The attending of lectures was not my strong suit. Most of the students who went did not behave too respectfully and the lecturers only did it as a chore to be carried out as part of a contract. Such an unsatisfactory state of affairs tended to exacerbate my tendency to oversleep. Thus when I did arrive at the laboratory in the morning the only person in residence would be Sherlock Holmes as the other students would either be at the lectures or in the wards. It gave us a chance to talk undisturbed and he could be quite open when he wanted to be.

On one particular day I went into the chemistry laboratory and Holmes was perched on his stool intently studying an experiment still in progress in the glass apparatus.

'If I did not know better, Mr Holmes,' I said jovially, 'I would say that you have been sitting there all night. You're in just the same position as when I left yesterday.'

Without turning his attention from the experiment, Holmes replied, 'If you had looked closely before you spoke you would have seen quite clearly that I have been here all night, Mr Stamford. I have thirty-six hours' growth on my chin and this distillation of belladonna takes at least thirty-five. To get the complete picture of the changes involved, as I wish, my presence has been essential. The pad of notes by my hand would also have given you a clue as each observation clearly has the time marked next to it.'

I was a little nonplussed by all this but I was able to reply, 'In that case, you should be finished by the time I have made the coffee.'

'Thank you, Mr Stamford. I would appreciate a cup of your brew.'

'Any sugar today, Mr Holmes?'

'I think two today, if you would be so kind.'

I set up the apparatus: a Bunsen burner, a retort, a clamp and two beakers. In moments the coffee was bubbling merrily. I was wondering whether a modification of one of Baron Liebig's condensers might be a better way of preparing the coffee but concluded that what was good enough for the alchemists of Old England was good enough for me, when I became aware that Holmes was sitting next to me. It was quite eerie how he could move without detection.

'I hope you've cleaned these beakers, Mr Stamford. Most of them have had poison in them at one time or another you know.'

'More of your obscure experimentation?'

'I cannot tell a lie.'

We both laughed at the obvious allusion. Holmes could be splendid company. I felt like asking him why he shunned society so much but thought better of it. It did not take much for him to return into his shell, and now that he was out I wanted him to stay that way.

'How do you do it, Mr Holmes?' I asked, as I filled his beaker with the hot coffee. His brows became a question. 'Know so much about everyone. I'm sure you don't go checking up on us all; so what's the trick?'

He gave a friendly smile. Good, I thought, I have not offended him.

'If I were to explain it to you, you would probably find it so commonplace that you would dismiss it as a mere party trick.'

'Please tell me.'

'All it amounts to is the observation of details and the logical deduction as to their origin. It has taken me some years to carry out these observations and to understand these details but I think I now have the basis for logical explanations for most things.'

'I am still slightly in the dark.' I lied. I was completely in the dark.

'Would you care for a practical demonstration?'

I nodded in agreement.

'Give me your hands.'

I held them out to him, palms downward. He looked for a moment and told me to turn the palms upward. When I had, he looked even closer for only several moments more. 'I think that will be enough, thank you, Mr Stamford.'

'Well, what did you see?' I asked.

'Only what you can,' he replied.

I looked at my hands. They were just hands to me, with fingers and thumbs and all the usual component parts. This was proving to be rather perplexing but at least Holmes seemed to be enjoying himself to judge from his expression of diffident amusement.

'Come on, old chap,' I said, adopting my most friendly tones. 'Aren't you going to tell me what you've been able to deduce about me from my hands?'

'There is little to say apart from the fact that you once played the 'cello but gave it up for the piano which in turn you now are seriously contemplating giving up as well. My advice would be to continue. I think that you may well have a talent for it. As to your study of medicine, playing of rugby and drinking of Kentish beer, they too are clearly marked but everyone knows about them without having to seek confirmation in your hands.'

My jaw dropped in disbelief and so did my beaker of coffee. Holmes was obviously prepared for such a reaction and caught it before it hit the floor. No one except my closest family knew about my musical studies. They had meant a great deal to me but I feared the ragging of my rugby chums if ever they found out. Music to them meant changing the words of various hymns and popular melodies to suit their own outlandish humour. It did not mean the interpretation of Chopin or Beethoven or Mozart. If Holmes had been alive two centuries before, the Witchfinder Hopkins would have soon been on his trail.

'Come on, Holmes, how did you do it?'

'Everything was, ahem, to hand as it were. You have certain types of calluses on the tips of your fingers that come from playing a stringed instrument. If you observe, I have some from playing the violin. Yours are different. They are wider but also not so well developed. Thus you played an instrument with slightly wider strings than the violin and even the viola, but you have not played it for some time, hence the softening of the skin. The piano? Playing the piano develops a different set of muscles. As your hands are so small you have found it a struggle to reach an octave – there are definite stretch marks on your thumb and at the bases of your little fingers. However, even they show signs of receding – thus you have not been practising so much of late. Hence your serious contemplation of ceasing your studies.

'It was then that I cheated slightly. I also looked into your eyes – you really ought to wear your spectacles at the hospital. There's nothing wrong with having to wear them, particularly as your infirmity was caused by a disease in your childhood which was no fault of yours. Your eyes confirmed what I had seen in your hands. A certain sensitivity that it would be wrong to neglect in preference to your other pursuits. Need I go on?'

'Thank you, Holmes, no.' I stammered, which reminded me of one of the cruel nicknames that I had had to endure when I was a small boy – 'Stammerford'. Holmes probably knew about that too. 'Actually I was going to ask you,' I continued, regaining my composure, 'to come to dinner at my parents' home next week on the 27th. The Kentish Brewers' Association, of which my father is President this year, is honouring a guest from France who happens to be a chemist. I thought it might be up your street as you obviously count chemistry among your many studies and you've mentioned France rather knowledgeably in your conversation before now.'

'I suppose you want me to do party tricks for my supper?' Holmes replied, a little testily.

'No, no, I assure you I thought that you would be an ideal extra bachelor for the party. On top of that you will be the only one able to ask our guest any questions that might be of interest to him.'

At that Holmes seemed to soften. 'Who is this chemist who has endeared himself to the brewers of Kent?' he asked with a knowing look.

'Louis Pasteur.'

'In that case it would be a pleasure for me to attend your gathering, young Stamford.'

I chuckled to myself. This man would prove to my family that I was not all beer and skittles. I also noted that Mr Sherlock Holmes was susceptible to flattery. That might be useful later too.

* * *

As Fate would have it, at the last moment several guests had to cancel so that Sherlock Holmes ended up escorting my sister, and I became the extra bachelor. That was how they first met.

Although M. Pasteur had an international reputation by then, the dinner which my father was giving in his honour was a small affair of only eleven people. My mother had felt that M. Pasteur would be quite exhausted by official engagements and so would appreciate a more domestic setting which would put him at his ease. And so it proved. The meal went very well and everyone seemed to get on with each other. In particular I noticed that my sister seemed to enjoy the company of the tall solitary man next to her. She was put off neither by his singularity nor the fact that it was her first proper dinner party.

When the meal was over M. Pasteur insisted on thanking the cook and his hostess for such an enchanting meal and was roundly applauded by us all. The ladies then adjourned to the sitting room and the port was passed around the table among the gentlemen. The conversation was quite general about all those subjects which see the light of day only on occasions such as these.

Everyone (M. Pasteur, my father, Josiah Vamberry, Alderman Roach, Sherlock Holmes and myself) was most charming but the vacuity of the exchanges satisfied no one except perhaps the Frenchman who was not entirely at ease with the English language despite the regularity of his visits to our shores in the 1870s. I decided to get the ball rolling and asked M. Pasteur to explain about his experiments in England for the benefit of Holmes who was a stranger to Kent but not to the chemistry laboratory.

Before our learned guest could answer Holmes spoke up, saying, 'It is not necessary for M. Pasteur to burden himself with an explanation of his experiments into the fermentation processes of beer that he has been carrying out on behalf of the British Government. I have been able to follow them in the appropriate journals and must congratulate you, sir, on the excellence and accuracy of your observations in proving the role of micro-organisms such as yeast in the initial stages of these processes. They form the perfect complement to your work on wine, vinegar and silkworms, if I may say so, and perfectly rebut the ideas of the late M. Pauchet and the work of Baron Liebig. However, I would point out that my own experiments suggest that not even your answer has given us the whole picture – yet.'

We all sat dumbfounded by this, not least M. Pasteur. Holmes translated for him and his eyes sparkled with delight. The only scientist of whom I had heard in Holmes's exposition was Baron Liebig and that was only in my coffee-brewing exercises which were not the inspiration behind the Baron's condenser. M. Pasteur and Holmes chatted away like old friends. My father was very impressed and nodded his approval to me. Josiah Vamberry seemed more intent on drinking all my father's port – they had never been that close but he had recently gone into wine from beer and so my father thought that he might be a useful guest to have with a Frenchman at the table. He would not be much use if he carried on attacking the port. Alderman Roach was little better, but his presence was dictated by business and social pressures.

I was just about to interrupt the conversation to ask the participants to at least speak a few words in English so that we could follow what was obviously a most lively and absorbing talk, but my father murmured to me, 'Let them carry on. I have a lot to thank M. Pasteur for and I'm glad to see him enjoying himself so much in my house.' I smiled in triumph; a look not lost on my father. 'Thank you for bringing him, son. Whoever he is.'

M. Pasteur had obviously seen our aside and started to speak in English again. At that my father tried to bring Vamberry into the conversation. 'You may not know it, M. Pasteur,' he began, 'but you are sharing a table with a man who has one of the largest stores of top-class claret in his cellars in the whole of England.' At that M. Pasteur looked across to the other guests. My father indicated Josiah Vamberry.

My father continued. 'When I decided to brew my beer according to your suggestions I won an export order from the British Government to ship it to all parts of the Empire. Your new process, M. Pasteur, has enabled beer to keep so much better that when it arrives in those far-off stations of the Empire our boys can actually get a taste of home instead of the bile they had to put up with before.' (Port had obviously loosened my father's tongue.) 'I beat Vamberry here to the government contract, but instead of going under – as we all thought he was going to – he took on a new lease of life and emptied his cellars of beer, replacing them with the finest Bordeaux. Didn't you, Josiah?'

'That I did, Stamford,' replied the wine merchant.

'You know France well then, monsieur?' asked M. Pasteur.

'Hardly at all,' answered the rubicund Vamberry.

'At least you know the wines of Bordeaux and that is probably France enough, eh monsieur?'

'I only know the ones to buy.'

'Which do you like best? I believe the Lafite '74 is greatly favoured in England.'

'So I believe, M. Pasteur, not that I have tasted it myself.'

'Ah, too young, yes? We French are accused of drinking our wine too young but you English always drink it when it is too old.'

'I wouldn't know about that, M. Pasteur.'

'Which wines do you have in your cellar, Mr Vamberry?' asked Holmes.

'I don't carry the list with me but they are all first growths representing all the vintages from 1874 to this year.'

'Such as?' persisted Holmes.

'Mouton, Palmer, Leoville, Latour, Yquem and plenty of others. They're all first class or, *"premier crus"* as they say.'

'Yet you have not sold any of them?'

'No. Here, wait a minute; how did you know that?'

'Your thumb, left knee, right sock and shirt collar.'

Holmes had done it again. Perhaps he was not intending to play party tricks but he certainly knew how to stop the show.

'Have you invested any money in any of Mr Vamberry's wine enterprise, Mr Stamford?' Holmes asked my father leaving Vamberry open-mouthed.

'Why yes I have, Mr Holmes. Not that I see that it is any concern of yours if I may say so.'

'If it is in wines already bought then you are safe. If it is in vineyards themselves then you must prepare for a loss if you do not get your money out now.'

My father had grown flushed with indignation at the interference that Holmes seemed to be making in his business affairs but was calmed by the unruffled way in which Holmes had spoken. Vamberry started to bluster.

'Now steady on, Mr Busybody. Who's the expert on wine around here, you or me?'

Holmes fixed him like an insect to a card with one look of his penetrating grey eyes. His words were like rapier thrusts. 'That you are in reduced circumstances at the moment is evident from the fact that you cleaned your own shoes before coming out tonight. You had already changed into your dining suit as is evinced by the smudge of boot black in your right thumb nail and the mark on your sock. The mark on your knee shows that you knelt down during this process. The state of your shirt collar serves to confirm my observations on your present reduced circumstances.

'As to the wines in your cellar they are indeed all first class if they are what you say they are, but they are not all *premier crus* if you count Palmer, Mouton and Leoville in their number. Yquem is of course first class. It is also a Sauternes not a Bordeaux. Even the most cursory glance at the classification of 1855 would have shown you that. Thus your advice on wine is not to be trusted, hence my advice to Mr Stamford.'

Vamberry looked like an animal that had been cornered. M. Pasteur came to his rescue.

'Perhaps Mr Stamford's excellent and most generous hospitality has made Mr Vamberry a little forgetful over details. They can be so confusing, even we French do not know where we are. Every winemaker believes his wine to be a *premier cru* no matter what the official classification might say. You may not be rich now but take my words for it, Mr Vamberry, you soon will be.'

M. Pasteur had spoken with such gravity and assurance that we all turned to him in amazement. Vamberry was not sure whether to bolt or stay. He stayed. M. Pasteur went on to explain. 'In the early 1850s the Bordeaux region wines were attacked by a small mushroom growth which attacked the vines and grapes when they were young.'

'Was that the *Oidium tuckerii*?' asked Holmes.

'That is true, my friend' replied the great scientist. 'It was first observed by an Englishman named Tucker in a greenhouse in your Margate on some plants that had come from one of your tropical colonies. How they got to France no one knows, but what destruction they caused when they arrived. Two whole vintages were lost to the Bordelais.

'Many remedies were tried. Sulphur proved to be a mixed blessing. It killed the mushrooms but much of the wine either tasted of it or went flat. Later, more efficient sprays were developed and the *oidium* was conquered. But there was one lasting effect.'

With the timing of the natural speaker M. Pasteur paused for a moment. A slight cough and he was off again. 'There was a very steep ascent in prices and they never went back to their previous levels, even in 1858 when there was a very large crop.'

'How does this affect Mr Vamberry?' I asked. 'Has the *oidium* come back?'

'If it had then we could conquer it again with our sprays. No, it is something much worse that threatens the whole crop and . . .' his voice lowered, '. . . even the entire economy of France herself if it is not controlled.'

We shot speculative glances at each other. Vamberry did not know whether to smile or not at the evident distress of the French scientist. M. Pasteur gathered himself and continued.

'It is a small creature. An aphid that can produce at least ten generations in a year. It attacks the sap of the vines. Sometimes these aphids stay in the roots and so they are not noticed until it is too late. Already Blaye, Libourne and St Emilion have been devastated but last year it was first seen in the Medoc. By next year M. Vamberry's wine may be worth more than rubies.'

I expected Vamberry to look pleased with himself. I had never liked him and knew that there was no love lost between my father and him. However, when I looked at him I was surprised to see not pleasure but complete incredulity as though he had bought a lottery ticket without much expectation of a prize let alone the jackpot which had fallen into his unprepared lap. Holmes too had noted this and turned to M. Pasteur.

'Monsieur, am I right in saying that it is the *phylloxera* that Professor Westwood of Oxford University first studied in 1863?'

'Ah, *phylloxera vastatrix*, Mr Holmes, is this fiend's proper name,' replied the Frenchman with passion. 'I should have realized that you would have known of it.'

'Is there no treatment for it?' I asked.

'There have been many suggestions but the Bordelais are a conservative people when it comes to their wine. They do not like untried methods.'

Holmes sat in thought for a moment. 'Speaking as an outside observer, M. Pasteur, I would say that logically there are only three possible ways of combating this menace.'

'Oh, M. Holmes, if you could save the vines, France would be in your debt forever.'

'Firstly, a chemical compound which attacks the aphids would appear to be an obvious solution.'

'We have tried ammonia and sulphuric acid, but with no real success.'

'What about a less obvious sulphur compound such as a bisulphide with copper or carbon? Better still, a potassium sulphur carbonate could be the answer.'

It was the turn of M. Pasteur to ponder. 'I see your point, M. Holmes. I will note it down and give them to my assistant M. Gayon. What are your other two suggestions?'

'Secondly, I would suggest a coal tar derivative brushed over the plants before the aphids can get into the sap. It will mean getting rid of those vines presently affected but new vines properly insulated might stand a chance.'

'It is true, it is true, *mon ami*. Are you saving your best answer until the last, M. Holmes?'

'My last suggestion is so obvious that I almost dismissed it.' M. Pasteur's face fell but he persevered.

'Please, M. Holmes, anything,' he said desperately.

'Obviously these aphids came from somewhere. Trace them to their origin and see how the flora have coped with them there. It may be that there is no more flora there as a result of the *phylloxera* but it is worth a look. Nature has a way of dealing with its malefactors,' said Holmes, looking at Vamberry who shuffled uncomfortably on his seat. Vamberry threw back the remains of his port and stood up on two unsteady legs.

'I'm not going to stay here to be insulted by some will-o'-the-wisp friend of college boys. I'm off.'

With that he lurched from the table. 'I shall want to see you about this Josiah Vamberry,' remarked my father sternly to his departing guest. 'Tomorrow will do nicely.'

'We'll see about tomorrow, Stamford. Are you coming, Roach?' He shouted at the alderman who seemed to have fallen asleep. When roused he joined the wine merchant in making his exit.

M. Pasteur turned to Holmes. 'I know that soon my assistant M. Ullysse Gayon is to take over the post of professor at the Station Agronomique in Bordeaux I recommended him myself. I shall recommend you to him also.'

Holmes smiled wryly, 'I thank you, M. Pasteur, but I have work in London that I cannot afford to miss.'

At this I pricked up my ears. What work was this? It seemed more a question of not being able to afford to make the trip. M. Pasteur beat me to it. 'M. Holmes, *mon ami*, I have only to whisper a word and the French government will roll a red carpet to your door. I insist you come.'

'It would be just the sort of problem for you, Holmes,' I enthused.

'In that case, M. Pasteur, it would be churlish of me to say "non".'

'Already France is in your debt, monsieur.'

Holmes was away for several months. At least I assume that he was as I did not see him for some time but then his visits to the laboratory tended to be sporadic. Thus it was with some surprise that I bumped into him one bright spring morning poring over an experiment as though he had never been away.

'Hallo there, Holmes,' I cried, very pleased to see him and anxious to hear his story. He did not immediately reply as his attention was fully directed to his work.

'Good morning, Stamford,' he eventually replied. 'Out of training, I see. Surely you're a cricketer as well as a rugby man?'

I chose to ignore his observations as I was too intent on hearing his news about the fight against *phylloxera* in Bordeaux. 'It's you I'm interested in, Holmes, not my sporting abilities. Have you succeeded?'

'Oh, yes. It was obviously chicken blood substituted to make it look as though there had been a struggle when in fact they had been in league from the start.'

'What on earth are you talking about, Holmes?'

'Mortimer Maberley. A mere trifle really but not without an educational value.'

'I wouldn't know anything about that, Holmes. No, I mean the vines and M. Pasteur. The *phylloxera*.'

'Oh, that. It was very straightforward.'

'Come, come, Holmes, if it was that simple M. Pasteur and M. Gayon would have solved it before they asked you to help. The French do not call on the British for help unless they are in *extremis*.'

'I would remind you, young Stamford, that I am part French myself, as I revealed to M. Pasteur during our conversation at your father's table.'

'Which one of your suggestions worked?' I prompted, resorting to flattery. Holmes responded.

'They all had some merit but it was my third suggestion of studying the source of the infection that seems to me the most likely to succeed.'

'Go on,' I urged.

'It appears that the *phylloxera* is native to the eastern seaboard of the United States and that when vines from that part of the world were planted in France they took the peat with them. There was an outbreak in the Herault district of the Midi between 1832 and 1840 which can be traced back to American vines.'

'So some had been brought over from the USA to the Gironde last year?' I asked.

'Certainly there were some then and just before, but as early as 1860 there were American vines in the general Bordeaux area. In fact one of the growers, a M. Laliman, suggested that the only way to save the vines would be by either replanting with the resistant American vines or at least grafting them to the existing French ones.'

'The French would not do that,' I cried.

'They seemed very reluctant. M. Laliman first made his suggestion about ten years ago. but as M. Pasteur said, the Bordelais are very conservative when it comes to their beloved wine. They say that American vines produce wines "*avec un gout de renard*" which is unacceptable to them. But I feel that this is the only alternative to widespread destruction. Several growers have already become bankrupt because of failed crops.'

At this my heart skipped a beat. Holmes realized that I was worried and shot a questioning look at me. 'Apparently after your revelations about Vamberry at the dinner party for M. Pasteur, my father and he had a terrible row and they have been daggers drawn ever since.' Little did I realize the irony of my words until I arrived back at my lodgings for lunch.

My landlady greeted me with a worried look as she opened the door. Standing behind her, looking the picture of a damsel in distress, was my young sister. She ran to me and blurted out her story between sobs.

'It's father and that awful man Vamberry. They had an argument. Later Vamberry was found dead – his throat cut. The police have arrested father. You must come immediately and bring Mr Holmes with you!'

I dashed off a note to Holmes and was on my way back to Lee in Kent with my sister within half an hour. It was a gloomy household that awaited us. Mother just sat by the fire, her face buried in her hands. I tried to comfort her but she felt that all was lost. She explained that father was invested heavily in Bordeaux vineyards taking Vamberry's advice as to the choice of the particular chateaux. Three had gone bankrupt and the other two looked as though they would soon follow suit. When he had heard the news father had gone to find Vamberry. He found him in his wine cellars and there was a furious altercation. The employees upstairs had heard it all. My father had even been heard to threaten to kill Vamberry, whose reply had been, 'Business is business, as you showed over the government beer contract.' Next thing there were the sounds of a scuffle and my father appeared at the top of the stairs with an ashen face and blood on his knuckles. The employees rushed downstairs and found their master with his throat cut. The police thought that they had an open-and-shut case, despite my father's protestations of his innocence. This was indeed a devastating chapter of events and I prayed for the arrival of Sherlock Holmes.

Holmes arrived within minutes of my mother telling me the story. She repeated it for Holmes who was tact and kindness itself to my mother in her moments of despair. Perhaps I have given the reader the impression that Holmes was arrogant and vain whose only weakness was a susceptibility to flattery. There were times when his machine-like ways and emotionless comments could hurt but to give him his due he was also susceptible to kindliness. It was that side that we all saw now. No wonder my sister had romantic thoughts for Holmes. Little did she know the man in charge of the machine.

He looked very serious after hearing my mother's story. He pondered for a few moments and asked how many employees did Vamberry have. 'Two, I believe,' my mother answered.

Then he said, with a warmth that reassured us all, 'I can see several rays of light but you must not build up false hopes. First I have to see Mr Stamford and the police inspector in charge of the case. Will you come with me, Stamford? I am a tyro in these affairs and a member of the family in attendance would probably help smooth the introductions with the official force.'

Inspector Craggs at the local police station looked on Holmes very suspiciously but was eventually prevailed upon to allow him to visit my father.

My father's haggard face shocked me, it was in such a contrast to his usual jovial expression. He rushed to greet me and hugged me without restraint. 'Thank God you've come and brought Mr Holmes with you,' he cried, pumping my companion's hand with both his own. Hope seemed to be rekindled within his breast and he began to look like his more usual self.

Holmes's first question lacked nothing in directness: 'Did you murder Vamberry, Mr Stamford?'

My father threw up his hands in despair. 'You must believe me, Mr Holmes, I did not. No, I tell you. I know it looks bad with the argument, my threats and the fight. But as true as I am sitting here begging for your help, Mr Holmes, Vamberry was alive when I left him in the cellar. He would have had a black eye and a bloody lip, but I left him alive.'

Holmes looked at my father's hands. If only he could achieve the same miracle that he had when he had looked at mine, I thought.

'You boxed in your youth,' remarked Holmes.

'Indeed I did, Mr Holmes. I was area champion for a time.'

'Then if you wish to thrash someone you have no need of a knife to discharge your purpose.'

'I suppose not.'

Holmes asked about my father's finances. He admitted that they had taken a severe knock with the failing of the various chateaux in which he had invested but he had not lost everything yet. The export contract with the Government was still intact and if economies were made elsewhere he felt that the crisis could be withstood.

'Then your wife's despair was merely concerning your arrest for murder?'

'Merely!' I cried, but Holmes would not be deflected and continued to address my father.

My father looked ill at ease. 'No, there is more, Mr Holmes.' He looked at me as though he had a guilty conscience. 'I had hoped to encourage my lad here back into the business by settling a rich endowment on him when he qualified. I also hoped to make a rich woman of my daughter at her coming of age. That is what tempted me into this speculation. There will now be very little for them when they come of age. I'm sorry, my son.'

'There's no need to worry about us, father. We shall pull through; it's you who is our worry now.'

'There's more, lad. I was in line for a knighthood and a royal warrant. I'll not see those again and I doubt that you will, even if you take over the business.'

Holmes gave a murmur which seemed to be full of philosophy as though he had seen it all before and was wondering why on earth we humans continue to make the same mistakes. 'The desire for wealth and social status,' he said, 'will destroy morality more completely than any *phylloxera* will wither a vine.'

'You must not think too harshly of me, Mr Holmes,' pleaded my father.

I had never seen him like this before. He had always been so self-assured but he had never been charged with murder before. Holmes made some reassuring noises and left us to say our goodbyes.

By the time I had reached the inspector's office Holmes was already in conversation with him. 'No, I'm afraid that I cannot allow you to do that. It's a Scotland Yard job now, sir,' said the inspector. 'I expect them at any moment.'

'Who is in charge of the case?'

'An Inspector Lestrade,' replied Inspector Craggs.

'I hope no one is taking my name in vain,' said a rodent-like man who entered the office without knocking. 'Well upon my soul, if it isn't Mr Sherlock Holmes.'

'Inspector Lestrade,' returned Holmes. 'How pleasant to see you again. Victor Lynch still at large, is he?'

The newly arrived inspector grimaced painfully at what I took to be a jibe by Holmes.

'You know each other then?' asked the bemused Inspector Craggs.

'Our paths have crossed,' volunteered the Scotland Yard specialist ruefully.

'I was just telling this Mr Holmes,' continued Inspector Craggs, 'that he can't go to the scene of the crime.'

'Don't worry, Craggs, he can come with me after you've told me the story and I've seen the suspect. Mr Holmes may not be a professional but he has his uses.'

'You are most kind, Inspector,' replied Holmes, with no small hint of humour.

We were forced to wait for over an hour while the Scotland Yard official interviewed Inspector Craggs and then my father. When he reappeared Holmes and I stood up in expectation of our departure to the scene of Vamberry's demise but Lestrade was obviously revelling in his position of authority and as centre of attention. 'Not so fast, gentlemen,' he said to us, 'I have still to read the statement of the two employees.'

'Oh you can do better than that, sir,' interjected the large, amiable-looking desk sergeant of the local force. 'We still have Mr Beal and Mr Wilson here in the off-duty room while my wife types their statements for them to sign. Shall I get them for you, sir?'

'That's a bit of luck. Yes, Sergeant. Send them to me in the interview room.'

With that Lestrade turned away from us without a word as he went about his official business. During this entire forced inactivity in the police station I had been unable to sit still in my state of perturbation. By contrast Holmes had hardly moved a muscle. He had sat as motionless as a statue, a distant look in his eyes and smoke lazily meandering from his pipe. However, as two powerful-looking men appeared from a side door, Holmes's face took on that eagle-like aspect that I had noticed before when he observed some phenomenon minutely. Far from being put out by Holmes's attention the two men swaggered past us with a sneer not far from their faces. As their backs disappeared into the interview room Holmes leapt into action. 'Who were those two men, Sergeant?'

'They're Mr Vamberry's two assistants at the wine merchant's, sir.'

'What do you know of them?'

'Not a great deal, really. I do know that they like a drink and a bit of fun.'

'How long have they been in Mr Vamberry's employ?'

'I don't rightly know, sir, but certainly a couple of years.'

'What are their names?'

'Beal and Wilson. The dark one's Beal.'

Holmes wrote out a note and handed it to the sergeant. 'Could you use your communication system to get this to Scotland Yard, Sergeant? It's very important.'

'I don't know about that, really I don't,' the countryman replied, slowly rubbing his large round chin with one hand and holding the note at arm's length with the other. 'I'll have to see.'

'Please, Sergeant, I am in deadly earnest,' pleaded Holmes with an openness that I had never seen in him before. I was deeply touched that it was my father's plight that had so affected him.

The sergeant continued to delay but finally he went into a back room, to emerge a few moments later smiling kindly to Holmes, 'I've got young Simpson onto it. It won't take long.'

As Holmes rejoined me, I asked him urgently, 'You have a theory, Holmes?'

'Four,' he replied, taking on his mantle of immobility again. Once more I was enmeshed in my animation.

Several minutes passed. Then, as the door of the interview room opened, Holmes sprang up and was over to it in a moment, crashing into the two assistant wine merchants in his haste. In the confusion he took Lestrade aside and whispered urgently to him. Lestrade replied to his words with a suspicious look. Holmes continued to remonstrate with him. At last Lestrade made his decision, motioned to a constable who disappeared to the cells, and called after the two assistants, 'Excuse me, gentlemen, before you go. I have to inspect the scene of the crime and I would greatly appreciate your assistance.'

'Of course, sir. Anything we can do to help,' they cried.

'I'm glad you said that. You have been model citizens and I knew I could rely on you.'

The two men exchanged a triumphant smile.

'Therefore,' continued Lestrade, 'Could I trouble you for your boots?'

The two men exchanged a nervous grimace.

'We were hoping to go out soon,' said Wilson rather limply.

'I'm sure you were, sir, but we shall not be long, Sergeant,' cried Lestrade. 'Make Mr Beal and Mr Wilson comfortable till we get back. One of your wife's cups of tea would be greatly appreciated, I'm sure. Ah, thank you, gentlemen,' concluded Lestrade taking up the proffered boots. The constable returned from the cells with what I instantly recognized to be my father's boots.

'Now, if we are all ready, let us be on our way,' commanded the rat-like policeman.

At last we were on our way to the scene of the tragedy.

'I'm risking making myself look a fool, Mr Holmes,' murmured Lestrade as we sat in the police van. 'Don't let me down, I can be a very tenacious opponent, you know.'

'Inspector I can only discover facts; not invent them.'

'I'm not after facts – I'm after the murderer.'

'And promotion,' I muttered under my breath.

'What's that, young fella?'

'Nothing, Inspector.'

When we arrived at the wine merchant's establishment, a very old building with a long and frequently dubious past,

Lestrade suggested that I might find the sight of a man with his throat open too much for my stomach. In return, I protested that my medical studies had made me proof against any such qualms. Holmes intervened, 'I would prefer it, young fellow. There's probably enough confusion down there already without you adding to it.'

Thus I had to wait upstairs. They were away for a good hour. At last they re-emerged, Holmes's expression one of good-humoured relief rather similar to that of a school-master who has at last been able to explain something very simple to an uncomprehending pupil and Lestrade's rather like a pupil who has at last been able to grasp something hitherto incomprehensible. He was vigour itself. 'Come on, men,' he shouted, 'back to the station. Look lively and have your truncheons, ready.'

Away they charged as though the Heythrop had just caught sight of a fox. They completely forgot Sherlock Holmes and young Stamford. I looked at Holmes bemused. He smiled back at me patting me on the shoulder. 'By the time we have walked back to the station, your father will be ready to accompany us back to his house a free man.'

I can't remember how I reacted, only the feeling of joy that I felt. Holmes, on the other hand, instead of the triumphant gleam in his eyes that I had expected, had that faraway look in them. 'What is it, Holmes?'

'There is more to this case than meets the eye. But come, let us hurry or we shall miss the fun.'

When we had regained the Lee police station it was alive with activity, the principals being Lestrade, Craggs and the desk sergeant. Lestrade was berating them for their incompetence and foolishness, they in turn were flushed of face and shuffling of feet.

'Thank God you're here, Mr Holmes,' cried Lestrade on

catching sight of my companion. 'These two have only let them go,' he gasped in despair.

'But, sir' returned the sergeant, 'they were in uniform, had a warrant and had the men's boots with them.'

'Then what are these?' roared Lestrade, holding up the assistants' boots.

'We were not to know, sir,' opined Craggs.

'Get out looking for them, or you'll be back on the beat permanently,' fulminated the exasperated Scotland Yarder. He then held his head in his hands.

'To think that I had Brooks and Woodhouse in custody and they let them go.'

Sherlock Holmes looked about him a picture of self-possession in the confusion. 'I think that the man you are ultimately hunting is extremely tall and thin. He has a prominent, domed forehead relatively untouched by the sun's rays. His eyes are dark and deeply sunken into his head. He has rounded shoulders but, most remarkable of all, his head has a curious reptilian oscillation that makes it constantly move from side to side in a slow rhythm.'

'Why, that's the very man who called himself Chief Inspector John Morrissey when he came for Beal and Wilson,' spluttered the desk sergeant.

Lestrade looked up at Holmes in awe. 'How on earth did you work that out, Mr Holmes?'

Holmes smiled. 'We amateurs have our methods too, Inspector. May I have a copy of these?' he asked, holding up some photographs.

'Help yourself,' replied the deflated Lestrade.

Half an hour later we were back in my father's house and the tears of happiness flowed as the family was reunited after such a terrible ordeal. Sherlock Holmes stood by impassively. My sister ran over to him to thank him for the miracle that he had wrought and even attempted to kiss his cheek. Holmes was unbending and the moment passed. We all begged him for an explanation which he freely gave as he sat by our fire, the blaze made more merry by our joy.

'I was anxious to examine Vamberry's wine cellar. No wine had been shipped since last March. Another shipment was due but I suspected that he had not bought this year if his contacts were as good as I suspected. Thus a year's deposit of dust would be on the floor and would leave many clues to the trained eye. There is no branch of detective science which is so important nor so much neglected as the art of tracing footsteps. I expected certain traces but I was resolved not to theorize until I had actually seen them for myself. Then the first of my surprises happened.'

'What was that, Mr Holmes?' asked my wide-eyed sister.

'When Vamberry's two assistants appeared I knew that I had seen them before but not as Beal and Wilson, assistants to a wine merchant. Disguises are a speciality of mine and so I have developed a method for looking through those of others. Of all the features of the face that are not usually altered in any way in a disguise it is the ears that remain true to the original. More than that, it is the ear lobes that escape the attention of the make-up artist, as Oichi in Japan discovered to his cost several centuries ago. Thus, whenever I have studied a face the lobes form my focus of attention and when Beal and Wilson passed us in the police station I knew that they were impostors.'

He then took the photographs from his pocket. 'I had the sergeant send for these to Scotland Yard.' He took up a pencil and drew on them. Then he held them up to us.

'Beal and Wilson,' cried my father.

Holmes then took an eraser from his waistcoat pocket and after working on them held up the photographs again. 'Brooks and Woodhouse, the murderers in the Queen Street Outrage of twelve months ago,' explained Holmes. 'They disappeared from the scene of the crime and have not been seen since. We now know that they have been able to operate from Vamberry's of Lee with impunity. Very clever.'

'I'll say,' I agreed.

'But it struck me as being too clever for them. Next we come to Vamberry's wine cellar. As I thought, there were plenty of footprints in the dust. I was able to demonstrate to Lestrade that Brooks and Woodhouse had gone down into the cellar after Mr Stamford had left because in no less than eight places their footprints clearly overlay Mr Stamford's. Thus when Vamberry's body was found deep within the cellar with none of Mr Stamford's footprints around him it was clear that this murderer was someone else, particularly as Vamberry's footprints were overlaid by his assistants and that many of those prints suggested a struggle.

'That was all clear enough, but who was the other man who had stood by and witnessed it all?'

We all gasped in surprise at this revelation.

'Not only that, but before Mr Stamford had arrived on the scene he had walked the entire length of the cellar with Vamberry and tested all of the barrels except for one in the far corner which was empty. That Vamberry was in awe of him was evident from his footprints which revealed reticence. On the other hand, the other footprints revealed resolution and from the distance that they were apart he was taller than myself. Yet he took no part in the argument when Mr Stamford appeared. In fact he went to great lengths to conceal himself. You did not see him did you, Mr Stamford?'

'Indeed not, Mr Holmes.'

'He blew out the candle and re-lit it using two Lucifer matches to do so when you had left. Obviously he was a very interested party in the wine. A buyer perhaps? Then why kill Vamberry? It would not decrease the cost of the wine. Thus was he a partner who wished to exclude Vamberry from the proceeds of their coup? This seemed a reasonable hypothesis.

'But how did Brooks and Woodhouse fit into this? Vamberry did not have the money to employ anyone thus they must be his partner's creatures. So this partner was not just a business man. He employed murderers to keep an eye on his investment. It is also noticeable that these murderers have been at work during their employ at Vamberry's. Would this be on their own initiative? I doubt it. Thus this man was probably the brains behind the Queen Street Outrage. He is obviously a dangerous criminal and you have had a fortunate escape, Mr Stamford.'

My mother clasped my father's hand.

'He also has a clear brain that can retain its clarity during a crisis. After your intervention in the cellar he had Vamberry murdered and you were the obvious suspect. Thus the testimony of the two assistants would have been enough to hang you.'

'But he reckoned without you, Holmes,' I cried.

'Without the dust in the cellar, Stamford,' he returned. 'As I told you, the study of footprints is a sorely neglected art.'

'But if it had been left to Lestrade, father would be up for trial now. It was you who explained what the marks in the dust meant, Holmes.'

Holmes looked genuinely pleased. Flattery again, I thought.

'It is obvious that there is a highly organized gang. Look how easily they sprang Brooks and Woodhouse from the police station,' added my father.

'Quite so, Mr Stamford, but this leader is far more intelligent than any man that I have ever come across in my study of crime. It is he who introduced *phylloxera* into the Medoc with the idea of winning a great profit from his investment and destroying the economy of France.'

We sat in a stunned silence.

'How do you know it was he?' I asked.

'The desk sergeant in Lee police station told me,' he replied. 'When I described this man he said that it was the same man who as James Morrissey had secured the release of Brooks and Woodhouse.'

'I still don't quite see the connection,' said my mother.

'When I was in France studying the *phylloxera*, I met a Pinkerton man from New York. He told me that there had been a man in the eastern states of the USA who had been asking questions about *phylloxera*. He said that he found him suspicious – no doubt the professional nose again that Lestrade believes that he has acquired – and traced him to France before losing him. He described his man and it was that description that I gave to the desk sergeant, based on an intuition and the footprints in the dust of a cellar in Kent.'

We all sat bemused by these riches. 'Who is this man, Holmes?' I asked.

'Aliases are something else that I have put my mind to; it is quite remarkable how many people when choosing an alias retain an initial, syllable or rhythm of one of their names. Beal and Brooks, Wilson and Woodhouse are obvious examples. Thus James Morrissey's true identity should not be too far from that name.'[1]

My father looked at Holmes with a very serious look on his face. 'I have to thank you for my life and liberty, Mr Holmes, but the more I think about it the more I feel that

---

[1] Sherlock Holmes took the name Sigerson on his travels during the Great Hiatus.

in saving me you have put yourself at risk from this man Morrissey. Such a man will bear no opposition to his plans. When he discovers your part in this affair it will only end when one of you lies dead.'

'Oh, pray don't say that, Papa,' cried my sister.

Holmes smiled grimly. 'I feel that you are right, Mr Stamford. Vamberry died because by trying to break you with his false advice he brought attention to himself and thus the operations of this gang. He had to be silenced. I shall be intrigued to see who comes forward to claim the contents of Vamberry's cellar but now I have some work to catch up on.'

I showed my father's saviour to the door full of gratitude for his inspired intervention. 'Holmes, what can I say, how can I thank you?' I exclaimed, almost stammering in my excitement. Holmes turned to face me.

'Surely it is I who should be thanking you, Stamford,' he replied imperiously. 'It was a pleasing little problem which although not difficult in itself has enabled me to steal a march on a highly accomplished adversary. I only hope to be able to maintain my advantage. His name, I must have his name,' he muttered, oblivious to my pleas.

There are two postscripts to this story.

Several days after Vamberry's death was announced in the London *Times*, a lawyer from Lincoln's Inn came forward claiming to represent an American client. All the documentation was in order including Vamberry's signature and so the wine was shipped to the USA where it made very high prices at auction. The lawyer was never heard of again.

When, in the fullness of time, Victor Lynch the forger was arrested, Holmes was more than instrumental in the operation. As a reward he was allowed to interview Lynch and so learn that he had forged Vamberry's signature on the documentation that had enabled the wine to be shipped to the USA for auction. Lynch refused point blank to reveal the name of the man who had required the forgery, becoming terrified for his life. Neither the 'carrot' nor the 'stick' could draw the name from him. Finally he told Holmes that, 'If you put an 'eart in Mr Morrissey then the name might come to you.'

The Adventure of the Old Russian Woman

'Would you object to breaking the law, young Stamford?'

'Not in the least!' I replied, and so became involved in the story of Olga Pleshkarova.

Sherlock Holmes was standing next to me as I removed the ruptured spleen of an old lamplighter who had been knocked down and killed by a runaway horse the previous day. The ruptured spleen was not the immediate cause of death but by the time I had been allowed anywhere near the corpse it was all that remained of any interest. As I turned to face my companion I realized that he was in a high state of excitement. His eyes shone from his gaunt sallow features and his every sinew seemed to be quivering with eager anticipation. He was wearing a capped greatcoat and close-fitting grey cloth cap. In his hand he carried a canvas bag that obviously contained some very heavy items.

'The tools of the trade,' he confided with a smile. 'I think you had better wash up before you come with me, I don't want to attract even more attention to myself.'

I looked at my rather stained hands and apron and hurried to the sink to clean up. In a few moments we were stepping out into the snowy January weather. Holmes's tall lean frame bending in to the wind. cutting through its opposition like a tea clipper's prow, while I had to run to keep up with his fierce stride, my cheeks growing pinker with the effort and the wind's buffeting.

We strode into the Clerkenwell Road and then sharp right down Back Hill. Holmes slackened his pace and held up a hand to arrest my charge. 'We must go quietly now. There may be opposition. We are now in enemy territory.' I was beginning to wish myself back in Bart's giving a cadaver my full attention but Holmes was such a strong presence that my enthusiasm was soon rekindled.

We paused in a darkened doorway. Holmes indicated a building across the street. It was obviously a poor lodging house much frequented by the unfortunates of society including students probably, I presumed. Holmes directed my attention to one of two dormer windows. There was a pale flickering light showing through its grime. 'That is our destination. I do not know what awaits us there. It could mean a fight or it could spell embarrassment. From the point of view of Olga Pleshkarova I hope it is the latter.'

Holmes paused, then whispered, 'Silence now, Stamford, silence.' While I was digesting this latest information Holmes was away like a hound that has slipped the leash. I rushed in pursuit not wishing to be left alone. We silently mounted the front steps and with a few deft prods with a thin gleaming implement Holmes had the front door open. Inside, a cheap oil lamp hung from the hall ceiling giving out a pale glow that concealed more than it revealed. Holmes did not seem to notice the gloom and was silently springing up the stairs. So that was why he had paused in the darkened doorway – to prepare his eyes for the darkness. I followed as best I could. The stairs were steep and double-backed onto themselves between each floor. As I passed landings I could hear muffled noises from the rooms. Who was in them? The darkness and my foreboding turned them into demons and I was afraid. For a moment I hesitated but I heard Holmes whisper sharply from somewhere above me, 'Come on, one last flight.'

I hurried to the imperious voice that commanded loyalty and instilled confidence even in a whisper. In a moment I was by his side. He gave me a heavy stick from his bag while he got hold of a strong crowbar. We advanced to the door of our quarry. We paused, straining our eyes and ears for any indication of activity behind the wooden barrier. Holmes was breathing very slowly and I followed his example, taking deep breaths to steady myself. Suddenly, like a shot from a bow, Holmes was at the door. The crowbar twisted and levered its way into the door frame. Wood, rotten with worm, splintered and the door swung open. We rushed into the room, weapons at the ready.

There was nobody to be seen. Holmes told me to keep watch by the door while he took out his lens and rushed around the small attic room like some strange animal on the scent of some poor beast for whom at that moment I had more than a tinge of sympathy. Sherlock Holmes was not the man I would choose to have on my tracks.

As Holmes carried out his search, I became aware of some voices murmuring below us. The noise grew louder and more confident. 'We are discovered, Holmes,' I whispered urgently.

'Just another moment, and we'll be away.'

After a minute that seemed a lot longer the voices started to form into heavy violent shapes that started to ascend the stairs. I turned to Holmes to warn him of our imminent danger but saw instead a rather large sergeant of police. In a moment he had my arm bent up towards my scapula. He carried Holmes's tool bag in the other hand. His grip was like the tensed steel of Dr Bessemer.

'It's alright, lads,' the sergeant bellowed in a voice that

came from somewhere very close to Bow Bell's clapper, 'I've got 'im.'

The menacing shapes murmured their congratulations and disappeared back into the gloom. The sergeant smiled and turned into Holmes once more.

Half an hour later we were sitting in the now deserted dressers' equipment store at Bart's having a cup of chocolate. Holmes was smiling to himself but made no attempt to communicate with me. At last I broke the silence. 'Come on, Holmes, old chap, what was all that about? It's not fair to take a fellow into mortal danger without telling him why.'

Holmes stretched himself in his chair and rubbed his hands together. 'You will be surprised to discover that it all started in the Reading Room of the British Museum.' I confessed that I was and bade him to continue his narration.

'As you know, I spend quite a lot of my time there but until four days ago I had not been there for some time. Thus when I returned, I found my usual place occupied and so had to seek out a fresh seat from which to order my books. The seats in the Reading Room radiate out from the centre of the room in rows like the spokes of a wheel. The centre area is a circular affair taken up by the staff and the bibliographies. There was only one place in my new row obviously occupied and so I sat several places along from this reader in order to be able to concentrate on my own studies and also to leave whoever it was in peace to continue with their work. The reader was away at that moment and so I was able to get down to work immediately.

'After several minutes I heard the shuffling walk of an old woman pass me. I glanced up and noticed that it was the old woman who empties the wastepaper baskets of the detritus of the failed inspirations of the readers. I had seen her many times before and in a moment I was immersed in my studies again only to be disturbed by one of the staff distributing the books that readers had ordered. It was a young man who appeared to be of sober habits although his love of cigarettes was clearly visible on his fingers, lips and teeth. The trolley that he was pushing, from which he dispensed the volumes, had a wheel which squeaked just loudly enough to be an irritant to the reader. The noise would stop as he gave out the books and then would resume as he continued his round. He stopped next to me and gave me my copy of Maupertuis's *Essai de Cosmologie*. His silence and fluidity of movement were in obvious contrast to the squeaking of the cumbersome trolley whose pilot he was. I hurriedly starting looking through the newly delivered work to find my cross-references and barely noticed the cessation in squeaking as the trolley passed the unoccupied place of the only other reader of row K.

'What seemed like seconds later but which on reference to the clock on the wall was a full twenty minutes I became fully aware of the return of the reader who shared my row. He let out a guttural shriek as he leapt from his chair holding a pin in one hand and his wounded buttock in the other. He looked at me with blazing eyes. I merely shrugged my shoulders and returned to my work.

'Moments later this same reader let out another deep-throated grunt as he fiercely crumpled a piece of paper in his large hands. Another idea on its way to the basket I thought, as he threw it aside but not bothering with the wastepaper receptacle. Obviously an unpleasant person but then he surprised me with the following words which seemed to be addressed to no one in particular. "They cannot me frighten. The truth will out even if only eventually it is".

'My curiosity was aroused. Who was this far from prosperous man (his clothes shone from over-use) with grizzled hair and beard whose accent and sentence construction made him of obviously Germanic origin? What had he meant by his statements? From his demeanour and obvious instant distrust of myself asking him would not provide me with my answers. The piece of paper that he had cast from him was an obvious clue. It lay in the centre of the space between us. For the next two hours we continued with our work. Luncheon was approaching so I picked up various papers and books in preparation for my departure back to Montague Street. I clumsily dropped a sheaf of notes and during my retrieval of them from the floor was able to secure the paper of my designs with ease. The other reader kept his eyes fixed on me throughout the whole show and watched me leave.

'Back in my rooms I was able to open out the paper and read it. It was most curious. At the top was a strange symbol Я and beneath this symbol were written the letters ARX. This was a pretty mystery indeed. What clues could I find as to the solution?

'Firstly, there was the paper itself. It was of a very fine quality, close grained with a very smooth texture. The watermark was well known to me as Shepherd and Fisher of Bond Street who supplied many of the crowned heads of Europe. That in itself was not without significance.

'Secondly, there were the letters. They had been written by hand in an elegant script that suggested a fine education. The ARX were in Roman but the curious symbol had something Cyrillic about it, particularly in the curvaceous quality of the feet.

'Thirdly, I put my lens and my nose to work. I sat back and pondered my conclusions. This note was written by a woman of Russian extraction who enjoyed both robust health and a French education. The strength of the application of pen to paper revealed the former and the perfume that clung to the weave suggested something of the latter.

'How had the paper appeared on the desk of the Germanic reader? There were two obvious candidates, the old woman who had emptied the wastepaper baskets and the young man who had delivered the books. Both were possible emissaries for a third party. Then of course the note could have been delivered before I had taken up my seat. There was nothing for it. I would have to return to the Reading Room after lunch and keep watch. At the end of the day's work I would have to reserve my books for the next day and arrive as the doors opened to ensure not missing the reader who was the recipient of this cryptic missive.

'Finally, and most importantly, what did it all mean? The symbol was new to me and I had no note of it in any of my indices. Neither could I find ARX in any of my commonplace books or dictionaries. There was something Greek about it to my mind, but I was open to other possibilities.

'Thus at two o'clock sharp I was back at my seat in the Reading Room hard at work. Several other readers had joined row K but my German was still as I had left him. Several times he broke his pencil in the fury of his writing. His work was obviously very important to him. Was that the reason for the cryptic message? Did his work have significance for others?

'The bell for the end of the session sounded and we all took our books back to the central area with our reserve slips in them. The German went to a different part of the reception desks so I could not see his name on the slips. It was of no great consequence, I would discover his name soon enough.

'At nine a.m. sharp the next day I joined the queue of readers, tickets at the ready, to enter the Reading Room.

Several were obviously regulars and the staff wished them a courteous "Good morning" which was returned with matching civility. Would that the whole world was so civil but then was I not on the track of some menace right in the heart of this haven of civilization?

'I hung back as I could not see my German reader. Eventually I went inside to look for him there. He was nowhere to be seen. Suddenly he came rushing through the door looking a little flushed. He hurried over to his seat and seemed thankful that it had not been taken. Was there a special reason for this or was he just like the rest of his race a creature of routine and method who did not care to have their circles disturbed? Or had he just been under attack and was glad to reach familiar territory again?

'On closer inspection I decided on the former. He had obviously walked a long way as his shoes, trousers and coat clearly revealed. That he was not very well off was also clear to see. He had obviously walked to the Reading Room owing to the lack of a bus or train fare. Thus whoever was after him was not after his money.

'After the usual preparations of papers, pens and the collection of books, the Reading Room settled down to the work of the day. I too had a lot of work to do but I was determined to keep an eye on what happened to the German.

'The familiar squeaking of the book trolley intruded on my thoughts. This time another librarian was pushing it, a one-armed naval rating who had last seen service, and presumably his left arm, in Jamaica just over a year ago.

'After that small interruption the work of the readers continued without disturbance until eleven o'clock when several left to stretch their legs or have a cup of something reviving. My German remained seated. So did I. Guericke's *New Experiments Concerning Empty Space* and various works by Lavoisier and Kirwan were delivered to me by the one-armed librarian. Soon after that he delivered some books to the German but I could not see exactly what they were.

'Several minutes later a cough and a shuffle of feet heralded the arrival of the old basket emptier. She had a mournful expression on her face. Why was that? Her ill health, the greater quantity of paper this morning, or was it because the German was still in his place and so she could not give him the message? She shuffled away.

'Both the German and myself stayed in our places until one o'clock at which time he abruptly stood up and stretched his legs before taking up his place again. One thing that I had noticed about him over the previous few hours was how he seemed to be constantly squirming in his seat. Was he nervous or did he suffer from some uncomfortable ailment?

'At two-thirty, his squirming reached a crisis point and he hurried away. Several moments later the squeaking trolley reappeared. I looked up. No longer was it the one-armed ex-Navy man but yesterday's cigarette smoker. He made his way along the row but did not stop at the German's place.

'If my theory was right the note – if there was to be another – would be delivered while the German was away. Nothing further happened. The German returned, cast his eyes over his books and papers and then disappeared again to order some more books. I could see him at the desk in the centre of the room and was aware that he was watching me also. I then turned to look back at his seat just in time to see the old woman going past it, her sack of waste paper trailing behind her. Had she done anything?

'My question was soon answered. The German returned and flicked through his books. He let out a snarl as he picked up a piece of paper, briefly scanned it before crushing it and throwing it aside.

'I went to the central area to see if the old woman was still to be seen but she had gone. I asked one of the librarians who the old woman was and was told that her name was Olga Pleshkarova, who had been emptying the wastepaper baskets for several years. She kept herself to herself but she was a willing enough worker who could be relied upon to do her tedious job no matter what the weather. "She'll be off home about now, she only comes in for a few hours before and after lunch. She normally leaves from the north door," my friendly librarian informed me.

'In moments I was away to the north side of the Reading Room and there just ahead of me the bowed figure of the old woman was leaving the building.

'I followed her all the way to the house in Back Hill that we entered earlier. I surmised that she had the top room as the light was the only one to be ignited as I stood outside and it was several minutes from her entering the house to the small glow appearing. A suitable time for an old woman to climb those many stairs.

'Now came a strange part. No other lights shone in any of the windows and the old woman's light continued to show but a young man stepped from the building in a very expensive coat and was away before I could fully study him. Which room had he come from? Perhaps one at the back whose light I could not see, but there was something about his clothing that made him appear not fitted to such sur- roundings or even to England. The fur collar of his coat was not English in style. It was somehow both brash and feminine.

'However, I now had the name and address of the old woman and had also been able to closely examine her footprints as I followed her. I took all this knowledge back to Montague Street and smoked a pipe over it.

'From what the librarian had said she was a Russian.

That fitted with my reasoning but her circumstances and the badly repaired shoes that had left very individual footprints did not square with the quality of the paper. Another curious matter was the footprints themselves. For a woman they were quite large and left a very clear impression.

'I returned to the Reading Room to reserve my books for the next day. The German was just leaving and I noticed that the paper was still on the floor where he had thrown it. I quickly pocketed it and returned home.

'My inspection of the note proved it to be in every way identical to that of the previous day in all details bar one. Instead of ARX, only RX was printed in Roman capitals on this one beneath the strange symbol. A new theory formed in my mind. I had to go and enlist some help.'

'So that's why you came to me,' I put in, having been too involved in Holmes's story up until that point to interrupt him.

'Actually, no, not on this occasion, Stamford,' he replied. 'Someone rather younger than you who with his friends forms a very effective agency for the surveillance of chosen subjects.'

'Sounds a bit irregular to me,' I mused.

'Indeed so, Stamford, indeed so,' returned Holmes with a broad smile on his face as though he were enjoying some private joke.

'Come on, Holmes,' I urged, 'what happened next?'

'At nine a.m. yesterday I was to be found on my way to my seat in the Reading Room. My German was already ensconced in his and so my vigil began. In between my studies of the chemical changes wrought by burning, my mind was a series of tripwires each prepared to sound the alarm at the least intervention of an old Russian woman, a German scholar or a squeaking book trolley.

'This time I clearly saw the old woman leave a note and

drop a pin on the seat of the chair. I waited until she had gone before I went to the wastepaper basket with some crumpled paper of my own, passing the German's desk as I did so. It was the work of less than a second to see the note and the name of the German reader on his book application counterfoils. I also thought it politic to remove the pin. As I regained my seat I felt a certain amount of elation. The note's contents were as I had predicted. The strange symbol was still there, but this time with only an X. Time was running out for the German. I went outside to check that my helper was in place. He was.

'Later that afternoon I followed the old woman to her house, only this time I was in disguise. When she reached her room I entered the house and checked on the back rooms. None were occupied at that time. Several of the front rooms showed signs of life and in my disguise as an Irish labourer with a slip of paper containing a name and address of a supposed acquaintance I was able to enquire at each door in turn. There was the sound of a key turning upstairs and the young man whom I had seen leave the building the previous day in the large fur-collared coat brushed past me. He had definitely left the front dormer room of the old woman. As he passed, he pulled his collar up. "It's cold today, sir," I said to him. He did not reply and was soon gone. I sniffed the air and a new theory formed.

'I had two choices. Go and see the old woman or follow the man. I chose the latter as I did not know where he came from and he seemed to be the motivator of the enterprise. In moments I was a poor parson just up from the country and in hot pursuit of the mysterious young man. Strangely we ended up near my own rooms, for the entered the imposing Hotel Russell Square. This was no cheap boarding house. Sherry is a shilling a glass there. I noted his room number and was soon able to divert the desk clerk's attention to read his name in the register. It was an Oscar Lundholm of Denmark.

'What was his relationship with the German reader? It felt as intricate as the Schleswig-Holstein question. I returned to my rooms.

'Sitting down over a pipe there came a knock at the door and my assistant informed me that all was well with the German. I paid him his fee and continued my smoke. Presumably this man was using Olga Pleshkarova to plant notes in the Reading Room and then meeting her afterwards to find out what had happened.

'One thing perplexed me and that was the footprints. Perhaps the snow was harder today but I was sure that they were deeper yesterday, and more fully formed. They were undoubtedly the same shoes with the patch on the sole of the left shoe but there was something wrong about them. I formed three theories and awaited fresh data.

'According to my calculations, today was to see the final chapter of the story. The German researcher received his note and became so agitated that he could not work. He left the Reading Room in a high state of ill-humour and made off for what I assumed was home. This time I followed him. We went through Woburn Place, across the Euston Road and made for Camden Town. As we passed into the Kentish Town High Road I felt a strong hand rest on my shoulder. "That is the man, officer. He has been watching me for days now," cried the German, turning to me.

'"Is this true, sir?" asked the police constable.

'"Do not deny it," shouted the German in a frenzy. I was taken to the local police station. By the time I had explained everything – which they did not believe, so it took accordingly longer – my German had long gone. Fortunately for him when the attack came he was not unprotected.

My "Irregulars", as you called them, were on hand and the assailant was soon put to flight.'

'The young man?' I asked.

'A young man certainly, to outrun my reinforcements.'

'What a way you have of passing your time, Holmes. Does this sort of thing often happen to you when you visit the library? Do you enjoy danger and the chase?'

'My greatest pleasure is in solving problems, Stamford. This one was most pleasing. I am sure that I have solved it but as you saw from the room our birds had flown. And this was all they left,' he said, holding up two balls of newspaper closely packed and slightly pointed on one side.

'I have lost the trail. No matter, it was diverting while it lasted. Thank you for your help, it was most appreciated.' He threw the two pieces of rolled newspaper into the bin and with that Sherlock Holmes was on his way. I tried to tempt him to accompany me to the Butcher's Arms but he said he had one or two things to look into.

'The Hotel Russell Square?' I suggested.

'Not a bad idea but my agents told me that that lead is also now cold. I shall not be in tomorrow.'

As Holmes went away he looked in marked contrast to the eager hunter of a few hours before. He seemed to have gone grey as though the life had gone out of him now that he had no diversion to occupy his mind. I was sad for him and resolved to visit Holmes the next day to try to cheer him up a little, but my watch told me that Sam Belcher was beginning to wonder where I was. Picking up my hat and coat I adjourned to the Butcher's Arms. The evening spent in the Butcher's Arms was a merry one. Sam Belcher, the landlord, was in a cheery mood, twitting me about some of my antics after one of the matches against Guy's. My chums joined in and I soon became the butt of many jibes and quips. Despite all this jovial good humour I could not get Holmes out of my mind. He had looked so deflated and crestfallen that I decided to visit a certain place in Jermyn Street and take him a present the next day which I knew he would appreciate. Extract of the coca plant, he had told me, was a very stimulating substance. My Kentish beer was enough for me but no matter, my mind was made up as to my course of action the next day.

The next day I rose early for a change and was actually on time for a lecture. This was followed by some laboratory work and finally a brief trip to the wards to see a patient who had been brought in from the Covent Garden fruit and vegetable market. He was a porter who had been bitten by a tarantula spider that had been hidden in a batch of tropical fruit. This was a rare chance for us to see such a phenomenon. Far from dancing a 'Tarantella' the poor man was at a very low ebb with a high fever and delirium. I feared that he had come to the hospital too late for us to help him. How often that was to be the case in my later life working in the tropics.

The visiting surgeon who had given us the lecture that morning had to be entertained and so a group of us took him to lunch. He turned out to have a very sardonic sense of humour and told us some very funny stories about mistakes in the operating theatre. Any patients overhearing us would not have found very much of it humorous, but medics, like sextons, can have a macabre turn of mind.

However, despite the great interest of the morning's affairs, Holmes was still very much in my mind. By the time I approached Montague Street via Jermyn Street it was gone three o'clock and there had been yet another fall of snow. Despite the bitter cold I walked. Walking has always been a pleasure to me; although rather slow, I always get there in the end. The cold made London more bearable as the streets tended to be less crowded with people who preferred to stay at home by their fire than face the icy blast of a north-easterly.

I pulled on the door bell but there was no reply. I tried again as I knew how Holmes could get in the dumps and not communicate with anyone for days on end. Indeed that was why I was there in the first place. After the excitement of the chase on the previous day I was afraid that he would suffer from some form of reaction. I tried the bell for a third time, but still there was no response. On peering through the window I could see no sign of life, then I remembered that his rooms were on the first floor so threw some stones against the windows. Still nothing stirred. At last I decided that my journey had been in vain. So that the journey should not have been wasted I put my present into an envelope, sealed and addressed it, and pushed it through the letter box. I hoped that that would at least cheer him a little and raise his spirits when he found it.

Just as I was leaving Holmes's steps I had another idea. I had just remembered that Holmes liked strong pipe tobacco, and as I had not seen him smoking too often recently it gave rise to the thought that possibly he could not afford to buy himself any at the moment. There was a small tobacconist just round the corner, or so Holmes had told me on several occasions.

Thus I resolved to go there and get Holmes some of his favourite mix. And possibly by the time I returned with it he might have returned to either his senses or his rooms – or both. It was a decision that saved Holmes's life.

The tobacconist's shop, although very small, was easy to find. Holmes had given very accurate details as to its whereabouts and the name of the assistant to consult on all matters relating to the mixing and rubbing of pipe tobaccos – yet another of his arcane pursuits it appeared. He never seemed to do anything without studying it in detail – not a trait that I could run to. I just appreciate, I don't have the need to analyse.

Mr Cyril Boddy turned out to be one of those pink-faced white-haired old men who have that inner glow that comes from a lifetime of diligent service to the needs of others. He smiled his greeting to me whom he addressed as 'Young sir' – 'young' really was becoming like a first name to me – his eyes sparkling at me over his wire-rimmed half-lens spectacles. For a moment the thought crossed my mind that he would make an ideal elf to help Santa Claus prepare for Christmas.

'Good afternoon, Mr Boddy,' I replied. 'I have come in on behalf of a friend. He has a particular mix of tobacco, I believe, not that I know what it is as I am certainly no expert on the subject.'

'And the name of your friend, young sir?' smiled the elfish figure.

'How silly of me. How could you know the mixture without the identity of your client? It's a Mr Sherlock Holmes of Montague Street. I've just come from there.'

'Well, how strange.'

'In what way, Mr Boddy?'

'He was in here only a few minutes ago. I'm surprised you did not bump into him if you have just come from there.'

This was rather annoying but I entreated Mr Boddy to mix up a pound of Holmes's mixture and keep it for him. I was just about to leave when Mr Boddy started talking. 'Very interesting young man, that Mr Holmes, if I may say so.'

'In what way?'

'He is always so precise and courteous which is always welcome in these days of constant rushing to and fro.'

'Oh, I see. Yes.'

'Another thing is his great interest in tobacco as a subject all its own. He asks the staff here all manner of questions about the different types of leaf, their smell before and after use, and even the different types of paper used in the manufacture of cigarettes.'

'Yes, he is certainly a student of many obscurities.'

'Quite so. Do you know what interests him the most about tobacco, young sir?'

'No, I'm afraid I can't begin to guess in the case of one so individual as Mr Sherlock Holmes.'

'It's the ash. You would think that he would like a good smoke but in actual fact he seems to smoke so much simply to see what the remains of the tobacco are like.'

'How very singular.'

'That's what I think, young sir. Although he likes his own strong mix of navy and shag number six to smoke just for pleasure.' I picked up a pinch of it as Mr Boddy continued his methodical mixing. Putting it to my nose it smelt like a combination of tar, rope and molasses. One man's meat, another man's Prussic acid, presumably, I thought.

'Last week,' Mr Boddy continued, warming to the conversation, 'Mr Holmes came in and showed me some notes that he has been working on all about tobacco. There were over eighty different types clearly listed. He told me that he was hoping to have coloured plates of the ashes to help people to differentiate between them. He sounded very scientific.'

'Oh, he is. He often works in the lab at Bart's where I'm a student. His knowledge of science is at once profound and idiosyncratic.'

'He's a doctor then is he, our Mr Holmes?'

'No, he's not actually. His ambitions are quite individual to say the least.'

'You don't say, young sir. Quite a little mystery.'

'Holmes is that all right.'

'Yet he's very friendly to me. When he brought his notes in to show me he asked me if he had missed any and I said at least forty that I knew of off-hand. He seemed quite surprised but instead of being put out he simply asked me if I would give him a list of those that he had not included so that he could start work on them. In fact that's what he came in for today. He didn't buy any tobacco – he's not had any for a while now, so he is probably quite low at the moment so I'm sure he'll appreciate your gift. He just came in to collect his notes and my list.'

'How odd,' I said.

'Yes, I expected him to buy some of the tobaccos that I had listed for him. But he didn't. He just smiled and said, "We shall have to wait and see what happens before I do that, Mr Boddy." Do you know what he could have meant by that?'

I confessed that it was as much a mystery to me as it obviously was to Mr Boddy.

Mr Boddy looked up from his work and gazed past me. 'Now there's another mystery,' he said abstractedly.

'What is, Mr Boddy?' I asked.

'Why, there goes Mr Holmes up that side street.'

I spun around just in time to see Holmes turn up a narrow side alley. From his walk he was not in the dumps at all but on the track of some quarry who had best look out for himself. I thrilled at this and rushed from the shop as Mr Boddy repeated. 'I don't know, people today, always rushing to and fro.'

I bounded after Holmes. He had already turned the corner and was well on his way up the side street. As I reached the corner I looked up the narrow alley. Holmes had stopped and there facing him was the old Russian woman, Olga Pleshkarova.

'So you think you have hunted me down do you, Mr Holmes? Well, it is the case of the hunter being the hunted. Goodbye, Mr Holmes.'

At that the old woman underwent a transformation. Instead of being a shuffling slow figure, she stood up tall and agile. There was the gleam of a knife in her right hand as she advanced on him. Tensing, Holmes seemed to sniff the air and spun round just in time to deflect an attack from a figure that had been hidden in the doorway close behind him. With a clever side-step he had his attacker rolling in the snow, his long stiletto rolling from his left hand into the alley's central gutter. The old woman now leapt at Holmes. Once again his speed of reaction was remarkable as he parried the attack. But despite Holmes's ability his assailants were determined and they outnumbered him. The figure from the doorway had by now recovered the stiletto and was advancing on Holmes's back. I bellowed something of a scrum nature and launched myself forward. My rugby tackle was perfect. With arms round the knees and shoulder into the thigh my opponent pitched forward into the snow and was well and truly winded.

The other attacker was so surprised by this new development that Holmes had soon bested her. It was then that I had the first of the many surprises that were to follow. Holmes tugged at her hair and it came away in his hands revealing the shiny locks of youth. Next he told me to be gentle with the prisoner upon whom I was sitting as it was a woman, his prisoner being her twin brother.

Fortunately, Mr Boddy had not been idle during our exertions. He had summoned a policeman and we all went to the local station to tell our stories.

That evening we were seated in the private dining room of the Diogenes Club, a hearty meal consumed and with a humidor of Holmes's mix between us from which he was filling his pipe as his brother Mycroft beamed in contentment. 'It was really most lionhearted of you, Stamford,' he said, between pulls on his pipe. 'You must allow me to repay you one day.'

'I am sure you will, Holmes, but really this adventure has been repayment enough.'

'That is most generous of you, but my brother is referring to your assistance not the present of tobacco,' interjected Mycroft.

'Enough of this. Tell me all about today. That was the old Russian woman, Olga Pleshkarova, whom we were after yesterday, or at least it was meant to be, wasn't it, Holmes? So who was the other woman with the stiletto? Where did she fit in? It's all very confusing to me, please explain it all to me.'

Holmes smiled a contented smile. 'It all started,' he began, 'as you know, in the Reading Room just around the corner from my rooms with a cryptic message and pin for the rather overwrought German reader.

'You know the story up until last night when I left you. This is the remainder of the adventure of the old Russian woman.

'When I got home. I was rather disappointed as to the outcome of yesterday's events. It looked as though the story was over and I had missed my prey. Thus you can imagine my surprise as I opened my front door and found a piece of paper exactly corresponding to those that had been sent to the German in the Reading Room. I opened it up and there was the symbol Я and my name with each letter crossed out. It was an obvious threat to my life. In the case of the German they had built up a climax by removing a letter from his name each day. They would have had to have spent a fortnight going over the same ground for me which was too dangerous for them now that they knew that I was on to them. They had to act quickly.

'I laid some plans of my own. I worked out a daily routine to make it easier for my enemies to know my whereabouts but also easier for me to prepare for attack. Thus each morning would be spent with my brother in Pall Mall. Lunch would be a walk around Trafalgar Square with, as a post-prandial stroll, a visit to Mr Cyril Boddy. After that would have been trip to the National Gallery or the British Museum's exhibition sections with dinner in the Diogenes with my brother Mycroft. Thus I was to have home advantage at all times.

'The morning passed pleasantly enough with a discussion on new German writers. Brother Mycroft here was able to enlighten me a great deal on that subject as well as warn me of the dangers that two in particular posed if their ideas were to be taken up in the future by men of extremes.

'We also discussed such subjects as footprints, cryptic symbols and Russian secret societies. As you probably know, the Tsar of All the Russias has made several visits to England recently for various reasons both private and public. There are of course blood ties between our royal families. Each of these visits has occasioned violence on the streets of London between various Russian secret societies who either support or despise the Tsar's regime. At first I thought that that was what this sequence of events was about. Once again my brother was able to use his superior powers to enlighten me.'

Mycroft dipped his head in acknowledgement and remained beaming, his look of abstraction a little disconcerting to one who did not know him well. He decided to join the conversation.

'Karl Marx, the German reader who was the subject of Olga Pleshkarova's notes in the Reading Room, has no connection with Russia but it appears that his work with its emphasis on class struggle could have dire consequences for any despotic regime if taken up by enough opponents of that regime. There is no monarchy in Europe more despotic than that of the Tsar. This other German writer, Nietzsche, could be just as dangerous with his ideas of a super-race. The writer's pen is indeed more penetrating than the soldier's blunt bayonet and the wounds more lasting.'

'But what of the two who attacked you today?' I asked Sherlock Holmes.

'Yes. Sherlock, I feel, was very foolhardy there,' interposed Mycroft Holmes. 'The footprints and the pins had plainly told him that there were two people involved in this affair and neither of them old yet he persisted in his plans. You even called off your so-called "Irregulars", did you not? Just in case they might frighten your opponents away.'

'We have Stamford to thank for that name,' said Sherlock Holmes.

'As well as your life as we have already observed,' remarked Mycroft Holmes dryly.

'Please,' I interjected, 'no more of that. Just tell me what happened.'

Sherlock Holmes continued the narrative. 'The footprints clearly showed that, although the same shoes were in use, one pair of feet was smaller than the other and the owner of those smaller feet was at least seven pounds lighter. When we broke into Olga Pleshkarova's room yesterday I found some pieces of newspaper in the bottom of the wardrobe.'

'The ones that you threw into the bin on your way out yesterday?' I asked.

'Observation is indeed contagious, young Stamford. Yes, you are right. They had been rolled into tight balls but were curiously pointed as though they had been thrust into a pair of shoes. It was interesting to note that when the lighter of the two was at work a pin was left for Mr Marx and not when the heavier of the two was at work. Obviously it was two people.'

'Why play such a prank as put a pin on a seat?' I asked.

'Why indeed – childishness, spite. Who knows?'[1]

'Go on,' I urged.

'Today, as you know, it snowed again. As I went to see Mr Cyril Boddy, there, as clear as day before me, were the footprints of the lighter old Russian woman. It was a game of cat and mouse but we came face to face in that side alley. I was expecting it to be the woman, as the foot size was smaller as was the weight, but when I got closer I was able to see through the disguise. I have trained my eyes to examine a face, not its trimmings. Being able to look through a disguise is probably one of the first qualities for a criminal investigator to have.'

'Among several others,' murmured his brother from the deep recess of his club armchair.

'That is true, Mycroft, but let us not go into that now. I was obviously facing the brother. Where was the formidable sister? There are seventy-five perfumes . . .'

'Eighty,' suggested Mycroft Holmes.

'. . . which it is very important that a criminal expert should be able to distinguish from each other. There had been one of that number' (here Holmes glanced at his brother) 'on the notes which had obviously been written by the female act in the duo and just at that moment I smelt it again, as I had when disguised as an Irish labourer. That had led to some confusion in my mind. The coat carried the perfume, not the person wearing it. Until face to face in the alley I believed that the one who dropped the pin was the

---

[1] Marx suffered from a painful complaint. Obviously Holmes was too much of a gentleman to mention it.

woman. It was in fact the man who was smaller than his sister as is often the case in Russian twins apparently. He had been wearing her coat as a further disguise.'

'So that was why you sniffed the air?'

'Quite so, Stamford. It was lucky for me that I noticed it so that I was prepared for the attack when it came.'

'But who were they both?' I asked.

'Mycroft?' asked his brother.

'Yes, I have the police reports here. They are indeed twins, Tsarist supporters who are so fanatical that their symbol is an Я which is based on the fact that they are mirror-image twins – you may have noticed that from the hands in which they held their weapons in their attack on Sherlock – and that the Tsars belong to the house of "R" or Romanoff. They were working independently of the Tsar, we believe, but they have been used by him on other assignments here in London, I believe. Do you agree, Sherlock?'

'Yes, I do, Mycroft. If I could have found a way of making a reagent which is precipitated by haemoglobin and by nothing else then they would have hanged last year.'

'Perhaps you will one day, Sherlock,' soothed his brother.

'There is one other question in particular that I would like to ask. Who was Olga Pleshkarova, simply a clever bit of make-up by these two fanatics?'

I looked towards Sherlock Holmes but his brother answered me. 'Sherlock was about to say "yes" but I think that the answer is "no". Olga Pleshkarova has worked in the Reading Room for several years. These twins have not been in England for more than twelve days. So what has happened to Olga Pleshkarova? I doubt that she will appear for work again. She knows the game is up and is probably out of the country already.'

'The twins, whatever their real names are – insist on

calling themselves Romanoff but they are not relatives of the Tsar – are very professional. I would not be surprised if they had planted a spy in the Reading Room to keep an eye on any subversive activities by the readers. They obviously thought Mr Marx's work too dangerous,' added Sherlock Holmes.

'Who is this Karl Marx?' I asked.

'At the moment – a nobody. He published an obscure work in 1848 called *The Communist Manifesto* which was out of date before it was printed. He has been a correspondent of a newspaper in America and in 1867 published a very difficult volume called *Das Kapital*, and the fact that it is referred to as Volume One suggests that he has more to say on the subject. He also helped to found the International Workingmen's Association but that was disbanded a few years ago. As a consequence he spends most of his time in the Reading Room. But none can predict the future, young Stamford.'

Sherlock Holmes had been absorbed in thought, but spoke up when his brother had concluded his résumé of Karl Marx's career to date. 'One thing we can predict is that these secret societies are a threat to law and order and need to be stamped out. If we do not, London will become like the Wild West with gun battles in its main thoroughfares.' On that dismal note we wished Mycroft goodbye and left the club.

The snow was now turning to dirty grey slush as we made our way up Pall Mall but my thoughts were on the watery grey eyes of the corpulent figure whose presence we had just quitted. This Mycroft Holmes was no mere auditor of accounts as Sherlock Holmes had described him as we had made our way there. He had had the police reports within hours of the crimes being committed. He knew about obscure German authors who were only just publishing their thoughts. He knew all about the Romanoff twins. He even told us as we left that he expected them to be deported without any publicity, but the way he said it suggested to my mind that he had organized it all himself. Who was this man and who was his equally singular brother now walking at my side? An eccentric adventurer or some sort of government agent?

I found myself thrilled at being so close to such high adventure and turned to my companion. 'Come on, Holmes,' I entreated. 'Who are you, what exactly is it that you do?'

He turned to me with a look of some exasperation as though I had interrupted an important train of thought. 'I doubt that you would understand even if I told you,' he remarked dismissively.

I bridled at this and persisted. 'Don't think that you are the only one with a brain in his cranium, Mr Sherlock Holmes,' I replied rather tartly.

'Indeed, but it is not the fact of possession but of application that is significant.' This was Holmes the machine talking. How I wanted to smash through that cold exterior to the man within. One day I thought, one day I will find your secret, but, as though to throw me off guard, he smiled and said, 'I have some work to do back at Bart's; perhaps if you come with me we can talk.' He had disarmed me but was he just humouring me? I have never liked being patronized and I was on my guard again. I was wondering if he would appreciate the present that was awaiting him when he returned. Little did I know what I had started.

The Singular Affair
of the Aluminium Crutch

(being a personal reminiscence of Mr Sherlock Holmes,
the world's first consulting detective, and told to young
Stamford in the chemistry laboratory at Bart's Hospital)

During my days of too abundant leisure as I waited for
cases to present themselves to me I had the opportunity to
compile the entries in my commonplace books. These were
to be my own indices of reference in which I collated those
obscure facts that I felt it best to have readily accessible to
me without turning my mind into a lumber room of inci-
dentals which might blunt my logical faculties. The sources
of this information were the everyday newspapers and the
most obscure manuscripts and palimpsests of the British
Museum on the other. Thus commonplace at first glance
appears to be an inappropriate title for them, repositories of
the recherché as they were. However, it was my plan to have
the most obscure facet of knowledge at my fingertips – in
other words to make them commonplace.

As all compilers of books of reference will know, certain
letters of the alphabet claim a disproportionate number of
entries. I soon had whole volumes devoted singly to C, B
and S whereas all the entries for the letters V to Z, W
excluded, could be comfortably housed in one volume.
Thus my entries took on a more personal aura. For example,
the V section came to include 'Voyage of the Gloria Scott',

and 'Victor Lynch, forger'. Not exactly a lexicographer's delight but as I created them for my own use and they fulfilled their purpose of rendering the obscure clear I rest my case.

For some years I had also busied myself trying to formulate rules as to the scientific study of detection. Genius has been described as an infinite capacity for taking pains. It is not a definition with which I hold generally – is there to be no place for intuition and its twin inspiration? – but I have to concede that it is a definition that can be applied to detection. The smallest detail may well be the most important in unravelling the apparently most baffling of problems. As indeed may the most obvious, which because of its very prominence becomes overlooked. This last is no original thought on my part, there have been people not able to see the wood for the trees for hundreds of years. But it remains a valid point to the detective and must never be forgotten.

In seeking to solve a case the first requirement is a set of facts. This can be obtained by the close questioning of a client and the witnesses, where there are any, but everything must be capable of corroboration or it remains open to question. For this my lens is my favourite and most reliable ally. Even the most unconsidered trifle needs magnification on occasion.

These facts, taken in conjunction with the crisis that has brought the client to my door, should enable me to work back to the causes of that crisis and thus identify the perpetrators. If the crisis is not the climax of a chain of events then I should be able to theorize as to the outcome of the prospective denouement and thus meet it fully prepared.

It is often said that the exception proves the rule, but in detection that is not so. Such an idea can only lead to inexactitude which is anathema to the logician.

The logician must analyse as though he were a machine. He must not be deflected by prejudice, praise, modesty or exaggeration. It would be as if Bach's music were to be played on a muted slide trombone. Most diverting, I am sure, but not in any way correct.

But of all the rules that I have formulated – and there are many – one stands out as the most complete and fundamental which should be engraved on my heart as characterizing my whole approach to the subject of detection. It is in the following story that I first fully evolved this basic law of detection and also had it most sorely tested.

The first case that I had been involved in was that of Victor Trevor's father and the 'Gloria Scott'.[1] After that I had returned to my Montague Street rooms to work on some more problems of organic chemistry before completing my last year at Oxford. I then returned to London to carry out my many and various studies in the pursuit of excellence in my chosen field of detection. I had a little money from my parents and my brother was on hand if all else failed. However, I was determined to make my own way in the world and I placed a discreet advertisement in several newspapers offering my services as the world's first consulting detective. Unfortunately – but for enquiries from the regular police force as to 'what I was up to' and from private detectives who did not want me to 'queer their pitch' – my advertisements brought me only one genuine enquiry. However, my solution was so unorthodox, albeit perfectly logical, that my client was entirely unsatisfied with my intervention. I received no fee, only disbelief and derision. It was a character-forming experience which served to confirm my faith in my most basic law of detection and harden my resolve for the future.

---

[1] See the *Memoirs of Sherlock Holmes*.

One hot August afternoon I was sitting cross-legged on my sofa puffing my pipe and keeping my P's and Q's up to date when there was a violent agitation of my doorbell. I sprang into action immediately, if only to save on the expense of replacing the chain.

As I rushed to the door I tried to fix in my mind's eye the identity of my assailant. Several theories crossed my mind as I ran down the stairs in triplets. Obviously it is an urgent summons in the mind of the caller. That could mean an accident in the street, but I had heard no commotion of coaches clashing with each other. Perhaps someone had fainted. Yet the fury of the summons seemed to presage something less prosaic. It was someone of some strength, determination, resolution and temper. Someone who had been thwarted in a design and who was not used to such treatment, hence the anger and continued ringing until the door was opened. A nobleman perhaps, or a ship's captain? A cavalry officer – they are usually far better with their horses than with their human companions. 'Or perhaps,' I said to myself as I opened the door, 'a woman'.

There before me stood a young woman in her early twenties. Her face flushed, her demeanour bristling with indignation, one hand still pulling on the bell, the other tapping her parasol on the step in an angry staccato.

'At last,' she cried. 'I wish to see Mr Sherlock Holmes, immediately.'

'It could not be arranged more quickly,' I answered, bowing to her. I was swept aside as she strode past me.

'At least you recognized that I was a woman. That is a start, although I would have preferred to be recognized as a lady,' she continued imperiously.

I smiled and bowed to hide my blushes. I did not realize that I had been speaking aloud as I had opened the door.

'Don't just stand there bowing, man. Where is your

consulting chamber?' This time it was her foot not her parasol that was taking up the staccato beat.

'This way, madam,' I replied as suavely as I could, motioning with my open hand to the stairs. She stood her ground but raised an eyebrow.

'Upstairs?' she queried in a voice loud enough to be heard in the Reading Room across the street. The thought came to me that this was an affair of the heart. My intuition had told me that here was a wronged woman, my reason had deduced as much from the violence of my summons to the door. Oscillation upon the pavement always means an affair of the heart. She would like advice but is not sure whether the matter is too delicate for communication to an outside party. This young woman had not oscillated for a moment. She felt herself seriously wronged by someone, presumably the man in her life, and sought not solace but retribution. She was dressed well if a little plainly but the engagement ring that she wore was anything but plain. It was a ruby of great lustre set in alternating tiny but exquisite diamonds and emeralds. There was no wedding band. Obviously there was some wealth involved here also. The result was a broken bell wire. It was something that I noted in my mind under the letter W.

All this thought had taken but a moment, but even such a small delay in answering this young woman – lady? I thought not – had reflected poorly on me in her eyes. So did the fact that I was still wearing my dressing gown. Her upper lip curled in disgust.

'These rooms used to be frequented by my brother but he has recently moved to Pall Mall and they have not been taken up by anyone else yet, so if you would prefer we may consult down here, Miss . . . ?'

'Miss Delicia Ogilvy. Yes, I think that would be better in the absence of a proper chaperone.'

She turned away from me and marched through the nearest door without waiting for me to show her the way or open the door for her. Surely not a lady but certainly a woman of some spirit. I awaited her return. She did not fail me. 'Good Lord,' she announced, 'are you so overworked that you keep a bed in every room?'

I smiled once more. '*This* way please, Miss Ogilvy. That way was my brother's old bedroom.'

With a proud toss of the head she was past me and into my brother's old sitting room. 'A moment, if you would be so kind Miss Ogilvy,' I remarked, as I showed her to her seat. Less than sixty seconds later I had returned from my room having changed out of my dressing gown only to find her collapsed on the floor of the sitting room,. It was quite stuffy in the room and I quickly pulled the sashes apart to let some air circulate. Next I carried her to a chair by the window and returned from my room in even quicker time with some smelling salts. She coughed and spluttered for a moment and shrieked out 'Cor blimey,' as I held them to her nose, but it was only for a few seconds before she had regained her composure. If every one of my cases was going to be so active in only the preliminary stages before I had been told the nature of the problem then I had chosen a very active career indeed.

'Excuse me, Mr Holmes,' she gasped, as she sat up more properly in her seat, but what you said were the exact words that my fiancé Algernon Berry used moments before he disappeared without trace. And then when you appeared to do exactly the same I felt that lightning had indeed struck in the same place twice.'

My attention was fully arrested by her words but the more 'proper' she became in her seat the less likely it became that I would receive the straight answers that I required to the four main questions that had already formed in my mind as I rushed to and fro, and which I felt would provide the solution to this young lady's unstated problem. Thus I had to gain the initiative, and there was one very effective way of doing so.

'Excuse me, Miss Ogilvy, before you tell me your story might I make one or two things clear?' Her reaction was agreeably muted to my offensive. 'I expect complete honesty from my clients in answering my questions. Without sufficient and correct data it will be impossible to solve the problem of your missing fiancé, Mr Algernon Berry. Thus, before you attempt to put me in my place by resuming your airs and graces I must point out that you are from Ilford in Essex, that you started your career as a seamstress but that you have recently gained proficiency in typewriting which has enabled you to move in somewhat higher circles than those of your origins. Hence your anger at losing such an eligible fiancé.'

That's better, I thought, as a look of wonder spread across her face which in turn became a question. I chose to answer it before she had time to ask it in order to complete the reversal in our roles.

'Your locket, fingernails, sleeves and slightly sharp vowels told me everything.'

At that she seemed to soften towards me.

'I see that I can hide nothing from you, Mr Holmes.'

'It would be better if you were frank, Miss Ogilvy.'

'I must confess to being in such a state when I got here that I almost forgot my manners completely. Do forgive me.'

'There is nothing to forgive. Your distress is obvious and understandable, Miss Ogilvy. Now, please, tell me your story as clearly as you can.'

I must confess that although I was eager to hear the details of this young woman's case, I was a little nervous.

At last, here it was. My first real consultation as the world's first consulting detective. One part of me wished to stand back from the scene and savour it in all its pristine newness. Fortunately the detective part of me took control and my mind cleared away the distorting euphoria. I was ready to solve the case of Miss Delicia Ogilvy's Vanished Fiancé.

'It all happened so suddenly not twenty-four hours ago. One moment I was with Algernon, the next he had disappeared and has not been seen or heard of since. I informed the police but they have been able to shed no light on the matter. Not even Scotland Yard in the shape of Inspector Lestrade has been able to clear the matter up. This morning I went to see a detective who was recommended to me by a friend, but all he could suggest was that Algernon had run away from me. He smelt of drink and as it was only ten o'clock in the morning I thought that his manner was offensive enough without ill-informed remarks reminding me of my fiancé's disabilities. I have spent the intervening hours scouring London for assistance. You are my last hope, Mr Sherlock Holmes.'

All this had been said with a crescendo and an accelerato. I felt incapable of stopping her, but as she reached her last sentence her eyes widened and moistened and she ceased speaking. My four questions had become five but I was still confident of success. I asked my first question.

'Where were you when your fiancé disappeared?'

'In his own house.'

I raised my eyebrows.

'I have been his secretary for the past two years. Although my typing is only twelve months old, I still took notes long hand for him before that. He is an inventor, a scientist. The works of Faraday, Galvani, Volta and Maxwell are his chief preoccupations and he has spent a lot of money on expensive scientific equipment to test his own theories of electricity and conductivity.

This was most interesting. A fellow scientist albeit in a field that was not my own. Obviously a man of some intelligence as well as means.

'You spoke of ill-informed remarks reminding you of your fiancé's disabilities.'

'Yes, he is crippled in one leg as a result of a riding accident in his youth. That's why I know that he did not – could not – have run away from me like that terrible drunken man had said.' At that she started sobbing helplessly again. This was going to take a long time if I was not careful. However, I kept my counsel and was soon rewarded by Miss Ogilvy once again controlling her emotions. 'Forgive me, Mr Holmes, this has all come as such a shock to me.' I nodded gently to her, my hands having unconsciously taken up a position with the tips of the fingers touching and my legs having crossed. Hitherto I had been unaware of such mannerisms, but hitherto I had not had a consultation. Miss Ogilvy was ready to continue but as she opened her mouth to speak tears were not far from her eyes. 'You see, all that remained of my fiancé, Mr Holmes, was his cripple's crutch. He could not have gone anywhere without it.'

'He had others perhaps? Walking sticks?'

'He had no canes or sticks, Mr Holmes. In fact, he did have one spare one but he never used it because it was so heavy and awkward. He always used his own special one that he had had made to his own specifications.'

'When was that?'

'Two years ago at least.'

'How old is your fiancé, Miss Ogilvy?'

She coloured slightly as she answered, 'Twenty-four.'

Does that mean that she is older and self-conscious of

the fact? What is that expression? On the shelf, I believe. It would a great loss to Britain if such maidens of character were to be consigned to such a limbo at five and twenty. However, that was not my reason for asking the question. I had to be sure that Algernon Berry had stopped growing. A picture of Miss Ogilvy's fiancé was emerging.

'Have you had cross words with your fiancé recently, Miss Ogilvy, or have you noticed him more subdued of late?'

'You may think me rather forceful, Mr Holmes, but that is one of the reasons that Mr Berry wishes to marry to me. We are devoted to each other. As a result of his disability he is very shy and rarely goes out in public. The theatre is his only joy outside his laboratory. He adores Irving and loved his Hamlet. It is I who am his link with the outside world. If you will pardon me, I am his legs.'

At that my heart grew cold. Did I sense something amiss here? A recipe for murder and a very cunning adversary before me? My faculties were taut with caution.

'Does Mr Berry's household consist of anyone else apart from yourself?'

'I am not a member of Mr Berry's household as such, Mr Holmes. I live with my mother. Originally I was employed to help out with Mrs Berry, my fiancé's mother. The father had been dead for some years and although comfortably off she had become increasingly bedridden and morose. She has a nurse and there is a cook. I was originally employed as a companion for Mrs Berry because of my ability with the needle and the crochet hook. I still see her every day. How can I break this news to her? I just cannot imagine.' At which she looked genuinely distressed.

'One more question, Miss Ogilvy. Had your fiancé received any communications recently that might have led to unexpected behaviour?'

'None whatsoever. As his secretary I went through his post with him each day – not that it was ever very much.'

I thought for a moment. We were not getting very far. There was nothing for it, I would have to examine the scene of the crime for myself and continue my questions there.

In a few minutes we were in a hansom rattling towards number 34 Percy Terrace, Shepherd's Bush. I estimated twenty minutes before we arrived. Time enough to think and rethink. I had five main theories and none of them were entirely complimentary to Miss Delicia Ogilvy, and several were not very complimentary to Mr Algernon Berry either. Whichever one would prove to be the answer – and I was sure that I had the answer among the five – I was confident of success in my first proper case. As the cab entered the Uxbridge Road and our destination grew near I felt the words of Henry V, hitherto a neglected dusty memory of school and learned by rote take on a new and vivid meaning – 'The game's afoot'.

The house was of solid red brick in a terrace of four with a double frontage of bow windows and mock verandas with the front door located centrally. Miss Ogilvy used her own key to enter – mistress of the house in all but name.

'Downstairs is Algernon's household, upstairs is his mother's,' Miss Ogilvy pointed out. 'On the left here is Algernon's sitting room and opposite is where I saw him for the last time.'

At first I thought she was going to start crying again but she contained herself and pointed out to me what had happened almost twenty-four hours previously.

'We had actually been out yesterday for lunch. It was a treat for me. Algernon said that I had been such a help to his mother and himself that he wanted me to know that they did not take me for granted. On the way back from our lunch he asked me to choose our wedding day. "Any day you like," he said. So you see, Mr Holmes, the last thing that was on our minds was arguing. We were both so happy. Then this . . .' Her voice trailed away

'Please, Miss Ogilvy, I must insist. Go on.'

She looked at me with great sad glistening eyes. As though in a trance she continued. 'We came inside. I said "Shall I make a cup of tea?" Algernon said "Why not. We can surprise mother later with the champagne." I laughed and put my arm in his to go to the kitchen. As we reached the door of his laboratory, opposite the sitting room door he said "A moment if you would be so kind, Miss Ogilvy," and disappeared into his laboratory and out of my life.'

'He called you "Miss Ogilvy"?'

'Yes, that was one of his little jokes. I was Delicia when I was his fiancée and Miss Ogilvy when I was his secretary.'

'Thus he saw you as his secretary at that moment?'

'I presume so.'

'Had he left an experiment in progress when you had gone out to your lunch?'

'Probably. There was always something on the go in there.'

I could certainly understand that from my own researches. 'What did you do when he said those last words to you?'

'I just laughed and went off to make the tea.'

'How long were you away? Please be exact.'

'Actually it was longer than I thought because I fell into talking with the cook to tell her my good news. When I came back I called to Algernon as I went past the door. It could well have been twenty minutes between our last words and my going to look for him in his laboratory.'

With that last statement I felt that the solution to the problem was at hand but there was still work to be done. It was my sincere belief that there were only two solutions possible. In one Miss Ogilvy was a cold-blooded murderess and a brilliant actress. In the other she was the victim of a hoax brought about by her own overbearing nature. There were two things left for me to do at Percy Terrace, if my methods were not to be faulty, and neither required the presence of Miss Ogilvy. First I had to examine the laboratory and then I had to interview the other inhabitants of the house.

I excused myself from Miss Ogilvy and entered the laboratory. It was well laid out with machinery to the left of the door including a large generator. It was switched off now, but had it been yesterday? There was a distinct smell of burning of a type that I had not come across before. It was a sweet smell and certainly a very unusual cigar if the aroma was tobacco-based. I felt all around the walls, shelves, skirting boards, picture rail and mantelshelf for concealed switches or levers which might lead to a hiding place. I checked to see if the carpet had been moved at all. All was solidly in place. I measured the room with my shoes and noted its dimensions on my cuff.

Next I inspected the hearth. Although the grate looked as if it had been unused for some time, as indeed there had been no need for a fire in a south-facing room in such a hot August, there was quite a large amount of ash on one side of the grate mixed with some specks of soot. I swept as much as I could into an envelope that I had brought with me, in which to collect evidence. That single action, unknown to me at the time, was to save Miss Ogilvy from the gallows.

Leaning against the mantelpiece was Mr Berry's crutch. How had it got there? I examined the crutch closely. The wood was teak so how could it be light as Miss Ogilvy had said earlier? I picked it up and was surprised to find it very light indeed. Even stranger were the marks on it. They were burn marks but not on the end as though it had been used absent-mindedly for poking the fire. Instead they were on the hand grip halfway down the shaft and on the leather pad at the top. They were quite light scorch marks difficult to discern against the darkly stained wood but my lens revealed them clearly enough. This was a mystery which grew deeper because they were obviously very recent marks owing to the fact that the leather cracked when I pressed it with my thumb and that some of the surface charcoal was still new enough to mark my fingers.

It was then that I noticed that the pad was loose. In fact it came away in my hand. Thus I discovered the reason for its unexpected lightness. The teak was merely a veneer. Inside it was completely hollow and lined with a dull metal. I scraped this metal and it revealed a bright silver-coloured metal beneath. It was obviously aluminium-coated with its naturally formed oxide. Next I turned it on its end. Nothing came out. What could it have been used for? This was an unexpected twist which had no place in either of my theories. On the far side of the room the other crutch lay dusty and neglected on the floor. I found it to be very heavy and cumbersome.

I went across the hallway to the sitting room and measured that. It was a perfect match to the laboratory opposite. There was no concealment here, but the house was quite large. Was there a conspiracy involving the whole house? My mind was full of new theories and suspicions.

I spoke to the cook, Mary, and asked if anyone in the household had asked for an extra helping of food during the last twenty-four hours. Not that she knew of, was her reply. I asked her where she had been when Berry had disappeared and she confirmed that she had been with Miss Ogilvy in the downstairs kitchen. She also confirmed how happy Miss Ogilvy had been and that she had not left her sight for at least a quarter of an hour. If Miss Ogilvy had murdered Mr Berry she had done it very quickly. Unless . . .

Quickly I mounted the stairs, taking note of the banisters as I went, to talk to the nurse, a Miss Slocombe. She did not live up to her first syllable at all as she was a constant fidget which she ascribed to the distressing events of the previous twenty-four hours and the harrowing responsibility of hiding the news from her mistress whom she forbade me to interview. As to her employer's son she described him as being a very slight figure who 'would not harm a flea' and who was goodness itself.

I concluded my questioning of Miss Slocombe by asking if Mary and Miss Ogilvy were particularly friendly to each other. 'I should think so, considering that they are mother and daughter!'

After this very unexpected news my mind was like a lattice-work of ideas and theories, each crossing the other before disappearing into another jungle of intersections.

As I returned to Miss Ogilvy I had two last questions. She had the grace to blush as she answered the first. 'Why yes, Mr Holmes, the cook is my mother. I thought that I had told you that.'

'You said that you lived with your mother,' I corrected her. 'You did not reveal her identity to me.'

Miss Ogilvy gave me a hard look. 'And your other question?'

'Did your fiancé make a will?'

She looked at me with triumph in her eyes. 'Why yes, he did. Would you care to see it? It is with Tewson and Billings. Here is their card.'

What did all this mean? Obviously she felt in the clear but I but I had to check anyway. I bade her farewell but told her that I would report back at eight o'clock that evening.

On my way out I took the aluminium crutch with me and made for the office of Tewson and Billings.

I was assured by the head clerk that only one will had been made by Algernon Berry and that two years before. It revealed that he left half to his mother and half to the Royal Society with some small provisions for his mother's household whom he listed as Nurse Slocombe, Mrs Ogilvy the cook, and his mother's companion, Miss Delicia Ogilvy. Obviously this was before any romantic attachment. Mrs Berry's will left everything to her son.

As I reached Montague Street I was deep in thought. A rough voice intruded as I crossed the pavement to my door. 'Oi, guv! What about the spondulicks then?' It was the jarvey; I had forgotten to pay my fare. As I took out the money from my waistcoat and handed it to him I enquired as to why a sailor from the prosperous tea clippers should work during his leave. A widower with a sister who has four children I suggested. 'That's right, guv'nor,' he replied before appreciating what I had said.

As I entered my front door I heard him shout after me, ''ow did you know...?' My door closed on the outside world before he could finish.

I strode upstairs, put on my dressing gown, filled my pipe, placed my commonplace books beside me, leant the aluminium crutch on the arm of the sofa and resumed my cross-legged pose of three hours previously. Now was the time for clear thought.

Was 34 Percy Terrace a house divided between a Berry faction and an Ogilvy schism? In which case what of Nurse Slocombe?

The nurse had seemed genuinely upset by the affair but what aspect of it exactly? The disappearance of the young man she had known since childhood, the condition of the mother, my presence to threaten any plot, or simply a concern for her future were all obvious candidates. Let me examine them one by one.

Nurse Slocombe had spoken very highly of Algernon Berry and so would be truly saddened by his loss; similarly she would assist him in any plan.

All seemed agreed that the condition of the mother was delicate and so a shock of this magnitude would have fatal consequences. Who would benefit? The missing Algernon Berry, not that he needs his mother's demise as he has been able to freely indulge his hobby so his mother's continued existence would not hinder him there. Miss Ogilvy? Only if Algernon updated his will for her benefit, but it is not Mrs Berry who has gone missing. Have the lovers faked his death in order to kill the mother off?

This was proving to be more Byzantine than I had thought. It was rapidly becoming at least a three-pipe problem. Facts, Holmes, what are the facts?

As told to me they are that one Algernon Berry disappeared from the face of the earth when he stepped into his laboratory. However, twenty minutes elapsed between his entry into the laboratory and the return of Miss Ogilvy. Algernon Berry and Delicia Ogilvy are engaged to be married. Algernon Berry is wealthy. He is also a cripple. Finally, he has a great interest in the work of Galvani, Faraday, Volta and Maxwell. Ah, not quite finally; he has another joy, Irving and his 'Hamlet'.

Not yet, Sherlock, no theories yet.

Miss Ogilvy is a rather forceful person who has got her eye on a better life and her hooks into a fortune. She did not tell me that the cook was her mother. Was she misleading me on purpose or has she become snobbish? If it is deception then is it true that Berry told her to name the day of their wedding? The cook confirmed the story but then a mother would. None the less, Algernon Berry disappeared as soon as they returned. Does this denote some sort of crisis for one or more of them?

What does all this reveal?

If Algernon Berry was trying to get out of marrying his fiancée why go to the trouble of the rare trip out to lunch and the talk of naming the day? It seems as though he were trying to raise her spirits and so to dash them suggests a spiteful nature which is not in line with Miss Slocombe's view of him. Perhaps it was his way of getting back at her for years of being the junior partner. If that is so, where did he go? I would wager what I have, which is not much admittedly, that he is not concealed downstairs. That means that he is concealed upstairs, but how could he have got there without either of his crutches? Unless he went up-stairs with a crutch and someone else brought it down for him. Nurse Slocombe? Is there hatred between the two households, the Berry and the Ogilvy faction?

The banisters did not reveal any strange new markings so he did not go upstairs without assistance – if that is where he went.

I turned to my commonplace book that contained the reference to Henry Irving, actor. I soon found what I was looking for:

> In 1871, [it read] when returning from the party which cele-brated his triumphant first night in 'The Bells', his wife scathingly asked, 'Are you going to make a fool of yourself like this all your life?' At this Irving stopped the cab (they were at Hyde Park Corner) and without a word or backward glance got out and never lived with his wife again. The wife was seven months pregnant at the time.

I wondered if such precipitate resolution was the reason for Algernon Berry's admiration of Irving. Miss Ogilvy had mentioned how he had 'loved his Hamlet'. I had seen that interpretation myself and although it divided the critics I felt that his reading of the Danish prince's actions, that he had failed to do the things expected of him not because of weakness of will but because of an excess of tenderness, was valid and showed humanity in the world of heroes. Perhaps that was what had attracted Algernon Berry. Nurse Slocombe would have agreed with that.

If he wished to get rid of the girl, why not pay her off or even go to court? Presumably (although to presume is very dangerous) bad publicity and a sick mother would prevent that, as well as the wrath of Miss Delicia Ogilvy. Not a thing to be trifled with. This brings us back to Miss Ogilvy. What could she hope to gain from the disappearance of her fiancé?

I was absorbed by my thoughts for several minutes. Unless there was a will giving everything to her then I could not see any way by which she could have benefited from Algernon Berry's disappearance. I felt slightly guilty at having been so ready to believe Miss Ogilvy to have been guilty of the crime of murder. I felt angry with myself for letting my emotions rule my logical faculties. However, I had not finished my investigations.

I picked up the aluminium crutch and abstractedly whirled it around between my fingers. The nurse had described Berry as being very slight and delicate since boyhood and his disability had not been compensated for by superior gifts to his other limbs.

What other possibilities were there? Aluminium has several properties. It is light, a good conductor of electricity and it does not rust owing to its natural covering of oxide.

Algernon Berry had a laboratory devoted to experiments with electricity and conductivity. He was also interested in the work, among others, of Galvani and Volta. My commonplace book told me that both these scientists believed that electric currents could stimulate dead limbs into life having based their opinions on work that they had carried out on dead frogs' legs. Was Algernon Berry experimenting on himself in order to cure his crippled leg? Aluminium is a very good conductor of electricity but silver, copper and lead are better. He could have afforded to line his crutch with any of them or even a combination if need be. but he did not. Why not?

Was it used for the concealment of something? A drug, perhaps. (Cocaine, I believe, has properties that can deaden pain. I must carry out my own experiments into that one day but until then I shall have to take the words of the German oculists.) I could smell nothing of a drug and could see no traces of any, even through my lens.

Thus there was only one answer to the riddle of the hollow aluminium crutch. It was so constructed because it was light. The teak veneer was for decoration only and presumably in an attempt to prevent drawing attention to it and therefore its owner. A case of not seeing the aluminium for the teak, I mused. At least my rules of detection were not empty.

But what of the scorch marks?

My reveries were shattered by another assault on my bell. Another case or the formidable Miss Ogilvy returned to belabour me? Certainly Miss Ogilvy was there but the bell ringer was a large sergeant of police who was accompanied by a plain-clothes man who looked rather small to be a policeman.

I ushered them all in, upon which Miss Ogilvy and the plain-clothes man starting speaking at once, she imploring my assistance, he trying to introduce himself. For once Miss Ogilvy was bested and stood crestfallen as the man introduced himself as Inspector Lestrade of Scotland Yard.

'I understand that you are acting for this young lady, Mr Holmes,' he said, his rat-like face constantly mobile. Miss Ogilvy looked at me with ever widening eyes.

'I have been trying to unravel the problem that she has presented to me, Inspector,' I returned.

'Well, there's no need to bother yourself any further, Mr Consulting Detective. We've found the body of the poor man floating in the Thames. I say body because there's not much left of the head. It's him all right Well dressed and crippled. Also I will trouble you for the evidence that you have in your hand.' His tone was a mixture of triumph and truculence. The sergeant relieved me of the aluminium crutch.

'Are you charging the young lady?' I asked.

'Identification first, then a few questions, and I am sure that something positive will follow shortly,' he said with a certain unctuous pride.

'What motive is there? How did the murderess get the body to the river? Where are your witnesses? Could it not have been a tramp wearing one of Mr Berry's old suits? The Thames claims many.'

'Not so fast, Mr Consulting Detective. The law must take its due course with deliberation.'

This man was proving to be most irritating. Miss Ogilvy was innocent, of that I was at that moment certain, but how to prove it there and then? At that moment I recalled the ash that I had swept into my envelope.

'Did you notice when you examined Mr Berry's laboratory that although we have had a very warm August and that the room is south-facing that there was fresh ash in the grate?'

'So what,' he answered gruffly.

'The fire itself had not been used for at least a fortnight and was clean apart from this ash on one side of the grate.'

'The servant did not clean it properly or Mr Berry burnt something. Papers perhaps.'

'Quite possibly, Inspector. There was indeed a smell of

burning when I entered the room twenty-four hours after the disappearance of Mr Berry. It must have been much stronger when you were there yesterday.'

'I must confess it did smell a bit, but I put it down to all those electric gadgets working away.'

'Then it was you who turned the generator off?'

'That is correct.'

'At least you have cleared up one small mystery. But here is a far more important one,' I said as I took the bulging envelope from my coat pocket. 'I was about to analyse it before you came to my door. Would you care to join me?'

With a long-suffering sigh the inspector sat down by my workbench. 'There's bit of a smell here too,' he observed, eyeing my bottles and instruments suspiciously. I took a tiny amount of the white ash from the envelope. I was eager to study it in order to compare it with the other ashes that I had already examined in the course of my studies. I looked into the microscope and adjusted the lenses. That it was not tobacco I already knew but I was not prepared for what it was. I sat back from the microscope in deep thought.

'Have your eyes deceived you, sir?' sniffed a rat-like mocking face.

'See for yourself,' I suggested.

'I don't go in for that sort of hocus-pocus myself. We have our own men at the Yard for that. Well, what did your clever contraption see?'

I looked at Miss Ogilvy and swallowed. 'It was just as you said, Inspector. Paper.'

'I thought so, sir. It takes a few years in the service but we professionals get a nose for this sort of thing. You might learn if you stay the distance. Come, Sergeant, we've seen enough of the new methods.'

As they were leaving, Miss Ogilvy cried out to me, 'Please help me, Mr Holmes. You're all I have left!'

My mind was racing, but I had a question for the inspector. 'Where was the crutch when you entered the laboratory?'

'Leaning up against the mantelpiece.'

'Did you put it there, Miss Ogilvy?'

'Why yes, I did. It was lying across the hearth when I went in at first.'

'Really, Mr Holmes, we must be going,' interjected the inspector. 'We have wasted enough time already.'

'Just one more question if you please, Inspector Lestrade.'

'Oh go on, but be quick,' sighed the professional.

'Describe the ring that your fiancé wore, Miss Ogilvy.'

'It was a plain gold band that he wore on the third finger of his right hand. It was quite thick with a scroll design on it and the initials EMB. It had been his grandmother's wedding ring which he said that he would give to me on our wedding day – if he could get it off. I can't remember seeing him without it.'

'If we may go now, Mr Holmes?'

'You allowed me to ask one question, Inspector. Does your corpse have a full complement of hands and fingers?'

'Not much head, but yes, everything else. Are you suggesting that we have to look for this ring and if it's not there it's not Mr Berry in our mortuary?' he said, the truculence returning'

'It seems a reasonable hypothesis, Inspector.'

The inspector became moody. 'I must admit I did not see any reference to a ring in the report. We shall have to go and check. Come on, Sergeant, bring the prisoner. There's work to be done.'

With that they rose to leave, but as they did so I assured Miss Ogilvy of my faith that she would soon be free.

When they had left I returned to my workbench and emptied out the rest of the contents of the envelope. Among the white bone ash lay a small thick gold ring with a scroll design and the initials EMB. I took out my lens and studied the ring. It was discoloured but not as a result of normal usage. It reminded me of heat discoloration.

There were now three verdicts open to me: murder, suicide and death by misadventure. Had Miss Ogilvy tampered with the machinery which had resulted in its killing Algernon Berry? She had acted as his secretary, had taken notes for him and was in fact as much an assistant as a secretary to him. She was clever enough and determined enough. But what was the point of her murdering him before they were married? If she were a fortune hunter it would serve her no purpose to do the deed before she could become his widow.

Suicide? Surely he had all he wished to live for, if it is true that he had asked Miss Ogilvy to choose the date of their wedding only an hour since. It seemed impossible. Perhaps she had said that she had wanted him to stop his experiments and this was a distorted way of getting back at her. If that were true then his mind would have to be very unbalanced. Also, where was the body? It is not possible to kill oneself and then go into hiding, unless . . .

Death by misadventure? An experiment in electric shock treatment that got out of control? Only if the charge were so great that it could reduce a body to a few ounces of ash. What was that that Miss Ogilvy said about lightning striking in the same place twice when we first met? There has been no lightning recently.

Getting back to the laboratory, the equipment was to the left of the door but the ash, ring and crutch were all on the far side of the centrally located hearth. Perhaps the shock threw him there, but for him to have been reduced to ash would have been impossible unless he were still attached to the machine. But there were no wires leading to the hearth. Miss Ogilvy could have cleared them away just as she stood the crutch up – the way women tidy up it could be the death of this one. No, that is still not good enough. Once again there is no motive for her to murder him – yet. Why is nothing else burnt?

Let us try again. Berry is attached to the machine for whatever reason. It is switched on. The current is so massive that it throws him across the room and reduces him to ashes. Miss Ogilvy comes in and cleans up, even standing the crutch up to make everything look pleasingly tidy to the female mind. Once she would have been premature to kill him. And of course why did she leave the generator on? If she had something to hide she would have turned it off, not left it for the police to do it for her. Also she went to the police, at least one private detective, and finally to me. That could simply be proof of her nerve or then again her innocence. Dear me, I must be missing something. But what?

That evening I returned to 34 Percy Terrace. Miss Ogilvy had not been released and it was a tearful Mary Ogilvy who let me in.

'You've gotta 'elp 'er, Mr 'Olmes,' she sobbed.

I assured her that all would turn out well in the end. On the way over I had stopped off for some assistance. It was a small black box. I attached it to the generator and switched them both on. My meter read 'low'. Even when the generator was turned up to its maximum the reading only just managed to creep out of the 'low' register. However else Mr Algernon Berry had died it was not as a result of his electronic equipment. It was clearly not up to it.

My suspicions that he was still alive became stronger. There was only one thing left for me to do.

At 2:45 a.m. there was a fire at 34 Percy Terrace. No one was hurt and help was soon at hand but not before the occupants had been forced to flee the building to avoid the choking smoke.

When I returned to Montague Street I knew that Algernon Berry was not hidden in 34 Percy Terrace. No one had seen him come or go and his crutches remained unused. Where was he?

I reflected on the day over a last pipe before turning in, although sleep was the last thing on my mind. There had not been a lot of success. True, I had been able to keep boredom from the door, and I had been able to use my powers of deduction to stun Miss Ogilvy and the cab-driver, but that was only very elementary work. By producing the ring on my way back from Percy Terrace I had secured Miss Ogilvy's release as well as the displeasure of both herself and the inspector for having withheld evidence, but I had needed a free hand at Percy Terrace to carry out my final investigations and who better to detain Miss Ogilvy than the police force? Not very gallant of me perhaps, but there was still the crime of kidnap to be investigated. She was innocent of that too. The cab-driver crossed my mind again and for the want of anything better to do I decided to consult my commonplace books to see if I had an entry for 'spondulicks'. I flicked through the pages and reached sp., spo., and then found the answer to the singular affair of the aluminium crutch.

I sat in dumb amazement at the simplicity of it all. My commonplace book had indeed made a commonplace of a most obscure occurrence. My mind went back to my youth in East Anglia. I was most annoyed with my stupidity. The aluminium crutch had told me all if only I had had the eyes to see.

'Then what has happened to Algernon?' Miss Ogilvy asked me as I called upon her that afternoon when she had recovered herself after her long day in police custody.

'I am afraid that you must brace yourself for bad news.'

'It is as I feared,' she replied, her head momentarily

dropping. I hoped that her mother had prepared the strong tea that I had requested as I came in. Her daughter was going to need it.

'Mr Algernon Berry is dead and he died in his laboratory shortly after you left him.'

'But how is that possible?' she cried, crushing her small lace handkerchief in her hand.

'I have made it a rule of mine, a first law if you like,' I answered, 'that once you have eliminated the impossible, whatever remains no matter how improbable must be the truth.'

'Go on, Mr Holmes,' she urged.

'Your fiancé died as a result of spontaneous human combustion.'

'What on earth is that?' she said, bemused.

'It is a very rare phenomenon. One that I have been very sceptical about. There are only three recorded cases of it that I have come across but none have been substantiated by proper eyewitness accounts.' Miss Ogilvy sat dumbstruck, her jaw sagging in disbelief and her brows knitting in anger. I pressed on. 'It occurs commonly enough in the countryside in ill-stacked hayricks that have been damp. That I have seen for myself.'

The explosion came. Perhaps she would not need that tea after all. 'Are you really expecting me to believe that Algernon simply burst into flames and disappeared in a puff of smoke?' she shouted angrily, her voice rising with each word that she spoke. 'Really, Mr Holmes, I am not an idiot!'

'Indeed not, Miss Ogilvy, but there is no other possible explanation. The generator was not strong enough to do it and if it had the current was still on and would have been a great danger to anyone else who entered that room. Yet both yourself and the inspector were unscathed. Everyone noticed the smell of burning. In the three cases that I have on record, nothing was left of any of the victims except in one case a shoe. There were no burns on the floor only a smell of burning and a small pile of ash. If Mr Berry had been standing on the hearthstones when it happened there would be no chance of any burn marks on the carpet. How else can we account for the ring found in the ashes, and the scorches on the aluminium crutch's teak veneer exactly in those places where Mr Berry made direct physical contact with it? The burns were so recent that the leather pad cracked in my hands. If they were old burns then it would have already cracked under Berry's weight.'

At this Miss Ogilvy rose from her seat, a very angry expression on her face and her whole being quivering with an unspoken rage. The words were obviously soon to follow.

'I thank you for getting me out of that police cell, albeit rather tardily, and for the work that you have put into this problem, this tragedy,' she said with admirable restraint, but the dam burst as her voice rose to a hoarse scream, 'but I would thank you even more if you were to get out of this house immediately! I find your humour in profoundly bad taste and I will not be engaging the services of the world's first consulting detective again. Neither shall I recommend his services to anyone else that I know. Good day, goodbye and good riddance, Mr Sherlock Holmes!'

So that was it. Holmes was a pryer into other people's affairs. I had assumed that he was one of those polymath minds whose knowledge is matched only by their wisdom, not a paid sleuth-hound who spies and intercepts one's mail. What a waste of knowledge, I thought, and told him so. He was unmoved. Typical!

A Full Account of Ricoletti of the Club Foot and his Abominable Wife

When first I came to London as a fully independent individual no longer resident at the family hearth in Kent, I spent a great deal of time exploring the vast, imperial metropolis. In those days it was far easier than it is now to detect the particular essential qualities of each of the districts even if they existed side by side, although I must confess that the first stages of the breaking down of such positive demarcations were already in motion. Now, to my mind, a pea-souper can pass as an apt description of the average Londoner as well as of his foggy weather. Individuality has been rendered down to soup so that only the most developed faculties can discern and appreciate the once separate ingredients. When Watson referred to London as a great cesspool he at least had severe injury and shattered nerves to justify his ill-humour. Perhaps my advanced age has led me to the same feeling of disenchantment. But to a young man healthy of limb and bank balance, London was a land of mystery and excitement. My favourite method of exploration was on foot as one sees so much more of people and places on Shanks's nag than through the window of a carriage.

There were two streets in London that were not far from Bart's which summed up for me not just London but what

I knew of England. They were Hatton Garden and Leather Lane. Although they ran parallel to each other they could have been from those different dimensions that Mr H.G. Wells believed to exist.

Hatton Garden was the centre of the world's diamond trade. The windows of the diamond merchants' premises were an Arabian Nights of riches beyond the dreams of mere mortals. Each establishment would have doormen caparisoned like field marshals to open their portals for the rich and favoured. Carriages emblazoned with armorial bearings were a regular sight, as were the red carpets unrolled to greet these honoured clients. These clients came not only from England but also from all parts of the Empire and the world beyond. I used to think that if I stood in Hatton Garden long enough I would see pass before me the crowned heads of every kingdom in the world – as well as the rulers of the so-called republics. The common folk of London could also be seen thronging the pavements but the only shopping they could afford was confined to the windows from which they were soon moved on by the policemen who patrolled this Hormuz in EC1.

Leather Lane was just as long as Hatton Garden, connecting the Clerkenwell Road and Holborn, but the contrast could not have been greater. For the well-heeled of Hatton Garden, Leather Lane had the bare-footed. For the wealth and exclusivity of the one there was the poverty and the open-stalled street life of the other. And yet there was a colour and an exuberance in Leather Lane that was totally lacking in its more distinguished neighbour. This vitality could be detected in so many ways, from the brightly coloured market stalls, reminiscent of a fairground, which were illuminated after dark by roaring lamps that threw up garish highlights and cast deep shadows in the gathering gloom, to the popular tunes of the organ grinders and those who gathered to sing along to these mesmeric orchestras of wood and wind or simply to watch the organ grinders' animals dance to their masters' tunes.

And what a cosmopolitan area it was too, in a fashion so different from that of Hatton Garden's international 'champagne and caviar' set.

The area was justly renowned for its craftsmen skilled in so many diverse ancient mysteries. These craftsmen came from many different backgrounds, from rural England to Huguenot France, or from the low-lying Netherlands where expertise was as diverse as diamond polishing and drain engineering. But more than anywhere it was from Italy, no longer merely a geographical expression that immigrants came. They seemed to have brought their Mediterranean sun with them so that they radiated a life force which enabled them to rise above the squalor of their immediate surroundings and overcome the depredations of an alien, inhospitable climate.

Just such a one was Guigliermo Feliz Ricoletti. Originally from Castellammare in the Bay of Naples he had lived for much of his early life in Naples whence he came with some relatives to London. These relatives soon disappeared leaving the young Guigliermo to fend for himself. Life was very hard for him because he knew only a smattering of English, because he was barely twelve years of age, but most of all because of his club foot. This affliction had been with him from birth, being hereditary. Of the four main types of talipes, Ricoletti suffered from *talipes equinovarus* in which the heel is drawn up and the sole of the foot turned inwards. That was in fact how a generation of students at Bart's got to meet this man for the first time.

One day he had delivered some food to the hospital and one of the chief surgeons had noticed his condition. He offered to operate on the young man, but when told it would mean missing a lot of work he refused. However, the surgeon prevailed upon him to visit the hospital every so often (for a fee) so that the students could examine such a clearly defined case. But I get ahead of myself.

When he was first left alone Ricoletti worked as a porter in Smithfield Market, a labourer on the roads and as a delivery boy for a baker (with this last job he could have the day-old bread free). These mundane jobs sustained him as he prepared for his chosen career – bare-knuckle prize-fighter. It was that work that he did not wish to miss by having an operation on his misshapen foot.

Guigliermo Feliz Ricoletti proved to be a very popular fighter with the crowds. Many believed him to be that rarity in those days of wagers and 'fixes' – an honest fighter; so that a bet on 'Happy Billy', as he was affectionately known from his ready smile, was never considered a wasted investment. If he lost, the punters put it down to 'just one of those things' or 'you can't win 'em all'. He fought in booths, on blasted heaths, in sporting clubs and on race-courses. A light-heavyweight of great strength and even greater courage he would often take on fighters far heavier than himself. Sometimes he would take a terrible beating but he rarely lost. 'Billy's Bumper' was the kiss that meant a full count to more than one over-confident, overweight opponent.

When he retired from the ring he was faced with the question that will always confront retiring athletes – what to do next? He had a certain Latin vanity and had grown to covet the centre spotlight of events. Thus it was no surprise that he went on the stage. Sometimes he would box an exhibition, on other occasions he would perform feats of great strength. No one noticed his club foot. Attention was on his rippling muscles and infectious smile.

Many rumours circulated about Happy Billy. These usually involved stories of money won and lost as well as women and wagers the same. Then he disappeared, no one knew where. Knowing looks and nodding heads agreed that it was the old demon, drink, that had 'knocked out the Neapolitan' in the end.

I had never met him, but then one day a man came into the hospital leaning heavily on a stick, his right leg swathed in grimy bandages from toe to knee.

'You know Surgeon Simpson?' he asked me, a smile on his lips revealing several gold-filled teeth.

'I am afraid not,' I replied. 'He was a little before my time.'

'Pity,' he sighed. 'He pay me to look at my leg. You a fighter, no, yes?' he asked, dragging himself closer to me.

'No,' I replied. 'Rugby football is my game.'

'Same difference,' he joked smiling even more broadly and revealing even more gold.

'Can I do anything for you, sir?' I asked.

'To be called "sir" by an Englishman would once have been enough, but now . . .' he raised his powerful shoulders and opened the palms of his hands to me in a gesture of resignation, 'I have this other matter.' He indicated to his obviously damaged leg. As he looked down I noticed that he was starting to go bald on the crown of his head, although his hair had been brushed and oiled to camouflage this development.

I examined the foot and found it to be *talipes equinovarus*. It had been very inexpertly operated on and was in a pretty poor state. It was then that he told me about himself and how he had been to Bart's before at the behest of Surgeon Simpson.

'You ever hear of "Happy Billy"?' he asked.

'Why yes, I have. Are you he?' I asked in wonder having heard my father mention him several times for his great bravery and honesty. My reaction obviously pleased him and the gold came on show again. 'My father won a packet on you against that American. What was his name again?'

'Yes, I make many men rich,' he remarked, a note of chagrin in his voice, but it soon passed. 'Gary Lieberhoff if you mean the very big Americano or 'Arry Jackson if you mean the gigantic one.' His good humour had returned and I found it infectious. We were soon getting on like old comrades swapping stories of sporting encounters.

Watson has immortalized me as being both 'young' and a 'dresser' and this is the only occasion that I shall have to be able to talk of my skills in the latter area. They were not considerable, as Ricoletti would confirm, but at least I made a clean job of it. Throughout his ordeal Happy Billy continued to live up to his reputation for good humour and bravery.

'I are sorry,' he said when I had finished my ministrations, 'but I no can pay you at the moment. But look, you have a couple of these. Bring some friends – a nice nurse, perhaps.' He winked theatrically. 'You all very welcome.' With that he thrust into my hand several tickets for a music-hall show at the Palace. 'They the best in house. I go now but I see you later perhaps, maybe, yes?'

When he had gone I reflected on my erstwhile patient. Had he fallen foul of drink as the rumours had said? If so he had made a sound recovery. His eyes were clear and he was full of life. Just talking to him had filled me full of vigour, but I feared that he would remain a club foot for the rest of his life. In fact the operation that he had had on it had nearly left him ruined. I felt duty bound to tell him and resolved to see him again. I turned over in my hand the 5s. tickets that he had given me and wondered who to take with me. Edith Wriggleton – probably not.

Several days later I was talking to Sherlock Holmes in

the chemistry laboratory as he purified an alkaloid solution of some pungency and I happened to mention Ricoletti's visit as well as my observations concerning Hatton Garden and Leather Lane. To my surprise he replied, 'I know what you mean. A walk along there finally made up my mind for me as to my future career.' He then briefly limned for me the events of December 23rd, 1874.

When he had finished, on an impulse I suggested that we revisit this influential site. It was late afternoon but with the season and the cloud cover London was already cold and dark. Holmes and I, buttoned up against the elements, put our best feet forward and were soon back in Leather Lane.

Another of the things that appealed to me about the area was the variety of sensations that it provided for the olfactory system. The artists of the school of Paris have captured scenes such as these during the period of which I write. The lurid artificial lighting, the sense of animation, the unexpected perspectives are now familiar to us from the canvases of Degas, Lautrec and their many followers. Very good they are too, no doubt, but no paint or pastel has been able to recapture that most evocative of sensations – smell. The fruits and vegetables so firm and crisp in the early morning, but by late afternoon they had become flaccid and their sharpness dissipated – although on colder days their tang would last longer. As their flesh corrupted there would be a sweet sickly smell that attracted the flies and the destitute, the latter being able to afford only rotting food. The cold fish on their icy marble slabs would give off an oily smell, whereas the crabs would still have the sharpness of sea salt about them. Then there would be the cheeses and the herbs; rich and aromatic, sharp and pungent; or as fragrant as a walled garden on an imaginary summer's day in Tudor England.

But it is always to the vegetables that my nose twitches in fond remembrance and, of them, three in particular – garlic, onions and tomatoes. I can remember only one type of garlic but that was enough with its lilac paper skin, leaky gas-pipe smell and the bracing assault on the tongue and tear ducts. The onions and tomatoes came in such a rich profusion that I never mastered them all. They were of different sizes, some as small as boiled sweets and others larger than cricket balls. The onions were golden or tawny, amber or mauve, their skins flaky and asking to be removed so that the stinging weeping flesh beneath could be prepared for consumption. Some glowed like glass balls from a Christmas tree, others sat fat and matt like contented Spanish prelates. The tomatoes brimmed with health like cardinals of the faith; from vermilion to scarlet to magenta and each giving off that delicate sweet pepper scent.

Then there were the smells of the food being prepared. In the streets there would be the aromas of bread freshly baked, with chestnuts and muffins heating over coal or wood burners each quite distinct from the other. Best of all would be the olive oil heating and then sizzling as it cooked a mixture of freshly chopped onions, garlic, peeled plum tomatoes and herbs, particularly oregano and tarragon.

What is there now? The products of Mr Austin and his rival Mr Morris giving us Chateau Exhaust '51. No doubt in years to come their individual aromas will unlock memories for a future generation grown old – I must confess that I rather like the smell of Morris interior – but somehow it is not the same. At least not to me, but I grow old again. Come on, young Stamford, Signor Ricoletti is waiting.

As indeed he was as Holmes and I made our way down Leather Lane and reached the corner of Greville Street. Much to our surprise he was turning the handle of a barrel organ, his face as usual one broad grin. A small crowd had gathered and we stood by to watch the entertainment. At first Ricoletti invited the group to join him in a song, then he asked if any individuals would like to try their luck. 'You never know,' he shouted. 'Sing well here, now, today and maybe the Palace perhaps tonight, tomorrow, eh?' One after another various singers came forward, usually young women. One was far better than the rest and she seemed to know it as she made her appearance towards the end of the show. Although her voice was obviously untrained in any professional sense and revealed a slight coarseness in the higher register there was vitality and spirit about it. I wondered if she was the same girl whom Holmes had seen that night in '74, but he was absorbed in his own thoughts and I left him to them. Ricoletti looked at her with clear admiration in his eyes. When she had finished her song the crowd had grown bigger and were extremely appreciative. Ricoletti shouted out above the din, 'Come to the Palace tonight and hear this young diva sing again. Tickets 6d. or less.'

The crowd cheered and cries of 'Good old Billy' filled the air. So that was what he was up to – drumming people up for the music-hall. He was very good at it. Ricoletti held his hands up again and shouted, 'Do not forget that there are funny men of the "comedias", other singers perhaps not as good as our diva here but they good too, and our new attraction: the "Missing Link!"'

The crowd stilled. ''Ere, what's that when it's at home then, Bill?' came a voice from the shadows.

'The Missing Link is the creature your Mr Darwin could not find to prove that we come from the apes.'

'Oh no. Not that again,' groaned another voice.

'We all know that you men come from apes,' screamed a woman's voice with a broad cockney accent. 'We don't need no proof on that one, Billy.' The crowd joined in the laughter.

Billy was smiling too when he replied, 'This one is a female.' All the men now laughed good humouredly. 'You better come now, ladies, to keep an eye on your men. I see you all now, later, yes?'

'One last song before you go, Billy?' they entreated.,

'Sure, sure. I play, you sing, yes?'

'Yes,' came back the happy chorus.

I turned to speak to Holmes but to my consternation he had gone. A moment later I felt a hand on my shoulder and turned to see the smiling face of Sherlock Holmes as he held up my pocket watch. 'Signor Ricoletti's not the only entertainment this afternoon,' he said quietly returning my property to me. 'The only question is, was he in league with the gang of pickpockets who were working the crowd just now?'

'I think not, Holmes. Billy Ricoletti is renowned for his honesty.'

'Let us go and have a word with him,' was all that he would reply.

By the time that we had got through the crowd the song had finished and Ricoletti was packing up his barrel organ ready to go back to the theatre for that evening's performance. When he saw us approaching he dropped what he was doing and rushed over to greet us. I held out my hand to shake his and to introduce my companion but instead of taking my hand he brushed past me and threw his arms around Holmes crying out, 'I am so pleased to see you again, Mr Sherlock. Oh, that straight left and cross with the right. You nearly beat me. Me! In front of all those people.'

Holmes smiled and introduced me to Signor Ricoletti who in his turn had the good grace to remember our last meeting and praised my skills beyond their true worth.

'Where have you been these last few years?' Holmes asked.

'I have travelled the globe, my friend,' came the less than precise answer.

'London was not earth enough?' I put in.

'It was not that, Doctor.' (That was the first time that anyone had ever called me 'Doctor'. I was very pleased.)

'Always I have wanted to travel. Columbus and Marco Polo were Italian; it is not just you British who travel the world.'

'Where did you go?' I added.

'Everywhere. Anywhere. Wherever my heart said go.'

'Did you find your Missing Link on your travels?' enquired Holmes.

'You could say that Mr Sherlock,' Ricoletti replied with another golden grin.

'You have been to Macedonia via Italy recently, I perceive,' Holmes continued. Ricoletti's smile disappeared but slowly returned so that the gold shone again.

'Always the clever one, eh, Mr Sherlock? Yes, I go to visit my family in Italy.'

'I thought you had no family.'

'Distant ones, new ones. We have big families in Naples.'

'When did you get back to London?'

'A week, two weeks ago. Who cares? But now that I am back I wish to entertain myself and entertain my friends. You come see my show tonight?'

'This Missing Link, what is it exactly?' Holmes queried.

'You come tonight, Mr Sherlock, and then you see.'

'Is there any chance that we shall be able to examine it afterwards?' I asked.

'Her, my good doctor, her. She live just like us. Have feelings just like us.'

'You haven't answered Mr Stamford's question,' Holmes interposed.

'Maybe. Maybe not. I go now. You come and see the

show. You still have tickets, Doctor? They are best in house.'

'Before you go I have something to tell you, Signor Ricoletti. It is not good news, I'm afraid.'

'Say it. Happy Billy will not be sad.'

'I'm afraid that whoever operated on your foot did a very bad job. You must keep the dressing absolutely clean.'

'What are you trying to say, Doctor?' His eyes narrowed.

My mouth was dry. This was the first time that I had had to break bad news and I did not like it. 'I am trying to tell you that you will suffer from your condition for the rest of your life. I am very sorry.'

Ricoletti looked aghast. My words had wiped the smile from his face far more completely than any punch had ever done. He muttered an oath and spat viciously into the gutter. 'This is why I come to England. Dr Simpson he my friend. He would have saved me.' He looked crushed as he trudged away as though I had sentenced him to death.

'What did you make of that, Stamford?' Holmes asked, as though nothing had happened.

'An understandable reaction in the circumstances, Holmes.'

'No, not that. I meant the story he had to tell.'

'He seems to have lived quite an adventurous life,' I replied rather half-heartedly, my mind elsewhere.

'You think so?' Holmes remarked. His cold manner was beginning to annoy me. I had not felt happy giving Ricoletti my medical opinion; the last thing I wanted was such an inhuman reaction.

I rounded on him. 'Why do you adopt that tone? Is the gold in his teeth only to be found in Birmingham, or did he have a piece of fluff in his ear that can only be found in Yeovil?' Holmes remained admirably impassive in the face of my invective.

'Not quite, but you are on the right track. When I met him several years ago the gold in his teeth was of far better quality than that he has now. Thus he is not so well mon-eyed now. Why not?'

'He's no longer boxing,' was my flat response.

'True, but he had great success with his act after he retired. In fact he retired earlier than most which in itself could be very significant. In fact the circumstances were curious.'

'Oh?' I said, my interest rekindled.

'He lost his last fight by not coming out to the scratch for the last round and yet up until then he was giving Thwaites at least as good as he got.'

'Were you there?'

'Yes, I was.'

'So you think Happy Billy's last fight was fixed?'

'Possibly.'

'But why should he have been a party to such a thing?'

Holmes shrugged his shoulders. 'Money. He wished to retire early perhaps In which case a fix could have been a short cut to wealth. It has happened before.'

'I can't really blame him,' I said expansively. He was probably tired of such a hard profession.'

'Possibly, but we must not forget his Latin pride – you yourself have noticed evidence of vanity. However, I must not speak further on this matter until I have more informa-tion. Suffice to say I have made it a rule of mine to look for possible alternatives and to provide against them.'

'You speak as though this was a case.'

'I got the distinct impression from Happy Billy that all is not well with him. My intuition tells me that something is going on and is about to reach its climax. I cannot say what it is yet. Perhaps we shall learn more at the show.'

We dined together but I remember nothing of what was said apart from the following: 'I have been re-reading Dar-win's *Origin of the Species* and have found his measured prose soothing to my mind whilst at the same time it is a work of great detection and thus a source of inspiration to me. Also I cannot help but reflect on the status of the work itself. Like so many works that have changed men's thinking the more famous, and consequentially influential, that it becomes the less it is read. I can think of no greater parallel example than that of the Magna Carta. It has become the symbol of freedom throughout the world wherever Britons have settled. Yet who has read it? Who can explain its form and syntax? Who can appreciate the motives of its original authors? If such knowledge was available to all I fear that the Great Charter would lose much of its influence and John Lackland would have a far healthier reputation.'

It was in this frame of mind that Sherlock Holmes watched Ricoletti's act from the front stalls to which my free tickets entitled us.

First he invited someone from the audience to bend some bars and lift some weights, none of which he could accomplish. Needless to say Ricoletti managed it with the greatest of ease.

Next his diva from Leather Lane appeared. Apparently she was a well-known character to many in the audience and her singing was greatly appreciated to judge by the volume of applause.

Finally, Ricoletti led his Missing Link on to the stage by hand. She appeared nervous but a few whispered words in her ear and she smiled. The audience applauded. She curtseyed and the audience applauded more loudly. Holmes narrowed his eyes and leant forward in an effort to see what was going on. The Missing Link was of ape-like appearance but her hairs were quite light. The forehead was low and slanting and the brows heavy and brooding. The nose was straight but broad of nostril and the mouth was heavy and sullen. She was about my height and quite heavy set although once her nerves had settled she moved with an almost feline fluidity.

She next performed various acrobatic tricks with great élan, much to the delight of her spectators. 'Now I show how human she is,' cried Ricoletti much to the delight of the baser elements in the audience. 'No, no. Not like that,' shouted Ricoletti, smiling as ever as he wagged an admonitory forefinger at the house which only increased its response. 'How many apes you know, apart from your husbands!' (loud cheers from the women) 'have blue eyes? Here look my friend, here. Blue eyes. Show them, show them. Show the people your eyes.'

At that the ape-like creature leant forward and the front few rows clearly beheld the blue eyes and several voiced their observations to those at the back.

'And no animal can laugh or cry like the human, yes, no?' The audience buzzed in confusion and expectation. 'My girl, she do both. I tell her a joke and you see what I mean.'

'But 'ow are yer gonna make her laugh, Billy,' guffawed a voice from the gods.

Unabashed Ricoletti told his joke in a gibberish that none of his audience understood although I felt that some of them should have done to judge by their antics. But as he spoke once again Holmes leant forward this time in an effort to hear what was being said. The Missing Link shrilled with high-pitched laughter. The audience was stunned into silence by the human girlish quality of the voice. Ricoletti beamed in triumph. 'I explain you the joke so maybe you laugh too, no, yes? It is about a shepherd who mistake a sheep for his wife. He slap her because he want to know who give her the fur coat. It lose something in translation maybe.'

Ricoletti sat the animal on his lap and cuddled her. The

audience let out a sympathetic breath, but suddenly Ricoletti jumped up and slapped the creature. She cried and the tears rolled down her face. The crowd murmured its disapproval and was about to start booing its former hero, when Ricoletti showed them blood dripping from his ear lobe. 'Look she bite me. She not realize her own strength. Nor me, mine. I sorry.' The creature had run sobbing from the stage and Ricoletti pursued her. Moments later they both returned smiling and bowing to accept the thunderous applause of the assembly.

After the performance Holmes and I went backstage to see Ricoletti. He was surrounded by admirers. The Missing Link was seated in the far corner of the room next to a heavy curtain and was being fed a bowl of nuts by the diva. All was laughter and merriment around the Italian but none encroached on the space around the animal. At least not until Sherlock Holmes made his appearance. He went up to the creature and peered directly into her eyes. She shrank back from this forceful scrutiny and whimpered away behind the curtain. Holmes tipped his hat to Ricoletti and we both left. As we departed I heard Holmes murmur to himself, 'Blue lions.' Ricoletti looked nervous.

'What was all that about?' I asked, having to run to keep up with. Holmes's fierce stride.

'I smell a rat,' he responded angrily.

'Oh come on, Holmes. No one believes that to be a real "missing link", although it's the best skin I've ever seen without a doubt.'

'Did you know that Ricoletti spoke to that creature in a rare Asiatic dialect believed to come from the High Himalayas? I have come across it in my religious studies. I was astounded when I heard it – you may have seen me lean forward in surprise. Even greater was my surprise when I translated his words: "Beware, my lady, of the tall one who looks".'

'You?'

'He was looking at me when he said it.' Normally I would have found such a conversation absurd but Holmes was in deadly earnest.

'Why should he warn his pet whatever it was about you?' I asked in all seriousness.

'Because while we were all watching Signor Ricoletti this afternoon it was not only your watch that was being stolen. I picked up an early evening newspaper and discovered that two Hatton Garden jewellers were robbed.'

'Well I never,' said I, somewhat uncomprehendingly.

'From the timing it is possible that the girl who sang with Ricoletti could have carried out one of the thefts but not both. If anything, the girl who took your watch could have done it but she looked rather young to be robbing Hatton Garden jewellers although she may graduate to such occupations if she takes no heed of my reprimand.'

'But why bring Ricoletti into it at all?'

'Because the site that he chose to set up his barrel organ was at the corner of Leather Lane and Greville Street which in turn leads off to Hatton Garden.

'So what of it,' I remonstrated. 'It was a sensible place to act up because that way he could get a large crowd and a better house later.'

'True, but it also meant that the resulting activity drew many of the police from their normal patrols in order to keep an eye on Ricoletti's crowd thus leaving their beats unguarded during the performance.'

'That would account for his pleasure on seeing the girl,' I surmised enthusiastically.

'You noticed that too?' Holmes remarked in a very deflating tone. 'Yes, if they were the perpetrators then when she appeared safe and sound he knew that the job had been done.'

'Unless of course he just likes her.'

'A possibility; it has been known to happen,' he observed rather stiffly. 'There is something going on and I don't like the implications.'

'What was that about "blue lions" that you mentioned backstage?'

'You misheard me, Stamford. I actually said "blue eyes and the smell of lions". You missed me saying "tail-less"'

'Don't be obtuse, Holmes. What does it all mean?' I asked rather impatiently.

'I am not prepared to say as yet,' he replied. 'I have several theories to test first. Good night, Stamford.'

With that he was off into the night. I decided to call on Mr Belcher in the Butcher's Arms. Holmes could be miserable company at times. He had not even thanked me for giving him one of my free tickets. He had taken it for granted that we would go and see his old pugilist friend in his new career with his fake monkey that had no tail. Holmes and I were heading for a confrontation.

The next day proved to be one of the most remarkable of my life.

It started remarkably enough with my being early to rise the following morning, but that was small beer compared with what was to follow. As I entered the cloakroom a figure lurched out of the shadows and grabbed hold of my lapels in his powerful hands. It was Ricoletti, his face a deathly grey and his eyes bulging bloodshot from his head, its baldness plainly apparent now.

'Where is Mr Sherlock? Where is Mr Sherlock? You his friend. You know where. Take me. Take me him. Now!' he screamed hoarsely, the tears pouring down his unshaven cheeks. He smelt of drink. I told him where to find Holmes but he would not let go of me. He kept calling me his friend and his doctor who had been so good to him despite his rudeness to me.

I led him from the hospital catching many disapproving looks as I did so. We called a cab and raced to Montague Street where we found Holmes about to go into his tobacconist's shop. 'Quick,' I hissed, 'Get in. Ricoletti's with me. He's all done in.' For once Holmes looked genuinely surprised but he leapt in immediately.

'Where to now, guv'nor?' cried the cabby.

Ricoletti called out the name of a very prestigious hotel which has still not acknowledged what took place there so I suppose it had better remain anonymous even now. How they kept it out of the newspapers I shall never know.

'Always the best for my Angelina and her Rose. Curse them both!' screamed the sobbing Italian. 'Abominata!'

By the time we had reached the hotel, Ricoletti had recovered himself and made a dignified entrance into the foyer. His key was to one of the finest suites. I felt rather out of place but Holmes was immune to such feelings. We quickly mounted the stairs not bothering to wait for the lift, and entered the rooms. Ricoletti rushed ahead and fell sobbing by a double door. So far the rooms had looked in perfect order. The only hint of trouble was an empty gin bottle under the sofa which Ricoletti had probably dispatched hence the smell of drink about his person. The horror lay beyond the double doors. Ricoletti started to claw the carpet with his nails and moan, 'Shame, shame.'

Holmes and I steeled ourselves before making our assault. Holmes turned the door handle. It was unlocked. We nodded to each other and, taking a deep breath, we swept noiselessly into the room as one. It was the master bedroom and all was peace and tranquillity. Our eyes wildly searched for a clue to help us solve this riddle. I let out a gasp as a cupboard door swung open to reveal the Missing Link, blood on its lips. Holmes sprang into his boxer's stance but it was only a skin. Holmes examined it, passing a finger inside it and nodding in triumph when he inspected the result.

Holmes then signalled to the bed and we approached with the utmost caution. Just as Holmes was about to pull the bedclothes back a sleepy arm emerged followed by a yawning face. It was Ricoletti's diva. The yawn froze when she saw us and it turned into a scream. The piercing noise seemed to rouse Ricoletti and he leapt onto the bed like a panther. There was a gleam of merciless metal in his hand and before we could move the screaming had stopped to be replaced by an horrific gurgling cough which sprayed the silken bedspread with blood as Ricoletti plunged his stiletto into the singer's throat. As the 'Leather Lane diva' pitched forward in her death throes Ricoletti turned to face us, his eyes the unblinking beacons of the madman. 'Now you shall see Ricoletti's shame.' His voice was a threat, a challenge and a cry of pain as he reached for the remaining bedclothes.

I never saw him reach them. Holmes and I made our charge. Ricoletti stabbed at Holmes. Holmes deflected the thrust but as he was doing so a wild left swing, more in hope than judgement, caught me full in the face. The last sensations that I could recall were the cracking of cartilage and the rush of warm blood to my face as my nose broke. I was unconscious before I had hit the floor.

When I recovered, Holmes was cradling my head and administering smelling salts in the region of what had been my nose. 'Easy, young fellow,' he said calmly. 'You caught a real "Billy's Bumper", that time. You have been out a long time.'

The mist cleared from my eyes and they focused on a scene of tumultuous dislocation. The bedclothes were ripped from the bed, chairs lay on their backs with their legs in the air, rugs were deranged, but most surprising of all not only was Holmes's hair out of place he also had a black eye and a bloody lip. He laughed off his flesh wounds and indicated Ricoletti slumped in a chair with all the dispiritedness of a French aristocrat awaiting his appointment with Madame Guillotine. Dimly I became aware that he was wearing handcuffs.

'Are the police here, Holmes?' I asked, still somewhat dazed.

'Not yet,' he replied, 'but they soon will be,' he continued, looking at his watch. 'I arranged for them to appear at ten o'clock so we have but ten minutes to unravel this warp and weft.' It was at times like this that I found it difficult to follow Holmes so it was best to let him continue.

'Now, Billy,' he continued, 'tell us your story and we may be able to help you, for you will surely hang unless we can speak for you.'

The crushed boxer shrugged his shoulders. 'I want hang anyway. I do my duty. There is nothing of Ricoletti now.'

'Then tell us what made you do this if only to get it off your chest,' I urged.

He frowned and sighed. Finally he sullenly spoke. 'I lose my honour twice over. My last fight — it was fix.'

'But you were always so honest,' I said. 'My father told me so.'

'That I was and all knew it. So by being dishonest in my last fight I was able to get much money on wagers.'

'But why?' I persisted.

'Many do it, why not Billy Ricoletti? I get the bruises but not the money. Where sense in that?'

'There's more to it than that,' intervened Holmes.

Ricoletti faced his conqueror. 'You right — as always, Mr Sherlock. I was to be married. I needed money to retire and settle down with my Angelina.'

'I did not know that you were married,' I said.

'In Napoli. All agreed by our families. We never meet until I go there. I raise more money by my show then I go back.' Here Ricoletti paused and smiled weakly. 'She was so beautiful but so young. Only a child. To her I was to be hero from faraway land. When she see me she see no hero, only club foot, flat nose and the cauliflowers, and the gold teeth. Her eyes had no love in them.

'I give her all I could. Money, clothes, jewels, house, servants. Even my teeth, I sell. Not enough. I advised to give her the children but it was not the time to do that.

'Then there are rumours. They say she steal. Is true. She steal anything. It's like she is the maniac for the stealing. But it was so strange. For her the stealing was all, not the having. She steal and dare to be caught. Then she throw the steals away. I could no understand. The doctors no under-stand but they take my money. I have to pay the hush-up money. In end we have to leave.

'You remember I tell you, Mr Sherlock, that my hero is Marco Polo? We go to Venice and follow his journey on the Silk Road. We see many wonders. One half of them you not believe, the other half you say I lie. But still she steal.

'Is then that we discover Missing Link. Here, I think, is something to make my Angelina love me. Now I can prove what your Mr Darwin did not. I become big shot.'

'You have read Darwin?' Holmes asked.

'No, no. You no need read the book to know his mind. He is all around.'

Holmes let out an exasperated sigh. 'Go on,' he urged.

'Two come with us. They say they like go to Italy. One die on the way. We skin her, and show skin to people but they only laugh. Angelina laugh at me. I have operation on foot.' It no good. We come to England to find Dr Simpson and to show Angelina how much I am hero here. We join show. Angelina likes that because she trained from birth for the circus as acrobat. Angelina she likes the crowds and Hatton Gardens. She steal.'

'That was when you first met Signora Ricoletti, Stamford,' Holmes pointed out to me.

I was confused.

'Your watch. I caught her but did not realize who she was. I thought that she was but a girl and so I merely recovered your property and castigated her; to no avail, I fear.'

'That is right, Mr Sherlock. She is sick. When you appear I was afraid. Of all people you would learn my wife's secret. Then what happen to us?' Here his Latin temperament took over again and he wept unreservedly. 'Then there were the other rumours,' he gasped between sobs. 'None dare say to my face. They too scared of Billy's Bumper. But they say behind my back that I am no real man. Where are the children they say? Then we help this slut!' he cried nodding towards the corpse of the murdered singer. 'My wife and her – Rose – they devoted. Guigliermo not mind, he happy Angelina is happy.' For several moments he was uncontrollable in his ululations. Finally he recovered himself as the clock on its side on the mantelshelf struck ten. Holmes checked it with his own timepiece and raised an eyebrow in surprise at its continued accuracy. Ricoletti recovered himself enough to blurt out his final words. 'Last night I find the rumours true. For such a crime there is only one sentence. Death.'

As he said the final word his head dropped and Tobias Gregson of Scotland Yard made his entrance. 'Good day, Mr Holmes,' opened the tall, hearty, flaxen-haired professional. 'What on earth have you been up to, Mr Holmes? This room looks as though a herd of wild animals has been through it. And murder too, is it?' he observed, his tone becoming more serious when he saw Rose's lifeless form.

'This is your man, Gregson,' said Holmes quietly.

'For which crime, this murder or the theft?' asked the tenacious Scotland Yarder.

'The murder; but go easy on him, there are extenuating circumstances.'

'Which are, might I be permitted to ask, Mr Holmes?'

'His temperament, his wife and something hereditary.'

'I'm afraid that they will cut very little ice with an English jury even if it's worth a plea on the Continent. But the Hatton Garden gems? Where are they?'

'They were stolen by Angelina Ricoletti during the show.'

'Where is she now?'

'I do not rightly know, but she cannot be far away. Her suit is hanging on that cupboard door and a young lady in a Venetian lace nightdress should be somewhat eye-catching at 10 a.m. in the streets of West Central London.'

Gregson was galvanized into action. He ordered an alert put out and a systematic search of the hotel. He then asked Holmes what he meant about 'her suit'. Holmes indicated the Missing Link skin.

'She wore that when she crept down the sewer below Grootze's and broke in through the drainage grille.'

'The grille?' boomed Gregson. 'Come on, Mr Holmes, that grille is too small for anyone to get through.'

'You will find that Signora Ricoletti is very small and more than capable of negotiating such a small aperture particularly when without the animal skin and wearing only her own greased one.'

'What!' cried a now nonplussed policeman.

'If you compare the grease on the grille with that on the inside of the skin you will see that they are identical.'

'Well, I'll be blowed!' gasped the detective.

'Stamford and I will leave you now, Gregson. You have plenty to do.' With that Holmes was on his way.

Once again I felt his manner too cold. I rushed over to Ricoletti and shook his manacled hand. 'Good luck, old man. That was a wonderful punch that floored me.' He smiled sadly back at me and nodded in recognition of my small crumb of comfort. I then rushed off after Holmes. There were one or two things that I wished to sort out.

When I caught up with him he was already sunk into one of those uncommunicative moods which it was best not to disturb. I disturbed it anyway. 'Do you always take handcuffs with you when you visit the tobacconist, Holmes?' I asked rather churlishly.

'Not as a rule, Stamford, but I had been to the Reading Room to confirm some of my thoughts and was on my way to seek confirmation of a point from Mr Boddy before coming on here. You intercepted me, not that it mattered in the event.' He was as unruffled as if he was reciting a timetable from Bradshaw to an inquisitive passer-by.

'What thoughts did you want confirmed?' I persisted, my tone still churlish.

'The only reference that I could think of to an upright tail-less ape was by B.H. Hodgson, the British Resident in Nepal, in his article of 1832. His porters thought that they had seen a demon but he thought that it was an orang-utan. Curiously he mentioned a smell, "like lions" was how he described it. I noticed that particular aroma backstage at the Palace again today about the skin in the cupboard, and this morning in Grootze's, though in the latter two examples the smell was not as marked as in the first. I had intended to ask Mr Boddy if it could have been a tobacco.'

'You have already been to Grootze's this morning?' I asked in amazement.

'Yes. After I left you last night I wandered the streets of London trying to clear my mind. I reached Hatton Garden and found that there had been no alarms. Obviously if no thefts had been discovered during the night then, if one had been perpetrated, it would only be discovered when the premises opened this morning at 8:30 a.m. I was there earlier awaiting the alarm. It came from Grootze's and I was able to investigate immediately. The smell was distinctive and the grease was conclusive when taken in conjunction with the contents of that cupboard later this morning. The rest of the facts about Ricoletti's wife seemed to confirm everything.'

'So who was on stage with Ricoletti?'

'Yes, it was when I looked into the creature's eyes after the performance that I realized that something was amiss.'

'You have not answered my question, Holmes.'

'Someone who understood Himalayan dialect, of course.'

'I can't possibly . . .' I stammered.

'You have to believe it. You were face to face with a genuine Missing Link in the human evolutionary chain when it was on stage. I had to find out what colour were Signora Ricoletti's eyes. I only found out this morning.'

'When was that?'

'You were unconscious at the time.'

'Where is it now? This is very important scientific discovery,' I enthused.

'I don't know where it is and as it has done no wrong I feel that I ought to occupy my time elsewhere.' From the direction of Holmes's tread we were on our way to Montague Street but I thought it more prudent to get back to the hospital before I was too badly missed. My nose also needed repairing for my breathing was becoming laboured as a result of its new shape.

I was about to take my leave when Holmes stopped abruptly, 'Yes,' he said, 'perhaps one day.'

'Perhaps one day, what, Holmes?' I asked.

'I must go there and solve this mystery once and for all.'[1] Already his mind was drifting to those far-off peaks. There was one question outstanding that needed an answer.

'What was Rose's crime that brought about the death sentence for her and for Signora Ricoletti if her husband could have carried it out?' prompted Holmes, as though reading my mind as was his wont. He smiled, 'You have seen much of life on the wards but not all it has to reveal. Their crime does not have a place in our statute books and will not have while Victoria is our queen.'

'Why not, Holmes?' I asked in genuine confusion.

'Because she does not recognize that it exists between women although she concedes it in the case of men.'

'But surely it is not a capital offence in Naples – whatever it is?'

'Not in their laws either, but to a hot-blooded Latin who is jealous of his honour, and even more of his virility, such things become paramount and in the end destructive.'

I shrugged my shoulders none the wiser and gave Holmes a dismissive wave. With that wave I bade goodbye to my special friendship with the world's first consulting detective. Who can complain about the man who came after – certainly not Sherlock Holmes.

---

[1] He did, during the Great Hiatus, but we have to await the publication of Sigerson's complete works before we know everything.

Part Two

A Farewell to Holmes

'Farintosh. . . . Ah yes, I recall the case: it was concerned with an opal tiara. I think it was before your time, Watson.'

From the *Adventure of the Speckled Band*

Matilda Briggs was not the name of a young woman, Watson. . . . It was a ship which is associated with the Giant Rat of Sumatra, a story for which the world is not ready.

From the *Adventure of the Sussex Vampire*

Mrs Farintosh and an Opal Tiara

It is with conflicting emotions that I take up my pen to write these lines. Sherlock Holmes has become justly celebrated for his formidable gifts and for his services to his fellow man in his unrelenting personal crusade against crime. However, I knew him before this celebrity and honour and found him to be not as the popular myth wishes him to be, either mentally or physically.

Let us take the latter point first. Both Watson and I have described what Holmes looked like and yet the mind's eye of the reader does not see what we so clearly saw. Instead he sees what Sidney Paget saw and drew based on his handsome younger brother whose name was, if I remember rightly, Walter. Let there be no mistake, Sherlock Holmes did not look like Walter Paget. Sherlock Holmes was ugly but it was an ugliness that was also fascinating. That Holmes was very tall and appeared to be even taller owing to his excessive leanness both Watson and I have clearly described, yet Paget's Holmes – i.e. the popular Holmes – conveys this impression hardly at all. Paget has made Holmes's figure too elegant.

However, the greatest falsification that Paget literally drew concerns Holmes's physiognomy. Both Watson and myself have described it in detail but perhaps the last word ought to go to Dr Conan Doyle who knew Holmes well from at least 1887 when he helped Watson to get 'The Study in Scarlet' published in *Beeton's Christmas Annual* of that year. He once described Holmes[1] at the first as having 'a thin, razor-like face, with a great hawk's bill of a nose, and two small eyes, set close together on either side of it.' Not quite the features represented by Sidney Paget, as I think you will agree. But popular myths are strong and I have no doubt that Paget will prevail over the doctors' triumvirate of Conan Doyle, Watson and Stamford.

Holmes's features were obviously not his fault but let us now look at the former point – Holmes's mentality. Once again I shall call upon Dr Conan Doyle to set the record straight. He characterized Holmes as 'a calculating machine . . . his character admits of no light or shade.'[2] I too have tried to convey this side of his character, and indeed it was his inhuman treatment of Ricoletti on whom he turned his back without a word once he had heard his story and presumably filed it for future reference that was the final straw for me as far as Holmes was concerned. In those early days he was indeed a calculating machine and became simply too cold for me. I had craved mystery and excitement and had found both with Holmes but in the end his frequent coldness I found not worth the candle.

As I reflect on all this, perhaps it was just the ardour of youth which can be more single-minded than a fanatic when in pursuit of a goal which made Holmes the way he was. Certainly my sister saw, or thought she saw, a more human side to Holmes, for example, his practical jokes in the Reading Room of the British Museum elsewhere recounted.[3] Even if he had not done those things the fact that he was creating an amusing diversion for his female companion does suggest some humanity at least. However, in

---

[1] In Collier's *The National Weekly*, December 29th, 1923.
[2] Ibid.
[3] See Vol. II of these papers.

the later cases that Watson recounted Holmes definitely reveals a love of practical jokes, nowhere more clearly demonstrated than in the *Naval Treaty* where he conceals the missing treaty under a breakfast cover and sets it before 'Tadpole' Phelps, the unfortunate official who had been driven almost frantic by its disappearance. Holmes almost drove him further with this dramatic flourish.[4]

As the cases accumulate we come to witness more sides to Holmes's character. The outburst of anger at the crisis point of *The Three Garridebs* sticks most in my mind as, I believe, it did in Watson's. Then, of course, there is the incident in the concluding paragraph of *The Six Napoleons* in which Lestrade on behalf of himself and the Yard pays Holmes a glowing tribute which made him turn away and Watson observe that 'it seemed to me that he was more nearly moved by the softer human emotions than I had ever seen him.' However, in a moment he was back to his more usual self.

That Holmes did not appreciate Watson including these human touches is clear from several complaints that he directs at Watson in an almost neurotic fashion, most notable in the *Sign of Four* and the *Copper Beeches*, but also clearly discernible in many other cases. This should not obscure the fact that Holmes definitely became less machine-like and more human as time went by. Some would ascribe this to his travels during the Great Hiatus of 1891–1894 in which he seems to have studied Buddhism. Others would point to the break with his old addictions. I point to Dr John H. Watson.

Perhaps you have got the impression from this book that I am very much a supporter of Watson. There is a good

---

[4]See also *The Mazarin Stone* where the author was clearly influenced by this earlier story.

reason for gaining such an impression. I am. He was a genuinely good man. Honest, loyal and chivalrous Watson. Holmes was very lucky to have had such a man as his companion and is it not clear in Holmes's own words how he had come to value his staunch ally? What humanity Holmes revealed in later life was, I feel sure, due to Watson's influence. Not only did Watson help cure Holmes of his addiction to drugs (for which he has got scant praise, so I do not apologize for repeating my earlier words) but by his example of being that 'one fixed point in a changing age' he kept Holmes's feet on the ground and prevented them becoming clay.

Thus I return to my conflicting emotions as I take up my pen to write these lines. This was the last time that I was involved in one of Holmes's cases so it is the close of an invaluable chapter in my life and one that I am grateful for being able to include in my own life's story. However, Holmes and I had become somewhat distant by then since the Ricoletti case so I cannot own to being too saddened by the occasion at the time. Retrospect has given it a different hue, as it so often does to things past.

My involvement in this case was, to say the least, peripheral and to recount it from my point of view would take very few lines and leave the reader in doubt as to whether there really had been a case at all. That in itself is ample testimony to Holmes's complete success in this delicate matter. That does not mean that Holmes was without his Stamford in this affair. The only difference was that the Stamford who assisted him on this occasion was my sister. It was she who told me about this adventure many years after it had happened, having been sworn to secrecy until that time. All the protagonists were by then dead of old age, the wars of empire or the attentions of Jack Ketch. In the record that follows I shall do my best to preserve my sister's words 'verbatim' but there needs must be several bridging passages in my own rough hand based on information gained elsewhere either by direct means or by implication.

Those of you who take an interest in English history will know that there has not been an English king (or queen) of England since the Battle of Bosworth in 1485; the Tudors being Welsh, the Stuarts Scottish and thereafter we have the German dynasties. That does not mean that English aristocrats died out, but they have certainly been reduced to a more supporting role in history's drama.

There was no more English a family than that which occupied Fleckingham Hall in East Suffolk. Lord Fleckingham claimed descent from Hereward the Wake's family, and his wife, Lady Katharine, had Plantagenet blood in her veins from at least four different sources. They had four children, three sons and one daughter who was also the youngest of the brood. Her name, Isabella Eleanor Plantagenet Fleckingham, might strike a chord with the society historians among my readers. From as young as fourteen she had been courted by some of the best families in the land and yet she married a Sicilian when she was eighteen. He was the young count of Noto-Palma. 'Why did she do it?' was asked. She was a radiant creamy beauty with a tumbling mass of auburn and chestnut hair threaded with gold that was a wonder to behold, vibrant emerald eyes and captivating lips of cherry. As she was the youngest of four and the only girl it might be expected that she was spoilt but that could not be farther from the truth. She joined her brothers as much as she could so that she could shoot and ride as well as any man and was more than capable of standing up for herself. Consequently some suggested that the old nobility of England found her 'too hot to handle' and left her to the mercies of a passionate Sicilian. Be that as it may, her marriage was happy and only cut short some twenty-five years after the vows were taken when the count was killed whilst hunting wild boar on his estates.

After the initial grief the Lady Isabella (as she was always called) lived a full life serving as a nurse on the Western Front, being a strong supporter of the League of Nations and the Suffragette Movement, as well as many worthy charities. She finally met her end aged seventy-two as she attempted to average 72 m.p.h. around the highly dangerous banked racing track at Sitges in Spain whilst driving a Bugatti 35C. As many said at the time: 'It was how she would have liked to have gone'.

Yet it is unknown to the world at large that the marriage was an arranged one of the most mediaeval type – they only met for the first time two weeks before their wedding having only exchanged paintings of each other beforehand (notice paintings, not photographs), and that the marriage was within a whisker of not taking place. Two things prevented this miscarriage of mediaeval strategy – love and Mr Sherlock Holmes.

The Stamford family entered the story on the last Monday of May 1880. My sister and I were in the sitting room reading. I was swotting up on my diseases of the nervous system, she was reading the latest edition of *Notes and Queries*. Every so often she would call out to me that she had found something that I would find interesting and then proceed to read out the entry to my unreceptive ears. However, I could forgive her much. She was a devoted sister and in a high state of excitement as in under two weeks she was to be a bridesmaid at the wedding of the Count of Noto-Palma and Lady Isabella of Fleckingham Hall, East Suffolk.

'Do you know the origin of the expression "as drunk as Blaizers"?' she enquired winsomely.

I did not and had no wish to hazard a guess as I felt that a knowledge of neuroma of the ganglion would serve me better in my approaching trials.

'Well, it comes from Greece where they celebrate St Blaize's day by drinking a lot of intoxicating liquor. Just like you and your pals after you've played rugger,' she added for good measure.

I looked at her over the top of my weighty tome. 'St Blaize being the patron saint of the throat having saved a boy who had a fishbone lodged there,' I riposted. 'His day is February 3rd.'

'That's not fair,' she cried. 'You knew all along, you beast.'

'Steady on, sister,' I rejoined. 'Didn't you know that we celebrate St Blaize's day at Mr Belcher's establishment?'

'I thought every night was St Blaize's night for you and Mr Belcher,' she replied testily.

We carried on reading.

'Oh, I never realized that,' she squealed. setting my ganglions jangling.

'Yes, monster?' I enquired as politely as I could.

'Snob,' came the reply.

'Snob?' I queried.

Fortunately I was saved by the door bell from having to listen to the next gem of trivia being so enthusiastically pursued by so implacable a Diana. I rose to answer the summons reflecting how it always seemed to be that such aimless threads and patches always seemed to become so firmly enmeshed in the memory when the important work that one has set one's mind on learning refused to take root. Perhaps I should be reading the *Notes and Queries* and my 'Diana' reading selected passages to me from my textbooks.

Before I had reached the front door the bell was rung again. For some reason I thought of Holmes – what was that that he had said about 'oscillation on the pavement', or some such thing? When I threw open the door there before me was the man himself.

'Good heavens, Holmes,' I exclaimed. 'You're the last person I expected to see out here. What can I do for you?'

'It's not you that I have come to see, Stamford,' he replied evenly. 'Is your sister at home?'

I was a little nettled by his coolness. Why did it make me get so hot under the collar? Still, what was this? I thought. A romance? Perhaps Holmes is human after all, I thought. I showed him into the sitting room and presented him to my sister. At the mention of his name and the sight of his frame she bowed her head demurely, but continued to sit on the rug next to the fire. Holmes, unconsciously, I am sure, took over my seat and I moved to another armchair closer to the fire, next to my sister.

'To what do we owe the pleasure of this visit, Mr Holmes?' my sister enquired of our visitor.

'Mrs Farintosh, late of Fleckingham Hall, Suffolk,' came the machine-like response.

'A dear lady,' replied my sister. 'A devoted servant to Lady Isabella Fleckingham of Fleckingham Hall, Suffolk.'

'I thought as much,' said Holmes. 'Then she is to be trusted?'

'From what I know, most certainly,' said my sister, slightly alarmed by Holmes's penetrating tone. I could see that Holmes's nostrils were slightly dilated and his eyes gleaming. These were battle signals that said a challenging case was in the air and Holmes was in pursuit.

'Can you tell us why you are asking these questions?' I interposed.

'Certainly, Stamford,' the detective replied. 'Mrs Farintosh has just been to see me in a state of great perturbation and I was hoping that Miss Stamford here could throw some light on the case.'

'This is remarkable, Mr Holmes; but if I can help you at all I shall be only too pleased to be of assistance in your enquiries,' my sister volunteered.

'Mrs Farintosh has carried out the roles of nurse, maid and governess to Lady Isabella Fleckingham for the last ten years or more . . .'

'That is so, I believe,' interrupted my sister, not aware that Holmes was telling her, not asking her.

'. . . and last Friday was her last day of employment at the family seat of the Fleckinghams.'

'But that is incredible, Mr Holmes. Lady Isabella is to be married in twelve days' time and surely Mrs Farintosh would be indispensable to her at this time.'

'Be that as it may; she was paid off and returned to her maiden sister's house in Wapping later on Friday evening. Can you think why she was dismissed, Miss Stamford?'

'Niccolo da Boninsegna, the Count of Noto-Palma, was due to visit the Hall on the Saturday. Perhaps Lady Fleckingham thought that Mrs Farintosh would not enhance the proceedings,' hazarded my sister.

'Why do you say that?' I asked.

'As you have met Mrs Farintosh, you should not need to ask that question,' replied my sister. 'She is the most well-meaning person in the world but she is also something of a pathetic case, as though all she can see is confusion and despair. To her it is a disaster if she drops a stitch, an absolute catastrophe if she has not warmed the pot before making the tea.[5] To her, life is a very small microcosm.'

I had never heard my young sister speak thus before and

---

[5] I wonder if it was Trevor's Natural Terai. (See next story.)

thought that she sounded very mature – something which I put down to the presence of our austere visitor.

'Thus you think she may exaggerate if something without should intrude into that microcosm?' probed Holmes, changing his tack.

'It is possible, I think. Why, what has happened to her that she should call on you? Surely not to solve why she has been dismissed, Mr Holmes?'

'Admittedly that topic was mentioned several times between the tears and the clutching of her lace handkerchief,' Holmes responded in his most machine-like manner, 'but the nub of her story was to ask why she had been followed for the last few days, her room broken into on Saturday, and she had been attacked and robbed of her sewing box this morning.'

'Good heavens,' I cried as my sister gasped a girlish, 'Gosh.'

'That sounds a pretty authentic set of reasons for getting upset,' I added.

'There is one other curious set of circumstances,' Holmes continued, seemingly more to himself than to us. 'On Saturday morning she found a note in her trunk which had just been delivered from Fleckingham Hall. It was on a piece of plain writing paper and had been cut from the *Western Morning News*. It read, "Take care. All rests on you".'

'How did you know that it was from the *Western Morning News*?' asked my sister incredulously.

Holmes showed that he was capable of being an ordinary fallible human being like the rest of us. He smiled warmly and replied, 'Once, when I was very young, I confused the *Leeds Mercury* with the *Western Morning News*. I vowed never to make such an elementary mistake again.' He had become the cold, calculating machine once more. 'That the trunk had come from the Hall was indisputable but Mrs Farintosh could not be sure about the newspaper. Presumably the *East Anglian Times* is the more usual newspaper in those parts.'

'Indeed so, Mr Holmes,' my sister replied. 'But it only goes to underline what I was saying about poor Mrs Farintosh. She has been a regular member of the Fleckingham household for a decade and must know that there is a small estate in the West Country to which Harold Fleckingham often goes particularly since the death of his older brother, Alured, who was heir to the family title and estates.'

'How did he die?'

'Killed on June 1st last year beside Prince Louis Napoleon in Zululand.'

'Thus Harold succeeds and has been getting to know the estates,' Holmes mused. 'Thus it is also likely that he brought a copy of the *Western Morning News* back with him.'

'Oh, no, Mr Holmes,' my sister interrupted. 'He has it sent to Fleckingham Hall every day so that he can keep abreast of local news.'

'Thank you, Miss Stamford. That is most helpful.'

'Do you think that he sent the message to Mrs Farintosh, Mr Holmes?'

'It is a possibility, Miss Stamford. How did Mrs Farintosh get on with the rest of the family?'

'I don't know about Lord Fleckingham. I doubt that they ever spoke; he is more interested in ornithology than in human beings.'

'Including his family, Miss Stamford?'

'You must not put words into my mouth, Mr Holmes,' replied my sister earnestly. I was quite enjoying seeing my sister being so mature. She seemed as though she would make quite a match for Holmes, in more ways than one. 'As to Lady Fleckingham I think that she found Mrs Farintosh very tiresome. Lady Fleckingham is a very austere woman to whom honour is all. Short-sighted, bumbling nurse governesses do not fit into her scheme of things.'

'Surely that is pride, not honour,' Holmes gently corrected.

'Perhaps you are right, Mr Holmes,' returned my sister, slightly flustered. So much for the match, I thought.

'What of the children?'

'Well, Henry, the third son, is in Afghanistan at the moment and has been for some months so I think we can discount him,' said my sister becoming more confident again. Perhaps a match after all?

'Quite so, Miss Stamford. Master Harold then?'

'He is quite a character. He never sits still for a moment; Isabella told me that he is like that because he is afraid of getting fat. His hair is carrot red, and he is heavily built, but it is his eyes that are most compelling. One is pale blue, the other is a mottled green – just like a plover's egg.' She seemed pleased with her thumbnail sketch. Holmes was not, as his exasperated eyebrows revealed.

'You have not answered Mr Holmes's question,' I prompted.

'Oh, I am sorry, Mr Holmes. Let me see. He was always very pleasant but I can't think of them as being friends at all.'

'And Isabella?'

'Mrs Farintosh was devoted to her. . . .'

'That was not my question,' interrupted Holmes irritably.

'Oh, I'm sorry, Mr Holmes.' She paused for thought, her brows knitting as though grappling with a great problem. Holmes divined its nature immediately.

'I must have the truth, Miss Stamford. Loyalty is touching, but it is also a bias which has no place in pure reasoning.'

'In that case, Mr Holmes, I have to admit that Isabella did find Mrs Farintosh a little irksome at times. Isabella is a very positive person who can give as well as she gets and so sometimes appears a little brusque. To her, Mrs Farintosh, although a dear, could be rather small-minded.'

'Yes, I recall your words about the pot and the tea,' remarked Holmes rather dismissively. 'When are you due there to take up your bridesmaid's duties?'

'This Saturday, Mr Holmes, but how did you . . .?'

'I have my methods, Miss Stamford,' said Holmes with a dry smile that was gone as soon as it had come.

'That may be too late. I myself shall go up this afternoon. When I have found suitable lodgings, I shall send you a wire so that we can keep in touch.'

'Do you think there is some danger, Mr Holmes?'

'I am not sure. The picture will become clearer when I receive the answers to my enquiries of this morning.' Holmes held out his hand, 'Until Saturday, Miss Stamford.'

'Saturday, Mr Holmes,' replied my sister, rising from the rug and almost dropping Holmes a curtsy. I escorted Holmes to the door. I had noticed that he had not invited me to join him in this venture. At the time I put it down to our estrangement but in retrospect he had probably seen my books and had deduced that I had better ways of occupying my time.

As I opened the door I repeated my sister's question. 'How did you know so much about my sister's connection with Fleckingham Hall? Did Mrs Farintosh tell you?'

'Only very indirectly. She told me that she had just left the Fleckingham's and my index did the rest. Then I saw that your sister and Isabella Fleckingham were both born in the same year and had gone to the same school in Heath for at least four terms it was a small matter to put two and two together and surprise Mrs Farintosh into giving me all the information that she could.'

'Same old Holmes,' I smiled. 'Good luck, and take care of my sister. And yourself.'

'Are you not attending the wedding?'

'No, I have not been invited.'

'But you do know Isabella Fleckingham quite well, do you not?'

'Yes. She has stayed here during the vacations and I have taken my sister to Fleckingham Hall once or twice.'

'And you got on?'

'Famously – but we boys left the girls to themselves despite Isabella's protestations to "join us".'

Holmes seemed rapt in thought. 'This is most curious,' he murmured.' So saying he wished me goodbye and set off with renewed resolve in his stride.

When Holmes returned to Montague Street there were several communications waiting for him. He read through them as he sucked on his pipe, their words suggesting more to his Byzantine mind than to any other man living. In several minutes he had packed his bag and was ready to start out on the next stage of his adventure. As he closed his door behind him a hoarse old voice called out to him, 'Are you Mr Holmes, sir?'

Holmes turned round to see an elderly post office messenger hurrying towards him on unsteady bow legs.

'I am,' he replied.

'Then this is for you, sir. Special messenger delivery. You have been popular this morning. It has been weeks since you last had a letter and now you've had four wires and a special messenger in one day,' puffed the worthy.

'Yes, things have been rather slack of late,' conceded the

detective. He took the special delivery from the messenger and send him on his way with a few extra coppers. The note was from Mrs Farintosh. She described how when she had returned to her sister's house the police had been there to look for her and she fully expected to be in police custody by the time he received the note. Holmes smiled to himself and reflected on the nature of the frightened creature who had come to seek his help. Not being used to the ways of the police she felt threatened by their presence and was probably worried about what the neighbours might say. He was sure that they only wished to ask Mrs Farintosh a few more questions about the robbery of her sewing box. He did not realize that Mrs Farintosh was to spend the next three nights in a police cell charged with the daring theft of an heirloom that was a part of European history.

That night he stayed in the Fleckingham Arms on the edge of the Fleckingham lands in the hamlet of Woodham Hoo. He soon got to talking with his landlord about the family after whom the public house was named. Others soon joined the conversation. All were agreed that Lord Fleckingham was a 'rum 'un' who cared more for birds than for people; that Lady Fleckingham was as hard as stone; that Alured had been a 'good lad'; that Harold was a 'rum 'un like his father and too fond of going to Newmarket for his sport – 'if you get my meaning'; that Henry was like his mother and would 'show those Afghans a thing or two'; and that Isabella was a beauty with a temper to match.

Talking of matches Holmes asked about the approaching wedding. No one knew the groom. No one had ever seen him before, and he was believed to be staying at the Hall lodge until the wedding in the old family church on the estate. The descriptions of this unknown foreigner revealed more of rustic intuition and imagination than of clear-eyed observation. He was a giant or a dwarf, a hunchback or a Hercules, a devil or a saint, 'or so they say', whoever 'they' were. Holmes bought a round of drinks and with it even more outrageous 'eye witness' descriptions. The entertainment was most diverting.

When the talk got back to ornithology Holmes revealed that that was why he was in Suffolk in the first place. He was on holiday and hoping to make a sighting of the rare avocets or long-eared owls that were to be seen in the area. At this the bar room worthies waved their dull pewter tankards in the direction of two men who sat apart in a settle by the door. 'Them's the fellas you want for that bird watching. They look after the trees for Lord Fleckingham 'isself,' they assured Holmes. 'Mr Myrland and Mr Reyde.'

Holmes went and joined them, taking a jug of ale with him. After the introductions and the distribution of the contents of the jug these two rather surly-looking individuals became very friendly particularly when Holmes revealed his great knowledge of the bird life of the area. Mr Myrland seemed to be the tree expert and rhapsodized about the firs that they had planted – especially for the long-eared owls pointed out Mr Reyde who was obviously the bird man. Then there were the elms with their rooks, the reeds with their bitterns, the ponds and meres with their moorhens and coots, and finally the estuary with the rare avocet. 'The most graceful of all waders,' enthused Mr Reyde, 'and that long thin – very thin – black bill that is curved upwards.' He seemed lost in reverie but he shot Holmes a look and said, 'But you're too early. They don't come in May to these parts. June to September if we're lucky.' He gazed on Holmes with suspicion.

'We only have forty-eight hours to go,' soothed Holmes.

'That's as maybe, mister, but we keep an eye on things. And that means you, if you come onto the estate.' Mr Myrland backed up his companion's words with a hard stare from over the rim of his tankard which he gripped in one huge hand.

'I was coming to that,' remarked Holmes as calmly as ever. 'Would you introduce me to his lordship tomorrow so that I might be able to visit his property?'

The two estate workers looked at each other. Holmes replenished their tankards. They agreed. 'Have to be afternoon, we got work to do in the morning.'

Holmes went to his room to smoke a last pipe of the day and ruminate over the information that had come to him from sources as various as the *Western Morning News*, the documents section of the Reading Room of the British Museum, Mrs Farintosh's trunk, the Diogenes Club, *Burke's Peerage*, his own Index, Miss Stamford, assorted denizens of the Fleckingham Arms, 'Brewer', Lloyd's and the Public Record Office. He had been busy.

Already a picture was emerging, but there was one thing missing – a crime. However, as the special messenger had observed things had been very quiet and Holmes had no other cases on so Mrs Farintosh's plea to him had not fallen on deaf ears in Montague Street as they had at her local constabulary. Holmes sifted through his information again. He knew that a crime had either been committed or was about to be at Fleckingham Hall and he hoped to clear it up with all dispatch before the regular force and thus win the plaudits of this old and, he hoped, influential family. He did not object to the regular force getting the public credit for any solution that might be required as long as this family knew his worth and could pass it on to their connections with a recommendation for dispatch and discretion. Then the affair at Fleckingham Hall would be just what the career of Mr Sherlock Holmes, consulting detective, needed.

One last time he went over the information that he had

amassed about each member of the family. Lord Fleckingham was a very keen ornithologist. So keen in fact that he had neglected the proper running of the estate and had turned it into a bird sanctuary for his own pleasure. He had sold off various parcels of land but had reached the edges of his forests and wanted to sell no more, any further encroachments would threaten the birds.

The oldest surviving son, Harold, had been something of a fast one at university having been asked to leave his 'alma mater' because he had spent a disproportionate amount of his time at nearby Newmarket. The estate in the west of England had recently been sold and had raised not as much as it was worth because it had been sold so quickly.

Lady Fleckingham was made of very stern stuff. She gave everyone the impression of a Gothic stained-glass window: an awe-inspiring vision of sculpted stone, durable despite its fine tracery and with a brilliance that was both cold and stunning. She had brought her own dowry with her when she had married Lord Fleckingham. 'Very mediaeval,' mused Holmes. This included many *objets d'art*, the vast majority of which was now in other collections. However, there remained some very rare illuminated manuscripts, books of hours, bibles, ivories, several paintings including a set of miniatures by Hilliard and a Velazquez of dubious provenance, as well as the justly celebrated tiara of Eleanor of Castile, queen of Edward I, the 'Longshanks' king who was 'Hammer of the Scots'.

This last item had a special place in the heart of Lady Fleckingham née Eleanor Plantaganet of Powys. She claimed direct descent from Edward's queen through his third daughter and her own mother, Margaret, who had claimed the right to use the name Plantagenet. This had been granted by Queen Victoria when first she had come to sit above the Stone of Scone, that symbol of rightful monarchy first wrested from the Scots by their 'Hammer'. Lady Eleanor's line was notable for the number of females that it had produced – hence the name falling into disuse if not the fierce pride of those who carried its blood. However, throughout these years of vicissitude one possession had remained sacrosanct – the opal tiara.

Although only a narrow band of Welsh gold it bore as pendants on small golden chains twelve of the finest opals that had ever been seen. Set above these twelve was a thirteenth whose lustre, or, to be more literal, opalescence, was a true wonder to behold and it would have been fit to take its place in any kingdom's crown jewels. It was an exceedingly rare black opal of great intensity. Legend said that they had first been brought to Spain in the eleventh century by a Hungarian knight who wished to fight the Moors alongside El Cid. He had no allies to bring with him, only his thirteen opals which were the finest in all Hungary. Thus it was said that they were fashioned into a necklace that first adorned the bosom of the Cid's wife, Dona Ximena, another woman of fierce pride, before becoming the property of the royal house of Castile and thus passing to Eleanor in the thirteenth century. Because the lesser twelve had a greenish lustre the tiara was sometimes called 'Christ on the Mount of Olives'. Others named it 'Las Lagrimas' or 'the Tears of Christ', although the females to whom it was passed always preferred to call it 'the Tears of the Virgin'.

This was another feature of the tiara's history. It was always to remain the property of the female line, no matter what might befall. This was highly unusual to say the least – particularly as the custom had originated in that most masculine of eras the Mediaeval period; but it was taken to be symbolic of the high regard in which Edward I had held his Spanish queen who had saved his life when on a crusade by sucking the poison from his arm after he had been stabbed by a paid 'hashishan'.

The tiara was always presented to the daughter of the holder's choice when she married. Had there already been an attempt on the tiara before it was taken to Sicily, pondered Holmes, or was that to come?

Another curious piece of lore caught Holmes's eye. Opals are said to be unlucky because the word is derived from the Greek *ops* (the eye). Thus if one comes into a house it is said to act as a spy, prying into one's privacy causing discord. For this reason the opal tiara of Fleckingham Hall was said to be kept on a statue of Eleanor of Castile in the orangery which was hard by the house itself. Did this make it easier to steal?

Holmes had started these last thoughts of the day from the point of view of the individuals of the household of Fleckingham Hall but it was curious to note how the opal tiara had taken over his thoughts. A powerful talisman resided at the Hall. If it was still there.

Next he thought of the third son, Henry, now in Afghanistan. Miss Stamford was right. He did not figure in these affairs.

Holmes had already learnt a great deal about the bride-to-be, Lady Isabella. One other point that he could add was that the serene and gentle Miss Stamford had become Lady Isabella's close friend. The fire of one and the water of the other, perhaps acting as opposite poles of attraction?

That left just two more to consider – Mrs Farintosh and the Count of Noto-Palma.

The Count obviously had two things in his favour in the eyes of Lady Fleckingham. He was said to be very wealthy, and it was claimed that he was descended from Robert of Sicily who in turn had been a scion of the House of Normandy that had produced the Conqueror.

That was pedigree enough even for that proud woman.

Finally, there was Mrs Farintosh herself. She had been a faithful retainer who had been rather poorly treated and, despite her apparent docility, she had both the motive and the knowledge of the household to carry out such a theft. Had she also acquired the resolve as a result of her treatment?

The next morning Holmes was up early getting the lie of the land and acting out his role of amateur ornithologist. Two avocets arrived thirty-six hours early and it was with a wry smile on his lips that he returned to the Fleckingham Arms to meet up with Messrs Myrland and Reyde. Instead it was Miss Stamford who rose to meet him as he entered the old inn. It was the first of several surprises that he was going to get that day.

'Mrs Farintosh was arrested last night,' she informed the mildly surprised sleuth, 'and is helping the police with their enquiries. Also the wedding is off.'

She handed him a telegram. It was from the Lady Isabella. 'Help me. Cannot marry. Come quickly. Issy.'

'Do you know why she cannot marry?' Holmes asked.

'There is no impediment that I know of,' she replied.

Just then Mr Reyde entered the building. 'You saw them birds, did you, sir? I saw you and wondered if you'd missed 'em,' he said, getting his retaliation in first. He looked warily at Holmes's female companion.

'Still coming up to the Hall, sir?'

'Certainly, Mr Reyde. We can escort this young lady there. She is one of Lady Isabella's bridesmaids.'

'Bit early ain't she?' Mr Reyde murmured as he led the way to the waiting carriage.

Well do I remember that long driveway, best appreciated from an open coach. The drive was an avenue of beech and poplar whose tips were slightly bent by the prevailing winds from off the North Sea. The Hall itself was a venerable Tudor pile of red brick but it was interspersed with the local rounded flint which gave it a more individual aspect. The chimneys were the usual expression of artful individuality and originality although lacking the grandeur of Sibberton Hall. The grounds immediately surrounding the Hall were a mixture of undulating plain and dark hedges with hidden vistas. There was a row of stately elms behind the Hall which provided not only a noble setting and a practical windbreak for the Hall but also homes for a vast number of rooks. The blue and silver green firs were a way off to the east surrounding a genuine Saxon church built with the local stone. The Hall had once been surrounded by a moat but all that remained was a large pond full of lilies and a serpentine undulation which gripped the house in its mute coil. The orangery was a shimmer of glass in the bright sunlight.

'Next thing, they'll be growin' vines here,' opined Mr Reyde among his observations on the bird life of the area. Holmes had been more intent on observing how there was a genteel air of decay about the whole estate, although this sense of decline was vitiated by distinct indications of defiance in the swept gravel and the grass, freshly mown that morning by the smell. It was a smell that hung on Mr Reyde. Obviously that was the job that he and Mr Ryland had been engaged upon.

'So much for footprints in the grass,' pondered Holmes. The west door was opened by a dilapidated retainer who showed them to a sunlit reception room. It was then announced that his Lordship was busy and would see no one that day. As he left the room Holmes bowed to Miss Stamford and said, 'Might we meet later this afternoon when you have had a chance to confer with the Lady Isabella?'

She gave her assent and they parted. Just as Holmes reached the door it swung open and he stood face to face with Lord Fleckingham and Inspector Lestrade of Scotland Yard. Mr Reyde stepped in quickly. 'My Lord, this is the gentleman birdwatcher that I mentioned yesterday.'

'Birdwatcher?' cried the Scotland Yarder. 'That's no birdwatcher, that's Mr Sherlock Holmes, the consulting detective.' He had obviously not understood Holmes's signals for silence. There was nothing for it but a frontal attack.

'Good afternoon, Lord Fleckingham. Lestrade. I offer you both my services in recovering the opal tiara, Las Lagrimas.'

The nobleman grew angry. His great white moustache shaped like a set of ram's horns seemed to bristle and his bald head seemed to glow. His lower lip hung heavy with spittle as he turned on Lestrade. 'I told you absolute secrecy. Now look what happens. Every Tom in the shire seems to know.' He returned his attention to Holmes. 'And you, sir! What do you mean by it? Pretending to be an ornithologist. And what are you? A reporter for some scandal sheet?'

'A consulting detective,' Holmes corrected.

'And a very good one too, Lord Fleckingham,' interrupted Miss Stamford who had been drawn from the reception room by the sound of raised voices.

'Miss Stamford? Are you in this too?' cried the nobleman aghast.

'Did you know that Mrs Farintosh has been arrested?' she countered. 'If there is any man who can save her it is Mr Holmes here. It is he who saved my father when he was accused of murder.'

'Mrs Farintosh? Good heavens, girl, she doesn't need saving. She stole the tiara. We have proof,' boomed the nobleman. 'Not a word of this, Reyde, to anyone, understand? Off you go and mind what you say or you'll not have a sinecure on this estate again.' Reyde disappeared towards the fir trees.

Lord Fleckingham looked at the three remaining visitors to his house, his face a mixture of emotions. Was it anger or was it bluster in his voice? Was there suspicion or was there fear in his eyes? Finally he turned back to Lestrade. 'What do you say, Inspector? Is this man to be trusted?'

'I would say so, Lord Fleckingham,' replied the now obsequious professional. 'He is a little unorthodox but as we have solved the mystery already there is no need to worry about him. His silence can be relied upon. Can't it, Mr Holmes?'

Holmes nodded his reply ironically.

'In that case, Mr Holmes, you might as well stay and hear what Inspector Lestrade has to say. As to you, Miss Stamford, I don't know why you are here so early, but Isabella is in her room. You know where it is. Come, gentlemen, this way to the study.'

As they entered the room a voice croaked loudly, 'Look out. Strangers!' It was Lord Fleckingham's pet jackdaw.

'I had best keep an eye on my watch chain,' joked Lestrade.

'Or the tiara,' mused Holmes to himself.

Once they were seated Lestrade made his report in which he pointed out that the last time that the opal tiara had been seen it was in the room which had been serving as an artist's studio while the Lady Isabella was having her portrait painted. The Lady Isabella had put the tiara away herself and had locked the box herself. The only other people in the room were Mrs Farintosh and the artist, a Mr Fomalhaut.

'Fomalhaut, Lestrade?' queried Holmes. 'Is that not a star in the constellation of the Southern Fish?'

'I don't know about that, Mr Holmes, but Mr Fomalhaut is from the Antipodes, I believe,' Lestrade replied. 'Exactly where I don't know.'

'Is he still here?'

'Yes, Mr Holmes,' Lord Fleckingham cut in. 'He has been painting a series of portraits of the family so that Lady Isabella can take them with her to Sicily when she has married the Count of Noto-Palma. There are also a series of portraits of her which are to remain here. I believe he's varnishing them this afternoon "when the light's right", whatever that means.'

'Have you questioned him, Lestrade?'

'Of course. And the Lady Isabella's and Mr Fomalhaut's stories exactly correspond,' returned the inspector.

'What precisely is your case against Mrs Farintosh?' Holmes pursued.

'She had a motive. She was being dismissed that day. The only reason she hadn't gone sooner was that the artist needed her as she was in his last picture.'

'May I ask the reason for her dismissal, Lord Fleckingham?' asked Holmes, his manner one of discreet assertiveness.

'Normally I would think it the grossest impudence to be asked such a question, but on this occasion I shall cooperate,' replied the indignant nobleman. 'She was now surplus to requirements. And that's that, my man.'

'Carry on, Lestrade,' continued the consulting detective.

'The box containing the tiara was left on the sewing table while the Lady Isabella and Mr Fomalhaut went to the window to watch the annual rook shoot.'

'That's where my son and I were,' said the nobleman. 'It's a tradition here to have rook pie on the estate every last Friday in May.'

'It gave Mrs Farintosh ample time to open the jewel box

and secrete the tiara in her sewing box. Her sewing box is one of those old ones with plenty of compartments and quite big enough to accommodate the tiara which is surprisingly small for an object with such a long history.'

'How do you account for the report that she gave the police of being followed over the weekend, that her room was broken into and her trunk rifled, and that on Monday morning she was attacked and her sewing box stolen?'

'A pack of lies, Mr Holmes,' replied the inspector dismissively. 'She did it just to try and throw us off the scent. Her trunk was hardly touched and she could have thrown her sewing box away. During the alleged attack all that happened was that she had her spectacles knocked off. She had no bruises at all.'

'As you probably know, Inspector,' returned Holmes, 'Mrs Farintosh is very short-sighted. Knocking her glasses off would be quite sufficient assault to leave her in disarray. It is to the quantitative not the qualitative that we must address ourselves.'

'And finally, Mr Holmes,' said Lestrade, drawing himself up with an air of triumph, 'we also have this ransom note which was delivered here this morning. Note the post mark – Wapping, where Mrs Farintosh is staying with her sister. And as only the immediate family knew of the theft when it was posted, and as they are all here, it can only come from Mrs Farintosh.' Holmes took the note. 'See how she has disguised her hand by using newsprint? Obviously she realized that she could not sell such a rare item and so she has attempted to extort money by other means knowing the importance of the tiara to the coming marriage. Don't worry, Mr Holmes,' Lestrade rattled on, 'she took me in for a bit with her pathetic ways. Typical feminine wiles; you get immune to them after a time.'

'Well done, Inspector, a good job well done,' enthused

Lord Fleckingham. 'Have you recovered the tiara yet?'

'Any moment, your Lordship, It's just a matter of time and patience, but we'll have it in time for the big day.'

'Could you please explain its significance for the wedding celebrations?' Holmes asked amid the general bonhomie.

'The Count of Noto-Palma insists, as does my wife, that the opal tiara forms the main item in the dowry of my daughter. You might think us old fashioned, Mr Holmes, but we are an old family with strong traditions. The opal tiara has been in my wife's female line for six hundred years, the Lady Isabella shall carry on the tradition. This might shock you, Mr Holmes,' continued Lord Fleckingham warming to his task, 'but the marriage between my daughter and the Count of Noto-Palma is an arranged one, just as her parents' marriage was. They met for the first time last Saturday. We happen to believe that the old traditions cannot be simply left to the whims of the young; they need to be directed by those who have more experience. In such a way they learn the value of duty and selflessness. We searched long and hard before we settled on the Count. The youth of today know nothing of duty and selflessness, but in far-off Sicily they at least know what's what. I have every confidence in the Count.'

The noble Lord was proud of his speech and opened a decanter of brandy to celebrate its completion. Despite being on duty, Lestrade accepted a tipple. Holmes accepted and noted to himself its inferior quality.

'A toast, gentlemen,' announced Lord Fleckingham rising to his feet. 'The wedding – as long as you get us that tiara back, eh, Inspector? If you don't – it's off.'

'Don't worry, sir, I expect it to be found at any moment.'

'Might I speak to the artist who has been painting your portraits?' Holmes asked.

'A waste of time. He's been here months. He's as trusted as any one could be,' beamed the nobleman. An odd scale of values, thought Holmes. Did Mrs Farintosh's ten years of service count for nought? It was rather like Brunton's summary dismissal after twenty years by Reginald Musgrave.

'All the same, if I might. Perhaps we could discuss art. My grandmother was a Vernet. The French artists?'

'Oh, very well, let's go and see him', said the Lord rather ignobly.

Lord Fleckingham led the way to the studio. The artist was hard at work putting the finishing touches to the paintings. Mr Fomalhaut was tall and slender. His hair was grizzled and his goatee beard was pure white. His long fingers worked quickly and with complete assurance in his medium. Holmes complimented him on his work and they discussed many obscure points of technique.

The opal tiara seemed a distant, forgotten topic. Holmes asked to see the last painting that the artist had been working on the previous Friday. The artist was justly proud of it. He had called it *The Wedding Morn*. It represented Lady Isabella sitting at her dressing table combing her hair, after having placed the tiara on her head. Her back was to the spectator so that the beauty of her hair was the main subject of the work but her face could be seen in the full and from both profiles as the table had three mirrors reflecting these different aspects of her face. In the background was Mrs Farintosh painted in a most summary fashion as to be almost unrecognizable. For several long minutes Holmes stood absorbed in thought before the painting.

'That's quite a compliment you're paying my work, Mr Holmes,' enthused the painter. 'I hope everyone likes it as much as you.'

'The painting?' said Holmes, rousing himself from his thoughts. 'Oh yes, the painting. Very fine. Conclusive almost.'

Holmes turned to leave but as he did so he came face to face with the formidable Lady Fleckingham. Everything about her spoke of austerity, pride and coldness. 'So you are the Sherlock Holmes that Miss Stamford has been filling my daughter's head with.' She spoke slowly, her voice edged with ice. She seemed capable of freezing water with a sigh.

Holmes was made of sterner stuff. 'At your service, Lady Fleckingham,' he smiled.

'Good day, Mr Holmes. I trust your journey back to London will be agreeable. Myrland is waiting for you at the door to take you to the station.'

'That is most thoughtful of you, Lady Fleckingham, but once beyond your gates I fancy that I can continue my ornithological holiday. The avocets have come early this year,' returned Holmes almost flippantly.

'Then Myrland will drop you at the gate,' continued the voice of frost in its chilling monotone. Did it emphasize 'drop you'?

On his way out Holmes picked up an old newspaper from the artist's workbench. 'For the train,' he remarked.

'I hope you find it interesting, Mr Holmes,' put in Lord Fleckingham, 'it's the *Western Morning News*. Probably the only one in East Anglia.'

'Could not be better, Lord Fleckingham,' returned Holmes with a smile. 'May I trouble you for some writing paper? I have left mine in London and there is none at the inn.'

'There's some on the table as you go out,' replied Lord Fleckingham, catching some of his wife's chill in his voice.

'Many thanks. Good day to you all.'

Half an hour later Holmes was putting the final touches to his plan when Lestrade came into his room. 'My word, what a woman that Lady Fleckingham is, Mr Holmes,' he said, rubbing his hands as though to get warm. 'She nearly froze my blood. I don't know how you kept so self-possessed. I'm glad to be away from there, I don't mind telling you.' He continued to rub his hands.

'Any news of the tiara?' Holmes responded brightly.

'No, nothing yet,' the Scotland Yarder replied glumly. 'Lady F. was very insistent with me that it had to be recovered or the wedding would be off. The Count is putting a lot of pressure on them apparently. It's a rum business, these arranged marriages, and no mistake, Mr Holmes.'

'By the way, Lestrade, I did not give you the ransom note back. Here.'

'Thank you, Mr Holmes. I was just about to ask you for it.'

'Don't put it away; check that it's all there.'

Lestrade took out the paper and opened it up. 'Is this some kind of joke, Mr Holmes? The paper and the newsprint are the same but the message is different. The one from Mrs Farintosh said, "Have the tiara. Ransom instructions to follow". This says, "I have you, Wainwright. Ransom. Instructions to follow". I don't understand.'

'That note will be delivered to Mr Fomalhaut, the artist, tomorrow. I expect the reaction to be profitable to our cause.'

'You mean that that artist is Wainwright? We've been trying to get him for the past five years. He's a master criminal without a rival. I wager that he could tell us a lot that we would like to hear. What a catch he would be.'

'Steady, Lestrade, he's not taken the bait yet.'

'You are sure it's him? This could mean the making of us, Mr Holmes, if we catch him.'

'You are welcome to all the credit and the promotion, Lestrade. I only wish to have the pleasure of solving the crime. You gave me the clue concerning his accent. He was no more antipodean than us. The brushwork was conclusive. Wainwright is no mean artist.'

'That is more than generous, Mr Holmes, but then I get all the criticism if it falls through, I suppose?' replied Lestrade ungraciously.

'Worry not, Lestrade, we sink together or you rise alone.'

Later that evening Holmes went for a quiet stroll and pondered his next move as he waited for Miss Stamford. She did not appear. It was not in his nature to conjecture without data but he felt uneasy. The heavy tread of the truculent Myrland nearby was another danger signal. He noted it and moved on.

All that afternoon Miss Stamford and Lady Isabella had sought to give each other strength. At first it was Miss Stamford who acted as the strong arm as Lady Isabella tried to give expression to her confused thoughts. She revealed many family intrigues some of them several centuries old but still alive today and exerting a strong influence on all their lives. Then Lady Fleckingham entered the room and it was Lady Isabella's turn to support her ally as the stern matriarch told her that she must not leave the Hall or see Mr Holmes until the wedding was over. Miss Stamford remonstrated that Holmes was the best man for the job. She told of his saving of her father's life, of the other adventures that she had heard of through her brother – not the most popular person at Fleckingham Hall which therefore counted against Holmes by the sin of association – and of her absolute trust in his discretion. The stern woman wavered but then she returned to her rigidity and would hear no more of Miss Stamford's entreaties.

The following day the most unexpected thing happened – nothing.

That afternoon Holmes decided to see for himself how the land lay. Myrland was still near the gates to the Hall's driveway but he was joined by his young master, Lord Harold, who held two snapping dogs on a short lead.

Holmes avoided them and dropped over the wall near the rookery. He had hardly gone ten paces when there was the loud report of a shotgun and a dead rook fell at his feet, the others raucously evacuating the elms in their terror. 'Mr Holmes, I presume,' said a firm young voice more used to giving commands than acknowledging them.

'Lady Isabella. How charming to meet you at last,' returned Holmes casually.

She was dressed in man's tweeds and even sported a spotted bow tie which was to become her trademark in later years. Her Purdy smoked from one of its barrels; the other was still cocked but the gun rested easy in her small hands. The wonderful mane smouldered.

'You are much smaller than I imagined,' said Holmes offhandedly.

'And you are much taller. I hope your legs are quick because that shot will bring Harold and his dogs.'

'What have you done with Miss Stamford?' said Holmes urgently.

'She is a little tired from her journey but she is in good hands and will be able to fulfil her duties next week. She sends that rather outgoing brother of hers her love. I can't think why.'

Holmes was not to be put off. He advanced. She raised her gun effortlessly. 'I will tell Crossy[6] that you were concerned for her. Now, quickly, you must go, I can hear them coming.' Her voice was now a plea. 'She is better than I am, Mr Holmes. How can I help Mrs Farintosh, my dear Mrs Farintosh, in that hateful cell? I cannot marry while she is there. I shall have no honour. But hurry, they are here.' Holmes fled.

---

[6]Miss Stamford's nickname at school derived from Stamford Cross (i.e. one of the Eleanor crosses that Edward I erected in honour of his wife when she died).

Later that evening Mr Fomalhaut called on Mr Sherlock Holmes. Mr Myrland stood outside the room holding a large stick as the two men talked.

'So you think you have me, Sherlock Holmes,' the artist casually began, but then his tone turned less amicable. 'Well, let me tell you something, you young whippersnapper. I've been in this business too long to be put out by the likes of you. You'll not scare me, and neither will your tame Scotland Yarder. And if you do get anywhere near me there'll be no marriage, no tiara and no Fleckinghams. Understood?'

Holmes continued to let the smoke from his pipe drift to the ceiling. He kept his counsel. There were several alternatives left open to him. Only one of them was legal.

'Nothing to say, Mr Pipe-Smoker?' snarled his adversary, the scent of victory in his nostrils. 'I hold all the aces; put that in your pipe and smoke it.'

So saying he marched from the room puffed with victory. He made for Fleckingham Hall but he did not reach it.

The next day Holmes went to the Hall to play his only legal card. He took Lestrade with him to ensure his safe passage to the Hall. Fomalhaut had not returned and Holmes felt that he could talk openly to the Fleckinghams. They grudgingly met in the library but before they started Holmes asked Lestrade to keep a watch outside for the missing artist. Then he began his declaration.

'Inspector Lestrade is outside these four walls for two reasons. Firstly, to prevent any interruption from a certain Fomalhaut, and secondly, to ensure that none of what is said here is official in any capacity. I speak as an unofficial agent although my conclusions might well be laid before the regular force if I do not receive satisfactory answers from yourselves. There may be details slightly wrong in what I am to say but I am sure that it is more right than wrong.

'Firstly, it is no secret that the Fleckinghams are desperately short of cash. Lord Fleckingham's estate management has led to a complete drop in income as is witnessed by the crumbling fabric of this building and the premature sale of the West Country property for a fraction of its true value.' Lord Fleckingham barked and yapped in protest but Holmes ignored his protestations.

'The Honourable Harold's love of the turf has only exacerbated matters.' Harold merely reddened. 'Thus the most pressing need of this family is to raise money. The only way left with any honour is for the Lady Isabella to marry a wealthy husband.

'However, simple wealth is not enough for the Lady Fleckingham. There must be nobility as well but not just recent nobility. It must be a family of long lineage. The most suitable candidate was the Count of Noto-Palma. His family is old and eccentric. Perhaps the son would be as well thus handing over the running of the family fortune to his bride.

'Despite her reservations Lady Isabella finally agreed to the match after hearing her mother list all the previous examples from the family history of such expediency. But, if I may say so, the female of the species, particularly one so young, is apt to change her mind. She confided her misgivings to Mrs Farintosh her only confidante. Mrs Farintosh could only offer words of comfort, not action, such is her character. But even that was dangerous. She had to go before the Count appeared so that Lady Isabella should have no support, no matter how fragile, in her opposition to the marriage, so that duty to the family and not her own personal happiness should win the day in any argument.

'Now we come to the artist. Mr Fomalhaut he might be

to you all but in truth his name is Wainwright. He is the leader of a notorious gang of cracksmen and ruffians. As you have all seen he is no mean artist and how his complex mind worked him into your household is not difficult to see. The only daughter of the Plantagenet who holds the legendary Las Lagrimas opal tiara is to be married. Thus the tiara that has not been seen for a generation is to be passed on to its next guardian. However, instead of a large wedding in public where a smoke bomb and some strategically placed co-conspirators could create confusion and snatch the prize from the head of the newly crowned bride, the wedding was to take place in a tiny church on a wooded hill within an estate. Any stranger would be a suspect. Thus Wainwright in his artist guise came to see you with his sample works and his recommendations from other houses of repute. Perhaps you sought him out before he came to you based on those recommendations. If so, all the better for him to work his plan.

'Thus we have a series of paintings culminating in *The Wedding Morn* which features the opal tiara. The prospective thief has been able to examine the object of his machinations from close quarters, estimate its worth, contemplate approaching a suitable buyer. The artist can be dangerously close to his subject.

'The tiara has to be stolen and who better to take the blame than the dismissed servant of ten years' standing, Mrs Farintosh? Motive and opportunity are both hers. Her fate is sealed. Everyone else has an alibi, each supporting the other. The weakest is left to perish.

'But now come the clues that reveal that all is not as it appears. The note in Mrs Farintosh's trunk which only one person in this room apart from myself knows about. Yes, Lady Isabella. You believed that Mrs Farintosh was going to get you out of having to marry after all by taking the tiara as you finished posing for your portrait. But she had not openly conspired with you to steal the tiara. You probably felt that she did not want to implicate you in such a crime so close to the wedding. Thus you had to send her words of encouragement but without revealing that you knew everything. What better way of disguising your familiar handwriting than by sending a note made up of newsprint? I am so glad that you chose a newspaper that is so rare in East Suffolk – the *Western Morning News* that your brother had sent to him each day until the recent sale of the West Country estate.

'How did you know that Mrs Farintosh had taken possession of the tiara? You had been wearing it for that final sitting. You then locked it away and, with Fomalhaut you went to watch the rook shoot. Unless you lied about your movements there was only one way – you saw her in the mirror of the dressing table as you rearranged your hair after the occasion before joining Wainwright at the window.

'But it was not Mrs Farintosh that you saw; it was Wainwright. You saw him and yet you allowed Mrs Farintosh to take the blame. What a way to treat your oldest ally.'

'That's not true; that is not how it happened,' groaned Lady Isabella, the tears streaming from her dazzling eyes, but her head was an unbowed icon. 'True, I saw Wainwright transfer the tiara into Mrs Farintosh's sewing box and she went to open the window or some such thing that Wainwright asked her to do. I presumed that they were acting together. My family was against me so I thought that my two friends were helping me. I was due to see the Count the next day and show him the tiara. If I did not have it the wedding was likely to be called off. I could not believe my good fortune. As neither had confided in me I said nothing. Mrs Farintosh was gone within the hour but

Mr Fomalhaut had to remain to varnish the paintings . . .'

'Something that he should have completed long ago, Lady Isabella,' Holmes broke in. 'He was fixing himself an alibi, not helping you.'

'So it would appear, Mr Holmes,' replied the young lady, recovering herself completely.

'However, I am afraid that there is more to it than that,' continued the relentless detective. He turned to the other three members of the family, the males of whom shuffled uneasily in their coats whereas Lady Fleckingham met his gaze with equal self-possession. 'Before I came here I checked up with my many sources of information. The premium that you pay to insure Las Lagrimas would make it worth over half a million pounds if ever it were to be stolen and not recovered. It was in the interests of the two gentlemen for the tiara to go missing and never come back. Nothing to say, gentlemen?

'Also there is the problem of the treatment of Mrs Farintosh. By which I mean her treatment in the painting of *The Wedding Morn*. It was very perfunctory. There was no need for her to stay that Friday. Wainwright's brushstrokes were conclusive on that point. Then why was she still there? In order to be framed by the whole Fleckingham family so that they could claim the insurance money and the freedom of the only daughter. Can you deny it?'

'You have done well but you know nothing, Mr Holmes.' The voice was like an icy blast. 'Neither of the men cared for the tiara. I am its guardian. Nothing can be allowed to stand in the way of my duty to it and the line. We are not talking of money. There are greater things at stake here . . .'

'Indeed, Lady Fleckingham,' Holmes broke in. 'A lady's good name.'

'I am pleased that you understand me, Mr Holmes.'

'I refer to Farintosh not Fleckingham, madam.'

'A minor inconvenience when measured against the other matters in this affair. She shall soon be free.'

'Will the marriage take place, Lady Fleckingham?'

'There is little to stop it. I have the original tiara. What was stolen was only a copy. A good one, but a copy none the less.'

Everyone, including Holmes, gasped in surprise.

'Las Lagrimas has been a lie for over two hundred years,' said the lady bitterly.

'I don't understand,' Holmes freely admitted. 'You have allowed a copy to be stolen so that a woman is under arrest, your daughter's marriage is in jeopardy and you are open to blackmail from Wainwright's gang. I assume the ransom note was from one of his London-based henchmen?'

'I might appear cold and hard to you, Mr Holmes, but I am something that neither you with your great intellect nor any other man can understand. A mother. My marriage was arranged for the same reasons that my daughter's has been. My husband is no better or worse than any other man but the marriage has lacked that spark which gives life a different, more joyous meaning – love. Some marriages begin in love, others grow into it – mine has never known it. I did not want that to happen to my daughter. I wanted her to have an escape route. You cannot believe how pleased I was when the Count insisted on the tiara being in the dowry or the wedding was off. All I had to do was have it stolen, knowing that I had the original all the time and could produce it if my daughter wished to proceed with the match. Which I hope she does as I have looked long and hard for such a man as he. It will be a perfect union.'

'Where is Wainwright?' asked Holmes.

'I have no idea,' replied the frosty icon.

The room was in silence. Each person was too pre-occupied by his or her thoughts to speak. Holmes spoke up first: 'You have a wrong to right with Mrs Farintosh. You have framed her, and she has lost her good name.'

'She will understand the reason,' came the unrepentant reply. 'She would sacrifice much for Isabella and she will be rewarded.'

Outside Lestrade was heard to say, 'Steady on, you can't go in there, young man.' A quiet, melodious voice replied in words too soft to distinguish within the library. 'In that case, sir, I shall wait here' said Lestrade as though still on point duty somewhere. There was a gentle knock on the door. Holmes and Lady Fleckingham exchanged glances. Holmes bowed to her.

'Enter!' cried the Lady of the Hall.

A young man entered. He was of medium height, very slim, dressed in a black suit with a vivid blue sash over his right shoulder. His hair was oiled and his olive skin shone with health. A smile played upon his lips and his large soft dark eyes glowed.

'Ah, Count. How wonderful to see you,' said Lady Fleckingham, for once warmly. 'I believe you know everyone here except for Mr Sherlock Holmes. Count Noto-Palma. Mr Sherlock Holmes.'

They bowed to each other. 'I believe I have something that you have been looking for, Mr Holmes, if my information is correct.' The Count handed him a small box. Holmes opened it to reveal the Las Lagrimas that had gone missing the previous Friday.

'And the thief?' Holmes asked. 'Where is he?'

'In Sicily we have ways of dealing with such people. Not English perhaps but effective. He will recover but will never return to East Suffolk.'

The vivacious young nobleman then turned to Lady Isabella. 'There is now no impediment to our marriage, my lady.'

Holmes cleared his throat noisily. Lady Isabella stepped forward. 'I am afraid there is, Count. This is not the real opal tiara.'

'I know,' he smiled. 'Your mother has the real one, I think she believes. This is a good copy made in 1661 in your Clerkenwell by Tuscan goldsmiths. But the opals are very inferior. Mr Wainwright recognized as much. That was why he tried blackmail as a means of extorting money from you. Now, Lady Fleckingham, I wish to see the real tiara.'

The Lady's colour was normally pale but now it had turned ghostly. She took out a leather-bound book from an open shelf and opened it to reveal a false set of pages. Concealed within was a small velvet bag with a leather drawstring. Pulling it open she poured the contents onto the table. It was nearly all dust with just a few larger shapeless pieces. Once again the atmosphere of the room was shot with surprise.

'This is all that remains of Las Lagrimas, Count,' Lady Fleckingham's voice now a sepulchral whisper. 'When the Puritans took over in England after the Civil War many Royalists were hunted out and more put to death than the records show. In an effort to save her husband, one of my ancestors – the accursed Matilda whose name has never been given to another of our line – gave the tiara as a bribe to one of the ruling council. After the Restoration she went back to claim the tiara and this was all that was left. The gold had been melted for coin and the opals, already old, had dried out and crumbled. This is what you insisted on as your wife's dowry.'

The young Sicilian smiled and snapped his fingers. One of his retainers entered carrying another box. The Count took it from him and held it up in front of Lady Isabella. 'I now return the true original to its rightful owner.' So saying he opened the exquisitely inlaid box to present the opal tiara, Las Lagrimas. The stones shimmered their approval.

'I don't understand,' said Lady Fleckingham, her voice hoarse with emotion.

'It is easy. Your Puritans were no fools. They sell it to Holy Father in Rome. They get more for it that way than by melting down,' he replied, his grammar deserting him in his excitement. 'The Holy Father in his wisdom does not reveal that he does business with the Puritans and they the same about him. That is why copy has to be made and this dust passed off as the original. It only came into my family very recently. I thought you had all died out. It was an answer to a prayer when Lady Fleckingham get in touch with my father. I then fall in love with a girl in a painting. So you see, Mr Holmes, I cannot hurt a man who has painted a picture that has brought me such happiness. You will catch him some other time perhaps.'

Need I add that Lady Isabella had fallen in love with him before he had finished speaking? The wedding day was advanced by six days and the happy couple were joined on June 6th, 1880.

Holmes meanwhile had turned to Lady Fleckingham. 'And Miss Stamford?' he asked pointedly,

For once the chill thawed, slightly. 'We all have a great deal to thank Miss Stamford for. If it had not been for her we would not have consented to listen to you, but she assured us of your tact, discretion and ability. She was right; I have been very impressed with you, Mr Holmes. Can I help to further your career in any way? As you know, I come from a very old line that has many contacts. Say it and I shall be able to set you on your way to a great career.'

Holmes did not hesitate, despite the temptation. 'Free Mrs Farintosh and give her her dues.'

Lady Fleckingham bowed. 'I see that you are incorruptible. It shall be done.'

'And apologize,' said Holmes coldly.

The great lady hesitated, then smiled. 'Yes, that too.'

Postscript: Mrs Farintosh was released from custody that day and was paid a handsome compensation by the Fleckinghams for her trouble. She moved to Surrey where she became friendly with Miss Helen Stoner and was able to provide her with Holmes's new address in Baker Street in her hour of need (see *The Speckled Band*), having continued to take an interest in his career after her one contact with the world's first consulting detective.

Matilda Briggs and the Giant Rat of Sumatra

'So you knew Holmes back in the Old Country did you, Surgeon Stewart?' said the large man with prematurely thinning hair seated across the low club table from myself. 'Well, well, what a small world it is becoming. We shall soon be bumping into each other on the moon at this rate.' He gave a deep chuckle at his own jest. I joined him in his merriment; it had been some time since I had been able to relax in the company of a fellow countryman.

'Do you know, it has been an age since I have been able to relax in the company of a fellow countryman,' continued my companion somewhat to my mild surprise. 'It's so nice to be able to use words of more than one syllable for a change. But listen to me – I have the whole rich lexicon of the English language from which to choose and I say "nice". Have I forgotten "stimulating", "refreshing" or "exhilarating" so soon? My brain must have atrophied in the foothills. Absence makes the perceptions less precise no matter what else it might do to the heart.'

We seemed to be getting on famously and the magic spell had been the mention of Sherlock Holmes. When my eye had first fallen on my new companion reading a year-old *Times* in the English club at Pilibhit I had thought him rather stiff and reserved, but mention of Holmes had changed all that. We had something in common and when that happens thousands of miles from home in an alien climate there is an instant rapport that is somehow more special than if the meeting had taken place on home territory. I am sure that there must be an increase in this specialness directly proportional to the number of miles that one is away from the Old Country.

I had in fact come in search of this man, for he was Victor Trevor, Sherlock Holmes's friend from his two years at Oxford. For reasons that you will discover later I had changed my name to Surgeon Stewart and while I did not wish to deceive Victor Trevor I felt it wiser to keep to my alias lest word of my true identity should be leaked back to the man who was my implacable enemy.[1]

We spent a very pleasant evening together at the club sharing dinner, a bottle of port and reminiscences of our mutual friend. As I told him of the adventures that I had had with Holmes he became quite garrulous and several times repeated, 'Just like my old guv'nor said, just like it'. By the end of the evening he had lost his stiffness and become the hearty man of earlier days whom Holmes had described to me. As we left to go back to our rooms he clapped me on the back with his great hand and arranged to meet up again the next day. The following morning, over kedgeree and devilled kidneys, Trevor invited me back to his tea plantation 'for as long as I cared to stop over', and with a heavy wink confided to me that he had a story of his own to tell about our friend Mr Sherlock Holmes.

We took nearly thirty-six hours to reach his tea plantation, having to spend a night on board his paddle-steamer *James Armitage*. It was then that I had quite a fright. In the captain's cabin was a glass case containing the most hideous looking creature I had ever seen. It was a type of rat whose

---

[1]See Vol. II of these Papers.

great size and evil expression made my palms clammy. I was very glad that it was stuffed.

When I asked him about it Trevor just gave me a knowing smile. 'All in good time,' were his only words on the matter. As we neared his property Trevor told me that he wished that we had some of Pennington's anti-malaria bark with us as the place was infested with the disease, although things had improved since he had cut down much of the long grass and most of the sal that had originally grown rampant in the area. The sal had been his first source of income until he had established the tea plantation.

Victor Trevor's property was a mixture of Terai plain and Himalayan foothill. That he had cut out his land from wilderness was obvious from the way in which his beautifully terraced plantation was flanked by swaying, untamed, wild long grasses and ancient trees, like new cloth in old raiment. He had chosen this isolated spot for its very remoteness. After his father's death in such tragic circumstances he had simply wanted to get away from England. By fighting to establish himself in this area he had rid himself of much of the torment that had haunted him since his father's death, although there was still a painful residue which would probably never be completely expunged, so deeply had he been affected by those last events at Donnithorpe. It made him feel closer to his father having set himself up by the work of his own hands just as Trevor senior had made his fortune by the calluses on his hands in the goldfields of Australia. I noticed that his steamer was named after his father's original name. Sherlock Holmes was his only happy link with his past and to meet another who had known him well was enough to create feelings of camaraderie far greater than is usual between Englishmen of casual acquaintance.

That evening we sat out on the veranda which afforded

us a full prospect of Trevor's plantation. The sun had just started its descent which my host took to be the signal for drinks.

'What do you care for, Surgeon Stewart?' he asked.

'Anything that you care to have for yourself,' I replied, lightly breathing deeply of the first cool draughts of the day descending to us from the snows of the high Himalayas and purging us of the oppressive heat of the afternoon.

'So you don't follow the advice of the moaning Minnies whose prescription for the tropics is either total abstinence or only the best that the Highlands of Scotland, the vineyards of Champagne or the swans' necks of Cognac have to offer us? Good, good. Capital.'

He summoned his attentive houseboy and ordered two large gins with water and limes. Before we had time to open our conversation the houseboy, immaculate in white jacket and colourful native trousers, had returned with our toasts to the going down of the sun.

Trevor chuckled at my eyebrows raised in surprise at such rapid service. 'Laxman Shiva is the best boy that I have ever had. He seems to know what I want before I do!' Laxman Shiva smiled and bowed in acknowledgement of the compliment. Trevor returned the courtesy and the houseboy withdrew to await his next summons.

'Cheers.' We drank heartily.

It was then that I noticed that the houseboy had left a few large buff envelopes on the table which also supported drinks. 'This is what I have brought you all these miles to see,' said Trevor, noticing my attention and picking up the large envelopes.

'What is it?' I asked, my curiosity well whetted.

'See for yourself,' he replied, handing me his first exhibit.

I opened it up and saw that it contained several letters from a firm called Morrison, Morrison and Dodd, as well as an official police report, several newspaper cuttings and some sheets written in Trevor's broad open hand.

'Go ahead, read them,' Trevor urged. 'They are all in date order. I have been thinking about writing them up and sending the story to the *Strand* or some such magazine. It's time that people knew about Sherlock Holmes.'

The first document was a newspaper cutting from the *Singapore and Malacca Signal*, dated to late 1880 (I forget exactly which month). It told of some freakish winds in the Straits of Malacca that had caused a great deal of damage to the shipping of the area. Several boats had been sunk and one had been washed ashore in Sumatra. It appeared that apart from two deckhands who had been washed overboard during the storms the crew had been saved. Unfortunately, two others had gone missing when the boat had actually run aground. They were a Dr Roberto H. Sinnotti and his assistant, Piero Cresczi.

The next cutting told how Cresczi had been found the following day sitting on a tree stump saying over and over again, 'He's mad, he's mad'. He was referring to Dr Sinnotti whom he had last seen rushing off into the hinterland in pursuit of his specimens which had escaped when the boat had made its forced docking. A search mounted soon after failed to find the missing doctor and the case was closed.

'Who was this Dr Sinnotti?' I asked my host. 'And what were these specimens that he was after?'

'As chance would have it I had travelled to Singapore on this boat, the *Esperanza*, just prior to the storm so not only had I had a lucky escape from being shipwrecked but I had got to know this Dr Roberto H. Sinnotti,' Trevor answered. 'His appearance was very striking. Hair bleached by the sun, eyes a piercing ice blue, and his face dominated by a large Roman nose. He was quite an eccentric whose peculiarities I will not burden you with now apart from saying that he had that nervous resolution and tunnel vision that so many academics seem to suffer from.

'He came from some university in the Mediterranean somewhere. I could never work out which,' he continued with the vagueness of foreigners so characteristic of Englishmen of the 1880s.

'What was he doing so far from home?'

'Apparently his university had given him some sort of travelling fellowship so that he could continue his researches out here.'

'Some fellowship, to be able to fund research out here?'

'That's just what I thought. It appears that his brief was rather like our man Darwin on the good ship *Beagle*. He simply sailed around the Bay of Bengal and the China Seas collecting examples of his chosen subject.'

'Which was?' I asked.

'Rats.'

'Rats?' I ejaculated.

'Yes. Any type would do. The more varied the better. As I heard it from his own lips, not that his English was any better than my Italian, originally he came from somewhere in the south of Italy like Brindisi, or some such hellhole, where rats are even more populous than the human inhabitants. As you can imagine, human health took a blast as a result. Thus it had become his life's work to study as many types of rat as possible in the hope of discovering ways of controlling them and the diseases that they so often carried.'

'Very laudable too, if I may say so.'

'I expected you to say that, Surgeon Stewart, but what I saw of his experiments – researches as he called them – tended to put me off him and his work.'

'What sort of thing do you mean?' I enquired.

'Some he would starve. Others he overfed. Some were

put into overcrowded cages and others completely isolated. Then they would be mixed together and the doctor would observe all this very closely so that his notes formed a massive set of volumes when I met him.'

'How long had he been at work on the *Esperanza*?'

'About three years; maybe slightly more. However, to get back to the experiments the one I liked least of all was where he secured the rats so that they could not eat, but worse than that they could not control the growth of their incisors which constantly grow throughout the life of the rat and are only kept in check by gnawing. When he did feed them it was with liquids so that they had nothing to gnaw on. Some of the incisors began to look like tusks.'

I conceded that I could not see the point of such 're-searches'.

'Neither could I,' continued Trevor, 'and when I said as much to Dr Sinnotti he flew into a rage calling me "Stupido" and threatening to attack me. Relations froze somewhat after that, although his assistant, Cresczi, continued to be affable enough if a little on edge.'

'What happened to Cresczi after the shipwreck?'

'He seemed to get over it after a few stiff drinks in the club but he looked a frightened man whenever he heard what he thought were rats. Then a complete change would come over him and he would start screaming like a madman. You know what these chaps are like. They haven't got our phlegm. We shipped him back to Italy with what remained of the equipment although that was the first of the strange events that started then.'

I was gripped by this revelation and urged Trevor to tell me more. He took up his story.

'Well, when we got to the *Esperanza* after the storms had subsided we discovered that just about all the equipment and Dr Sinnotti's notes had disappeared. They had not been lost during the storm and so someone must have removed them.'

'Dr Sinnotti?'

'There was no trace of him. As I've already said he was last seen chasing after his precious rats into the hinterland of Sumatra.'

'What happened next?' I asked eagerly.

'Well, the next document is a bill of sale made out in April 1881 signing the boat over to the Association of Terai Tea Planters. In other words – me.'

'Why did you want the *Esperanza*?' I asked in surprise.

'Having travelled some way in her I realized that she was a good vessel and would be very useful for shipping our tea down to the dock in Calcutta from the Terai. The price was low because of the storm damage, not that that was very serious, and I could see that I had a bargain on my hands.

I looked at the bill of sale. It was notarized by Morrison, Morrison and Dodd with offices in Old Jewry, London, Mookerjee Street, Calcutta, and Port Street, Singapore. They had also checked the machinery of the ship – she was described as a steam-paddle freighter – and given her a clean bill of health.

The next document was dated a month later, registering the *Esperanza* with Lloyd's of London and changing her name to *Matilda Briggs*.

'Thus the Terai Tea Planters now had a boat of their own with which to ship their produce without having to rely on anybody else. It was quite a coup and I felt very pleased with myself.' It was then that a cloud seemed to pass over his brow and his voice dropped to little more than a whisper as though he was suspicious of being overheard. 'Now begins the next chapter of mysteries,' he announced dramatically.

He took the envelope from my hand and drew out a

handful of newspaper cuttings. It was then that I remembered having heard the name *Matilda Briggs* before. Each of the press cuttings which Trevor had laid out on the table in front of me described in varying detail and tone the strange incident of July 7th, 1881. Those of you with long memories will recall how the *Matilda Briggs* was found in the Bay of Bengal sailing at full steam ahead without one member of the crew on board. There was a full cargo of the finest Terai tea on board which was used in only the most exclusive blends of Asian tea that reached the shores of Britain and the tables of royalty and government throughout the English-speaking world. None of it had been removed. What had happened?

Here is a sample of one of the newspaper reports:

Deserted *Matilda*

There was no waltzing on this *Matilda*. The steam freighter *Matilda Briggs* of the Terai Tea Planters' Association was found at full steam ahead heading out to sea in the Bay of Bengal yesterday. Not a member of the crew was on board. Police sources say that they are baffled.

The evidence points to the crew abandoning ship in a real hurry. Food was still cooking and the lifeboats were unused.

There were no signs of violence and nothing was missing, so pirates have been ruled out.

Also the weather was fine so only freakish conditions could have had any bearing on the mystery. British naval sources have no sightings of pirates or any peculiar phenomenon weatherwise or otherwise at that time in that area.

Owner Mr Victor Trevor of the Association of Terai Tea Planters said that it was a complete mystery to him.

Mr Vernon Maclure, the well-known American mystery writer, has offered £100 to anyone who can solve the mystery of the *Matilda Briggs*.

Australia Press Agency – Bruce Duggan

Victor Trevor then took up the story. 'The *Matilda Briggs* was taken back to Calcutta where the agents of Morrison, Morrison and Dodd pronounced the ship to be in perfect working order. The police force made a very thorough investigation and came up with a strange scenario, most of which was withheld from the press for reasons that will become evident later.' Trevor then handed me a copy of the police report.

The report revealed that there was ample evidence for believing that the *Matilda Briggs* had been overrun by rats. There were various prints of their feet, one particularly macabre one being found in a splash of blood. When the tea was inspected it was contaminated with dead rats and their droppings. The loss of the shipment had been a blow but not a crippling one, Trevor informed me. However, as he told me this I noticed that he seemed to be in the grip of a strong emotion. His voice was hoarse, the colour had left his face and he tightly gripped his glass. He waved my enquiring look aside and I finished off the report as he drank deeply of his drink.

Questions had remained. What had happened to the crew? Presumably they had jumped off the ship and had been unable to regain it as it was moving so fast. The police concluded that they must have perished at sea.

Then there was the question of the rats. When and how had they got on to the ship? Why had they so frightened the crew that they had abandoned ship? What had happened to them? The police report came to no conclusions apart from pointing out that if any of the rats had left the ship they had over one hundred miles to swim before reaching the nearest landfall. It was not known if rats could achieve such a feat. The report was signed Owain Bress of the Hooghli River Police, 12/7/81.

I turned again to Trevor who seemed to have controlled

himself, but his voice remained a hoarse whisper. 'You are the first person that I have told this to face to face, and I did not realize that it would affect me so strongly. Do forgive me. What comes next is strictly off the record, and is known to only a handful of men alive today.' He took a deep breath and told the rest of his story.

'As I was in Calcutta already – it had been the first time that we had taken our tea to Calcutta in the *Matilda Briggs* and I had wanted to check the unloading – I went with the police to inspect her and so was privy to everything that happened during that inspection.

'As we searched the quarters which had been Dr Sinnotti's experimental laboratory we became aware of the loud squealing of an animal as though it was in great pain. Cautiously we searched the cupboards and lockers. I then realized that the noise was coming from the doctor's enormous rolltop desk that had housed his vast volume of papers. We approached with batons raised and hands on our guns. Bress advanced to open the desk – it was locked. As chance would have it I had a key for it; it had been Dr Sinnotti's spare, the original having gone missing with its owner in Sumatra on a chain around his neck.

'I stepped forward with the key. I don't mind telling you, Surgeon Stewart, every one of us was afraid of what was beyond that desk top. I could hardly put the key in its hole in my nervousness. When I did succeed in turning the key my companions cocked their guns and took careful aim.

'At last the lock turned and the desk top flew open. I shall never forget the sight that met my eyes as long as I live.'

For a moment the large man beside me shuddered and closed his eyes. Laxman Shiva quietly reappeared with the gin bottle and was silently gone before his master had opened his eyes. When he did, he saw the green bottle and filled his glass to the brim, dashing half of it down his throat before he could bring himself to continue his narrative.

'Inside the desk was the mutilated head of the captain of the ship and a group of rats. But these were no ordinary rats. They formed a sort of rat king of seven rats, their tails inextricably knotted. Worse than that they were enormous brutes, each one the size of a small dog with incisors both long and razor sharp. They had torn great strips of flesh from the captain's head in their pain and savagery. When the desk lid flew off they were blinded by the light and sought to avoid it but in their attempts to run away they pulled on the tail knot which made them scream all the louder.

'They tumbled from the desk bringing the bloody head with them with a sickening liquid thud. They then adopted a sort of crab-like movement and advanced on us, their skins glistening with fresh blood and their teeth and whiskers dripping as they advanced on us, snapping and squealing.

'Instead of the volley of gunfire we were turned to stone by the sight of the horrific seven-mouthed beast, like something from a nightmare. It was as though they had overpowered us by their evil. Their beady eyes were like red dots of pure hatred.

'At last Bress recovered himself and roused us all into action. We fired and batted the rats in a frenzy of fear and loathing, reproaching ourselves for our erstwhile cowardice. A shot must have severed a tail because one of them got free and leapt up at one of the constables biting a great hole in his stomach before we were able to destroy the beast.

'By the time we had finished, the cabin was a shambles of blood and foul, loathsome stenches. Not a few of us, including myself, were sick with the horror of it all.'

Trevor sat trembling, recalling the scene. I poured us

both another drink. When he had recovered himself I asked him what had happened next.

'I got in touch with Morrison, Morrison and Dodd in Mookerjee Street. As representatives for many tea brokers they would be concerned about mysterious rat infestations, as would their clients. They came to the conclusion that the problem was quite beyond their purview which meant communicating with their head office in Old Jewry, London, although they frankly doubted that they would be able to help unless they had recently appointed a specialist in 'acts of God'. It was then that I suggested Mr Sherlock Holmes of Montague Street.

'True to their word they sent off all the information that they could, and I was able to add what had been withheld from the press. Now all we could do was wait.'

Victor Trevor then took an envelope from the inside pocket of his jacket and handed it to me.

'This was the reply that came to us via the Calcutta office of Morrison, Morrison and Dodd.'

I opened it and read it out aloud: 'Either tsutsugamushi or bubonic. Isolate boarding party. S.H.'

Both these diseases were well known to me. Both were rat-borne and both resulted in horrible deaths for those who contracted them. 'I see you know them, Surgeon Stewart,' Trevor broke in. 'As it happens it turned out to be both. The constable who was bitten died of tsutsugamushi or scrub typhus as we call it here. Two others contracted bubonic plague. The doctors said that they were the most virulent cases of those deadly diseases that they had ever come across.

'I wired this information to Holmes and returned here, where there was another consignment of tea to supervise. It all went through without a hitch and three months later I was returned to Calcutta. This time I did not leave the

Matilda Briggs for a moment in order to ensure that all went well.

'As we arrived there was a representative of Morrison, Morrison and Dodd waiting for me at the quayside. He informed me that he had been able to find buyers for our tea through a new firm named Muirhead and Co. Ltd,[2] tea brokers of Mincing Lane. The price was very advantageous to us; in fact it was so good that we would be able to recoup all our earlier losses. There was one drawback. The tea had to be taken to Trincomalee to be loaded onto a Shanghai clipper before being shipped to England.

'I pointed out that the crew had only signed on for the Ganges to Calcutta trip and that they were not ocean-going sailors anyway.

'"Not to worry Mr Trevor," I was assured. "We have a new crew as well as a representative from head office to supervise everything."

'None the less I insisted on going along to see who this representative was and to meet the new buyers in Ceylon. My tea has a fine reputation and I did not want it to be mixed with an inferior grade. There were also my outlets in London to consider. I was strongly assured that the new buyers were equally concerned that the exclusive nature of my tea was scrupulously maintained; but I was still uneasy.

'I was strongly advised not to go but I insisted and awaited the new crew on the bridge. No wonder they did not want me to see them, I thought, as they appeared. They were the most murderous bunch of cut-throats that I have ever set eyes on. One in particular was tall and thin with a cast in one eye and a great hooked nose. He gave me a sidelong leer and then smiled at me revealing horribly

---

[2]Later Ferguson and Muirhead (*The Sussex Vampire*).

discoloured teeth probably caused by too many pipes of opium. My blood ran cold.

'The representative from head office turned out to be Dodd's son. It was good to see another Anglo-Saxon face but more doubts were raised in my mind when I saw that he was armed. My resolution faltered, then hardened. I would see it through.

'The journey south was completely without incident, although there was a certain tension in the atmosphere particularly when we put into Madras to refuel. However, nothing happened to raise my alarm any higher, and we continued to our next stop of Trincomalee.

'As you probably know, Surgeon Stewart, the harbour at Trincomalee is one of the greatest natural harbours in the Empire. One thing that I had not realized about the area was that the almost land-locked bay known as Lake Tamblegam is full of oysters and pearls. In fact some parts of the water are so shallow that the natives can actually pick them up with their toes. Unfortunately for them the pearls are of such poor quality that they are not good enough for the European market. Watching them at work eased the tension for a while. A lull before the storm, I wondered?

'We drew into our berth and the harbour master's staff checked our credentials and our cargo. After a delay of some hours the unloading was ready to begin but there was no sign of the buyer. The tension rose again. It was to be dispelled by a small fat man waddling to the quayside holding a Chinese lacquered umbrella and begging a thousand pardons for his tardy behaviour. He then presented us with his authorization papers and the full price in a bag of gold! The tea was moved with a will when the men saw the cash. When they had finished they went ashore for some refreshments.

'Dodd shook my hand and told me that he was returning to England in the Shanghai clipper. We divided the money and parted company. He also informed me that he would be taking some of the crew.

'When the time came to leave I saw that Dodd had taken the roughest fellows of the crew including the tall thin pirate with the wretched face. That was something to be thankful for.

'The journey back to Calcutta and up country to the Terai was equally without incident. Giant rats and the mystery of the *Matilda Briggs* seemed a lifetime away.

'Back in the Terai, I was able to ponder the many unanswered questions and postulate as to Holmes's conclusions all those thousands of miles away.

'The questions were many and various. There were the riddles concerning the deserted *Matilda Briggs* and her missing crew, the rats, the tea, the captain's head in the locked desk with the king rat, the type of rat, the diseases that they had carried: how had Holmes known about them? Then there were questions about Dr Sinnotti: had he survived, what exactly was his research, and what had made Cresczi so nervous? Finally, who was this mystery buyer from Trincomalee who had paid so handsomely for my entire crop?

'Another three months passed and I returned to Calcutta on the *Matilda Briggs* with some tea from another group of planters. As I stood on the bridge supervising the unloading, a messenger from Morrison, Morrison and Dodd appeared and gave me this.'

At that Trevor again dug into his jacket's inside pocket and brought out another envelope. It had been franked in Trincomalee but there was something very familiar about it. I opened it and read the following:

The British Residence
Trincomalee
Ceylon
30th May 1882

My dear Trevor,

Thank you for your most diverting little problem. It has now been completely cleared up although I fear that certain dire consequences are still possible, if not in our lifetimes then in the not too distant future.

The information that you originally sent me was useful but incomplete for the creation of an acceptable theory. You did not explain Dr Sinnotti's research clearly enough but I was able to trace his work to the University of Salerno which was able to give me a clearer outline of their travelling Fellow's work.

Finding his assistant, Piero Cresczi, was not so easy. That he was found at all was owing to my brother's influence with the Italian authorities.

When I visited Mycroft at his club and showed him your communications he nearly choked on his port. He told me that there was a flap on at that very moment in the very highest circles of government concerning the *Matilda Briggs* and the Giant Rat of Sumatra.

Apparently the British Government had received a box containing one of these rats which created quite a stir in the House's postal department as it was still alive and very hungry. Shortly afterwards a letter arrived stamped at Singapore. Its writer had wished to remain unknown but based on the deductions of my brother and myself arising from various indications in the letter itself the Singapore officials were able to recognize in our resulting description the person of one Li Xian Kyuong ,a well-known criminal mastermind of the area who uses a rubber plantation in Sumatra as a 'blind' for his operations.

The letter described in most full and graphic detail what had happened on the *Matilda Briggs*. It was so detailed an account that the police report seemed a very pale document in comparison. Li Xian went on to say that he had wished to prove to the British Government that human agencies had carried out the attack and not the supernatural as the popular imagination wished to believe. Hence the captain's decapitation and his head being deposited with the rat king in the locked desk. That it had been opened, the head and rat king placed inside and then locked again clearly suggested that Dr Sinnotti's key, if not the man himself, was still in existence. Stoking up the boiler to full steam ahead was another indication of human intervention. Not that Li Xian objected to the public's desire to turn it all into a supernatural mystery. It served his purpose as it acted as a screen to his true intentions, for the time being at least.

The Chinaman went on to say that he required £1 million sterling in gold or he would kill the entire ruling class of Great Britain.

At first it was taken as just another madman's fantasy that is addressed to Westminster or Windsor from time to time; but reading on, the threat became less fantastic and more realistic. Li Xian continued that a giant Sumatra rat infected with plague fleas could easily be let loose in the sewers of London – its brother was in London Zoo by then – but the resulting plague would harm only the people, not the higher echelons of society who would withdraw from the capital as they had done in the past. No, death was to come to them in a most exclusive and unexpected way if his demands were not met, so he informed us.

This I learnt after I had sent you my first wire. It was your second wire to me that confirmed my fears which Mycroft's disclosures were also endorsing.

When he was traced, Piero Cresczi gave a full statement concerning Dr Sinnotti's activities to which I shall now refer. Dr Sinnotti's work had been the study of rat-borne diseases. On the *Esperanza* he was carrying out pioneering work on the isolation of viruses, their storage and subsequent use in the development of vaccines.

As ever, money was a constant problem as the fellowship was not enough to meet the expenses of such a sophisticated floating research laboratory. Paying customers around the Bay of Bengal were an important source of income (as you know from personal experience) but the most generous patron of the work was a Chinaman from Sumatra who owned a large rubber plantation there. The reason for his generosity was that Dr Sinnotti had gone there to study the rats of that island and this Chinaman complained to him that there was a type of rat that, in its efforts to keep its incisors at a manageable length, would gnaw his precious trees causing a great deal of damage. Dr Sinnotti was able to help him, hence the generosity.

What Dr Sinnotti did was to release some of his own rats, which were sterile, onto the Chinaman's plantation. The reason that they were sterile was that Dr Sinnotti had developed a strain of tsutsugamushi that brought about sterility as a side effect. The rats mixed and died out.

The Chinaman, whom Cresczi thought was called Sheyan, proved to be very interested in Dr Sinnotti's work and the doctor and his assistant became regular visitors. Unfortunately a new strain of rat developed that was immune to this side effect. Dr Sinnotti was able to isolate the virus and then discovered that it was capable of living apart from its host. Furthermore, if it was properly dried it could remain dormant until reheated when it would revive and be as dangerous as ever.

Dr Sinnotti was on his way to the Chinaman to tell him of his latest discovery. As fate would have it, the storm blew the *Esperanza* aground and several infected rats escaped, hence Dr Sinnotti's anguish. When the search party arrived all the important equipment had been removed including these new dried cultures of tsutsugamushi and bubonic. In his worthy efforts to defeat a disease the doctor had created a monster which could threaten the world in the wrong hands.

Now, my dear Trevor, it was a question of finding out how you fitted into the scheme of things. Was your tea shipment attacked simply to demonstrate the truth of Li Xian's words? Had you upset him in some way? Did the ship still contain a clue to Dr Sinnotti's work — a cure perhaps? There was one theory that seemed to fit everything.

Obviously the attack on the *Matilda Briggs* was a test run for the new strains of rat and diseases. It also served to demonstrate to the British Government that Li Xian's threats were not idle boasts.

The threat was now real and it was to come from you, Mr Victor Trevor.

Your Trevor's Natural Terai mixture is the most exclusive and expensive tea in London. It has enjoyed an even greater vogue of late as your last shipment never reached our shores owing to the attentions of the giant Sumatran rat. I would not be exaggerating if I said that the whole of London awaits your next shipment with bated breath and parched lips. Every member of the Royal Family and Her Majesty's Government enjoys our tea. With Dr Sinnotti's dried disease in it, every cup would potentially be the drinker's last. Thus even teetotallers could have a demon in their drink. I wonder if Li Xian has a sense of irony? For what could be more ironic than Britain's favourite reviving beverage being the cause of its downfall?

Thus Li Xian, having created even greater demand than usual for your tea, had to ensure a regular supply, preferably a monopoly. To do this he had to buy at a very high price and mix it where there is another source of good tea. Kenya? Not really, when Ceylon is *en route*, and your tea is used in Asian blends.

It was a gamble. Had Dr Sinnotti lived and Li Xian exacted his secrets from him? It seemed likely in view of the purloined equipment and the location of Li Xian's rubber plantation. Now was our only chance to catch him and his gang red-handed, hence the presence of Dodd and various undercover agents on the *Matilda Briggs* when you went to Trincomalee.

The gang was caught red-handed mixing the contaminants with your tea, but Li Xian was not with them. The Singapore police went to his Sumatran plantation but he had already fled. They found Dr Sinnotti in a pit suffering terribly from the attentions of the rodent he had once studied. Before he died he was able to tell the police that Li Xian had taken with him one giant rat of Sumatra – but it was a female and pregnant. Li Xian's last known whereabouts were south-west China. Our agents there have already reported a larger epidemic than usual of the plague and warn that it could easily develop into a pandemic.

Disease or germ warfare has been used before, Trevor, I regret to say most notably by smallpox-ridden Europeans in their conquest of the New World. As yet, the world-wide, devastating potential of this form of warfare has not been fully realized. Let us hope that it never is, by Li Xian or any successor to him.

To turn to other matters, old friend. Did you notice that the tall thin pirate to whom you took an obviously instant dislike had a cast in his right eye on the first day out from Calcutta and in his left for the rest of the voyage? Pennington would have seen through that, I fear.

S.H.

Postscript for posterity: the last pandemic of bubonic plague was in the late nineteenth century. Its origin was believed to have been south-west China.

Publisher's Note

Readers who have enjoyed *The Elementary Cases of Sherlock Holmes* may like to know that further extracts from young Stamford's papers will be available from the same publisher. In *Watson's Last Case*, Stamford not only tells in his inimitable fashion of Watson's service to his country during the Great War, but provides some fascinating background information on the early days of Sherlock Holmes.